*Seth looked dow [...]
had just rescued.*

With all the layers of mud and dirt covering her, it
was difficult to tell what she looked like. Tangled,
wet hair clung to her neck and shoulders, and her
face was badly smudged. His eyes traveled
downward and caught sight of her swollen ankle.
Without any fuss he picked her up and said, "I'll
carry you to my camp."

She nodded weakly. She slipped her arms around his
neck and rested her head on his shoulder. When his
small campsite came into view, Jessica decided she
had never seen anyplace so warm, welcoming or
charming.

"Before you get too comfortable next to the fire,
how about getting cleaned up a little?" he suggested.

Her free hand flew to her hair and face. She was a
mess! Before she could answer, he was carrying her
across the small clearing to a spring.

"Take off those wet clothes," he growled.

Dear Reader,

Each and every month, to meet your sophisticated standards, to satisfy your taste for substantial, memorable, emotion-packed stories of life and love, of dreams and possibilities, Silhouette brings you six extremely **Special Editions**.

Now these exclusive editions are wearing a brand-new wrapper, a more sophisticated look—our way of marking Silhouette **Special Editions'** continually renewed commitment to bring you the very best, the brightest and the most up-to-date in romance writing.

Reach for all six freshly packaged Silhouette **Special Editions** each month—the insides are every bit as delicious as the outsides—and savor a bounty of meaty, soul-satisfying romantic novels by authors who are already your favorites and those who are about to become so.

And don't forget the two Silhouette *Classics* at your bookseller's every month—the most beloved Silhouette **Special Editions** and Silhouette *Intimate Moments* of yesteryear, reissued by popular demand.

Today's bestsellers, tomorrow's *Classics*—that's Silhouette **Special Edition**. And now, we're looking more special than ever!

From all the authors and editors of Silhouette **Special Edition**,

Warmest wishes,

Leslie Kazanjian,
Senior Editor

JANET FRANKLIN
The Right Mistake

Silhouette Special Edition

Published by Silhouette Books New York

America's Publisher of Contemporary Romance

To my children, Aaron and Donyale,
for their love and support while I was involved
with other "people."

SILHOUETTE BOOKS
300 East 42nd St., New York, N.Y. 10017

JANET FRANKLIN

has been writing for years but until recently never put an entire book together. Becoming a published author is something she always wanted to do; finally her dream has come true. She is a longtime resident of Georgia, and when she isn't busy writing or working or attending nursing school, she enjoys music, needlework and reading almost anything.

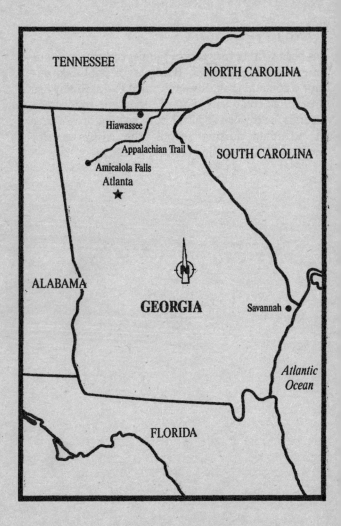

Chapter One

Jessica Buchanan paused a moment and tugged at the straps on her shoulder, readjusting the weight of the backpack. With a deep sigh, she began walking again. It just wasn't working this time.

The sense of peace and freedom that normally came to her when hiking wasn't there. She wasn't relaxing and she wasn't finding any answers. All she felt was endless anger and resentment. Anger that made her steps jerky with unleashed fury. Resentment that robbed her of the peace being alone usually gave her.

She forced herself into a steady rhythm, forced her shoulders to relax under the weight of the pack. Shaking her arms to ease the tension and consciously unclenching her fingers, her body at last fell into a more natural rhythm, but her mind continued to seethe with fury.

Black and dark, the anger blocked out the dull gray sky. Her eyes registered where her feet went, but she failed to watch the path or appreciate the scenery. A chill breeze threatened rain and falling temperatures, but her preoccupation kept her from noticing the cold when her light blue windbreaker flapped open. Again and again she went over the recent events in her mind. How could she have been so blind and stupid? How could she have thought she would get the promotion? How could she have thought Gerald Daniels wouldn't let her down?

She was standing at the edge of one of the reporters' cubicles, small units that contained a desk with two drawers and were surrounded on three sides by thin plywood to give the impression of individual work areas. A warm hand had touched her back, then shifted, the thumb stroking the nape of her neck beneath her hair. Startled, she had turned quickly. Gerald Daniels, the station manager, smiled at her.

"Jessica, I'd like to see you in my office."

She was pinned between him and the partition. Slowly he dropped his hand, letting it slide down her arm until his fingers brushed hers. Jessica shuddered at the touch, a shudder she could see had been misread by the reporter whose eyes were missing nothing. "I'm busy at the moment, Mr. Daniels." She would not turn and follow him like an anxious puppy, no matter how much she wanted that promotion. "I'll be free in an hour if that would be convenient for you."

"Mr. Daniels?" he mimicked softly. "I thought we had become much closer than that, Jessie."

She glanced nervously to the side, seeking an escape route from the close contact. It was either stand still or sit on Bill's lap and Bill's lap was beginning to look very inviting. Daniels deliberately misinterpreted her look.

Straightening, he stepped back slightly. "Yes, Miss Buchanan, an hour will be fine."

Jessica watched him saunter away, feeling used and wishing she could take a shower. He was the most revolting person she had ever had the misfortune to know and she hoped she never met anyone like him again. He had deliberately said that to give the impression... Well, he could just give all the impressions he wanted, it didn't change the facts. She turned back to Bill. "I think if we take this story from a different angle..." She continued talking, but her mind wasn't on Bill or the problems they were discussing.

Had Daniels made a decision about the news director's position? Was that why he had insinuated that they were more than just boss and employee? Had he done it because he was going to offer her the job or had he done it just to make her life miserable? Knowing Gerald Daniels it could be both. She was crazy to sit around and take that kind of harassment for a job. Any job. And he certainly wouldn't be *giving* the position to her. She had earned it.

When she finished discussing the problems Bill was having, she returned to her office and quickly checked the lineup for the six o'clock news. Then, after making sure an hour had passed, she left her office and walked through the news department and upstairs to the second floor. Today the plush corridor that was home to management seemed longer than normal. Despite her anger, she knew she had let her hopes climb. She had put too much into getting this promotion. She arrived at Daniels' office and took a deep breath. His secretary motioned for her to go in.

Gerald Daniels was smoothly handsome, like a movie star. Everything about him was planned. His thick, light brown hair was always neatly combed. His tanned face was smooth and closely shaven, even this late in the afternoon. The clothes he wore were impeccable—expensive and tasteful suits that molded his shoulders and chest, silk shirts that looked as if they cost a fortune. Everything about him was meant to be appealing and seductive. Even the faintly musky scent of his after-shave was suggestive.

Jessica knew he applied similar tactics with men using charm and power to which no one seemed immune. As she crossed the plush carpet to his desk Jessica wondered why she could find nothing attractive about him. Her thoughts ran to words like oily and slimy. But he had power. That she couldn't deny.

"Please, Jessica, sit down." He rose from his leather chair and came around to perch on the edge of the desk.

"You wanted to see me?"

"Yes." He smiled. "I don't see enough of you." When she didn't respond the smile faded slowly. "We haven't really had a chance to discuss the news director position."

Jessica felt her heart thud heavily in her chest. "No, we haven't," she agreed, fighting the urge to wipe her hands on her skirt.

"I was wondering if you were free tonight. I'd like to talk about it over dinner."

"I'd rather answer any questions you might have here."

Daniels studied her a moment. "You know, you're still very young and I think, shall we say, inexperienced."

Inexperienced maybe, but not naive. After the demonstration in the newsroom she wasn't going to give him any more opportunities. "Are you saying I'm not going to get the job, Mr. Daniels?"

"No," he assured her quickly. He slipped from the desk and sat down in the chair next to her. "No, not at all. But I do feel discussions like this are much better held in a less—" he glanced around the gleaming office "—restrictive environment."

"I think we both know what I have to do to be seriously considered for the position."

With a satisfied smile Daniels leaned back in the chair, then reached over to lightly touch her arm. "I wasn't sure you fully understood the terms."

Jessica straightened, fighting the bile that had risen in her throat. "I understand your terms." She let her voice become cold and didn't try to hide the repugnance she felt. "I think, rather than being too young for the job, I'm much too old."

"Don't be too hasty," he went on, unruffled. "The choice is between you and one other person, a corporate man they're pushing on me. I can get the job for you if you really want it." His eyes slid across her face to the front of her jacket. "I think you owe it to yourself to at least discuss it."

Jessica rose stiffly. "Your terms are too high." His eyes had begun to wander down her body, slowly and methodically. Jessica closed her eyes and swallowed. She turned to the door, took several steps, then turned back. "For your own personal reference, I find you absolutely disgusting."

Daniels stood in a swift movement filled with cold anger. "You'll regret that remark, Buchanan. This job goes to the man and you can forget ever being more than the executive producer with this station or any other that Garver Broadcasting owns."

"Yours isn't the only television station in the world. I see that as no obstacle." After a tense pause she asked, "So, what's the official reason for my being turned down? Lack of experience? Uncooperative with management?"

Gerald grinned, leaning back against the edge of the desk. "Probably both of them. But we both know the real reason." Again his eyes slid over her, making her skin crawl.

"Do you know what sexual harrassment is, Gerald? It's a form of rape, and you do it very well."

He completely ignored the insult. "You've played the game before."

Cold chills raced down her spine, but she wouldn't let him see how deeply the words had cut into her. "I never have and never will sleep with you or anyone to get a job."

His eyes glittered viciously, and his expression changed to one of satisfaction as he saw the anger on her face. "I do my homework, Buchanan. It's something you need to learn. You shouldn't try to play with the big boys until you have some practice."

"Thank you for your invaluable lesson today," she retorted, and left the office.

As she entered the news department she heard someone say, "This time I approve of Daniels' tastes in afternoon delights." Head throbbing and stomach churning, she left the building five minutes later. She stopped by her apartment and wrote a note to her roommate telling her she had gone hiking because she needed time to think.

Only she wasn't thinking. She was reliving those moments over and over.

She had wanted that job. She had pinned her hopes on it, counted on it. For weeks she had eaten, slept and dreamed being news director. So much thought and energy gone into a wasted effort. She should have known she wouldn't get the job. Even if she had acquiesced to Daniels' unspoken demands she wouldn't have been promoted. If the corporation wanted to send in a wonder boy to work miracles with the ratings, she was out. It was as simple as that.

But it had been rape. Not rape like being dragged down a dark alley but a mental and emotional assault. His touch had been revolting. How could anyone . . . She shuddered at her own thoughts.

"You have to stop this, Jessica. It's ridiculous."

She had known what Gerald Daniels was for a long time. And she knew television. Why was it bothering her so much now? She had avoided playing footsie and kneesie under the table with him before *and* she had managed to keep her cool and remain unruffled. She had adroitly sidestepped his advances and remarks. Until now. What had happened that was so different this time? Why was this incident upsetting her so much?

Her desire for the job. Her shoulders sagged beneath the weight of the pack. She would have put up with his innuendoes to be news director, and that was the difference. That was what she had run from. Herself. Somewhere in the past two years she had lost sight of her priorities. No job was worth selling yourself, even by implication.

Jessica sank down on the ground and cried, only the whispering pines and stark bare trees witness to her defeat. Finally she dried her eyes and stood, adjusting the straps of the backpack, and started walking.

For the first time in hours she began to see the forest around her, to note the evergreens and skeletal trees, the gray sky and gusting wind that carried the promise of rain. It was time to find a place to camp for the night, get a fire started and set up the tent. Her steps slowed again as she really looked at her surroundings.

She was no longer on the trail! Stopping, she looked back and to her side. Silent trees stood guard over the trackless terrain. When had she left the trail and how? Her feet knew these paths better than her mind. Not quite believing she had done such a careless thing, Jessica turned and backtracked for a few minutes, but still she found nothing familiar, no well-worn path, no trees with trail markers, nothing. She glanced at the leaden November sky again.

There was no sense of panic or fear, only disbelief that she had let herself leave the path. The mountains of north Georgia were not an isolated wilderness in which she could roam forever. Tomorrow she would simply go downhill. She had food and shelter and dry clothes in her pack. She only needed water to have all the comforts of home. First, she had to find a suitable place to camp. Almost laughing at herself, she started in a diagonal line down the mountain, hoping to find a spring or a stream to use for cooking and making something warm to drink. Without the water her supper would have to be chocolate bars and raisins. She felt chilled and wanted the comfort of something hot inside her while she pondered her problems.

At last she heard the sound of water. It was a tumbling creek at the bottom of a deep ravine. Sighing, she turned downhill and began to follow the bank. The sides of the ravine were steep with occasional rocks and one or two small trees that projected at odd angles. There seemed to be no place where the stream was accessible. A quick glance at the sky told her she wouldn't have much longer to walk. It would soon be too dark for hiking to be safe.

Hoping one last time that she would see a place where she could reach the water, Jessica stepped to the edge of the bank. She leaned forward to look down, and the earth abruptly gave way beneath her.

She was falling, sliding face forward down the steep bank. She grasped frantically for anything to stop herself. Briars tore at her hands and face. Damp earth found small openings in her shirt and clung to her breasts and stomach. Struggling against her downward motion, she reached desperately for anything to stop the endless slide.

A large boulder loomed in front of her. She tried to roll over, but the backpack blocked the move. Desperately, she swung her legs to the side, but the rock caught her right foot and ankle. Moments later she hung head down over the edge of the last drop. Her foot, wedged under the boulder, was the only thing keeping her from falling the last few feet.

Jessica tried to wriggle back so that her body would be on the ground, but the heavy pack added too much weight for her to complete the maneuver successfully in her precarious position. Her entire body, from her hips upward, now hung suspended in space. It was a straight drop into the shallow, rocky stream ten feet below her.

The blood was beginning to settle with stinging force in her face and neck. It was rather like the sensation she had gotten as a child when she hung upside down on the gym set too long. She definitely wasn't going to spend the night in this position. Slowly, she released the buckle that held the pack and slipped it from one shoulder and then the other. Using all the strength in her arm, she flung it behind her, only to watch helplessly as the pack slid past her into the water below.

For the first time Jessica felt a twinge of fear. The pack was her survival kit. It contained her food, clothes, tent and sleeping bag. It also contained first aid supplies—antiseptic that her stinging hands would need, a bandage that her throbbing ankle would need. But first she had to get her body up onto the slope. She would worry about the pack later.

She braced her foot to use it as a lever to help herself back. Pain shot from her ankle to her knee, pain that took her breath away and made her break out in a damp, cold sweat. She refused to think about the possibility that the ankle was broken. Clenching her teeth, she heaved herself back, landing with a solid thump against the hard ground. The blood slowly drained from her face. She lay still as the feeling in her leg gradually changed from a piercing stab of agony into the dull throb of misery.

When at last the pain had settled into a more bearable state and the nausea had passed, Jessica opened her eyes again. It was nearly dark. Had she fainted at some point or was it just the cloudy sky stealing the last of the light too quickly? She tried to sit up, but the rock moved. She froze. If the rock went then she would go as well. "You wanted time to think, Jessica. Now you have all night." Her voice sounded eerie and strange in the utterly silent forest.

Lying back carefully, she arranged herself as comfortably as she could. She wouldn't be here forever. Her roommate, Emily, knew where she was going and would send out the marines when she didn't return on time. And the ache in her ankle at least let her know she was alive. Pulling the lightweight windbreaker closed, she lay still to wait for morning.

Soft rain woke her. A gentle, cold rain that fell like mist soaking her hair, dampening her clothes and the ground. Jessica pulled the nylon jacket around her neck and huddled into a small ball, unable to stop the shivers that shook her. She wasn't sure all the wetness on her face was from the rain.

A gray, foggy dawn slowly lightened the area, revealing shadowy shapes that took on form and definition to become pieces of a real world. Moving slowly, both from cold and caution, Jessica surveyed her situation. Her right foot was wedged into the base of the rock. The slope was steep and wet after the rain, and there were no handholds. It would be a tortuous climb and probably impossible with the pain in her ankle. Going down was equally unfeasible. It was a straight drop into the rocky streambed with the very strong likelihood of breaking another limb, and she definitely needed the three she had in good working condition.

To her right and up the hill several feet was a small tree that might be useful. Stretching slowly and carefully she could just reach the trunk. It wasn't often that she thought about her height, but at the moment being almost five nine was a blessing. She clasped the small sapling and pulled hard. It held. Easing off her nylon windbreaker, she worked it around the tree, leaving the sleeves dangling. With the sleeves gripped tightly in her hands, she tried to free her foot. The rock slipped and suddenly it and some of the ground that had been her bed throughout the long, cold night fell into the stream below. Her heart pounded in her throat for long minutes while the only thing that kept her from following the small boulder's path was her grip on the nylon material. Using a strength she didn't know she possessed, she pulled herself up to the tree until she could wrap her arms around it. Then she maneuvered herself into a sitting position, the trunk clutched tightly in her arms. At last she released her death grip on the sapling and looked at her ankle.

If it wasn't broken it was the next thing to it. The skin was stretched with swelling, her shoe cutting painfully into the bulge. Several dark bruises showed where she had kicked the rock. "Pretty, very pretty." The unnaturally high sound of her voice frightened her and she fell silent. Still holding the tree, she turned and looked up the steep embankment. If she let go, tried to climb and slipped she might not be able to catch herself again. But sitting here for several days also seemed out of the question. Common sense said to sit still and wait.

"Hello! Can anyone hear me?" she called out as loudly as she could. The only sound was her own voice echoing back.

The day dragged on. It was gray, damp and misty. Every few minutes she called out, but only an echo answered. Each time she got no answer she considered trying to climb up the steep bank to the top, and each time she forced herself to be calm and rational.

The sky began to dim again, and Jessica tried to resign herself to another night on the damp hillside. She called one more time, sending a last pleading hello out to trees that didn't care and wouldn't answer.

"Hello?"

Had it been a voice or wishful thinking? "Hello. Over here. Can you hear me?" Don't get your hopes up, she told herself sharply.

"Over where?"

A lovely, deep, male voice. Never had so few words sounded warmer or friendlier or stronger. "In the ravine." Moments later a figure towered at the edge. "Don't get too close or I'll have company," she warned as he leaned over the side. She sighed with relief when he took the warning seriously and stepped back, then dropped onto his hands and knees.

"If you didn't want company why did you call?"

Jessica half giggled, whether with relief at having help near or at the question, she wasn't sure. "Just being perverse, I suppose."

"You look comfortable," the man teased. "Saving the best campsite for yourself?"

"It would be absolutely perfect if I had a rope," she responded, trying to keep her voice light.

"I have one. Would you like to borrow it?"

"Yes, please, but just one end." He was wonderful, absolutely wonderful.

"Being perverse again? Well, whatever will make you happy. Don't move. I'll be right back."

"I'll be right here," she promised with another laugh. She wondered how long the wait would be, but it didn't matter. She leaned against the tree. In a few minutes she would be out and maybe he would have something hot to drink. Tea, coffee, cocoa. Even hot water would be good.

"Here it comes." Jessica looked back and watched as he slid one end of the rope toward her. With shaky fingers, she caught it and for a moment, couldn't do more than just hang on. "It would help if you tie it around you."

She did, fastening it tightly around her waist and tugging fiercely at the knot. No more slips. No more mistakes. She was all too ready to give up her campsite. "Okay, I think," she called, and began to inch her way backward up the steep slope, pushing with her foot and using her hands to lift herself up.

"You might be faster if you tried both feet."

"In a hurry?" she called without turning.

"Always," he chuckled.

She smiled to herself as she inched up again, the rope tugging gently on her waist, reminding her that she wouldn't go tumbling down. Suddenly, strong, warm hands caught her under her arms and dragged her backward onto flat ground. Jessica collapsed, breathless, and safe at last.

Seth looked down at the woman at his feet. What with layers of mud and dirt it was difficult to tell what she looked like. Tangled, wet hair clung to her neck and shoulders. Her face was smudged and dirty, and there were lines on her cheeks, evidence of tears shed earlier. Her clothes were torn and damp, clinging to her body, outlining the full curve of her breasts, which were rising and falling with her panting breaths. His eyes traveled downward and caught sight of the swollen ankle. Kneeling, he began to unknot the rope. "Do you think you can hobble if I help or do you want me to drag you?"

"Just drag." She pushed herself up to a sitting position. "Or you can leave me here. Just being on flat ground is marvelous." Jessica looked up into soft, honey-brown eyes. Thick, dark hair fell over his forehead, curling softly behind his ears and around the collar of his flannel shirt. His face was angular, almost hard. His jaw was sharply defined and covered with the late-afternoon shadow of a man with a heavy, dark beard. Wordlessly, she reached for his hand and half pushed, half pulled herself upright. Gingerly she put her right foot down. Pain rocketed up her leg.

Seth saw her face go ashen beneath the layers of dirt as she clenched her teeth. Without a word, he lifted her, one arm under her legs, the other around her back. "Only to the camp. Tomorrow you walk." She simply nodded this time, not bothering with a quick comeback. No retort, no smile. Her arms slipped around his neck and she rested her head on his shoulder.

When his small campsite came into view Jessica decided she had never seen any place as elegant or lovely. Never had any house been as warm, welcoming or charming as this spot with its blazing fire and blue dome tent. It was heaven. He helped her down next to the fire and she held out her hands to the warmth. It was pure bliss. There was nothing more she wanted in the world.

Seth watched as she extended reddened hands to the fire. Her nails were broken and encrusted with mud and dirt. Scratches covered the backs, small red lines from the edge of her jacket to her fingers. Her knuckles were skinned and bruised. She was going to need some attention and first aid. "Would you like anything to drink?"

"Oh yes, please." She looked up. "You wouldn't have any hot chocolate, would you? I couldn't think of much else all night."

"All night?" How long had she been there?

"Mmm." The fire seemed to lose its warmth as she remembered the long hours alone. Dark silence had enshrouded her. The pain in her ankle had been her constant but silent companion.

Seth fixed the chocolate and bent to hand it to her, noting the scratches on her face and a bruise on one cheek. "How bad is the ankle?" That seemed to be the worst injury as far as he could tell.

"I'm hoping not as bad as I'm thinking," she said, glancing at the swollen foot. The dizzy euphoria at being found drained away as the realization that she was really safe sank in at last.

Seth saw the sudden change. Setting down the cup of coffee he had been drinking, he began to gather some supplies. "Before you get too warm and comfortable next to my fire, how about getting cleaned up a little?"

Her hand went to her hair, feeling the tangled, wet length, and then she touched her face. She was a mess. Filthy. And so tired. Before she thought to answer, he had pulled her upright again and was carrying her across the small clearing to a spring. He helped her down and handed her a cloth and some soap.

Jessica's teeth chattered as she washed her face and hands in the icy spring water.

"Take off those wet clothes, too. I'll find you something to put on."

Jessica looked up at the man. "I'm fine. I really don't need—"

"You're wet and cold. You should get out of those clothes so your body isn't chilled more," he said, turning and striding away.

He returned a moment later with one of his shirts. "Here, let me help you put this on."

"I'll do it myself." She accepted the shirt and waited until he had left her alone again before undressing. She washed as much dirt off her body as she could, and then slipped into the soft flannel shirt, feeling soothed by the clean, dry material. At her quiet call the man reappeared instantly.

Seth carried her back to the campsite and, putting her on her feet again, said, "Jeans too." Jessica started to protest. "I want to hang them near the fire so they'll be dry in the morning."

Glancing down at the long shirt, Jessica unfastened her jeans and pushed them from her hips, but was forced to accept his help in getting them off.

Seth eased her down onto a small log and knelt by her. Carefully he untied her shoes and tugged them from her feet, supporting her injured ankle. He slid the jeans from her legs and hung them near the fire. Turning back, he studied her foot.

For a moment he felt slightly sick at the amount of swelling and bruising. He gently touched the taut skin, but could feel no displaced bones. He picked up her hand. It was small and slender, and now that it was clean he could see the scratches were deeper and more numerous than he had first thought. A tiny sound made him look up and then turn her hand over. The palms were deeply cut and bruised as well. "What did you do?"

"Nothing much. Just grabbed a few briars to try to stop my forward progress." She shook her head, thinking of

Daniels. "First I grab one to pull me forward and then one to stop," she mumbled.

"What?"

"Oh, nothing." She looked at the cuts on her hands. Suddenly everything ached and felt sore. Every muscle in her body protested sitting there half-dressed. She was cold and tired. "Do you have a blanket or something?" She wanted to crawl away somewhere dark and warm and sleep. A nice little cave, protected and secure, where she could banish all her thoughts and worries and just rest.

"Tired?"

His back was to her, and she couldn't see what he was doing. "A little."

"After I put something on those cuts you can get in the tent. I'm afraid we'll have to share the sleeping bag. It may be a little crowded."

"I don't think—" The words died as he turned, his eyes stern, his expression unyielding.

Seth shook his head. She was upset. She was also in pain, possibly suffering from shock and exposure. He curbed the retort that had formed and knelt next to her. "We don't have a choice tonight. It's too cold and wet. You can't afford to be in the open and tomorrow..." He left the sentence unfinished. Tomorrow would bring a whole set of new problems.

Jessica knew he was right. It was cold and the ground was soaked. If she refused to share the shelter he offered she might be totally helpless by tomorrow. Her ankle throbbed incessantly and all she wanted to do was sleep. "After clinging to a rock all night I think it'll be fine."

"That's twice you've said all night," Seth said, sitting down by her. "When did you fall?"

"Late yesterday afternoon, just before dark." She winced as he cleaned the scratches on her face.

"What happened?"

"I was hoping to find water before I had to camp, and that stream was all I could see. I got too close to the edge. Some dirt gave way and I fell."

Seth picked up her right hand and turned it over. "What stopped your fall?" The bank had been bare of any handholds except her tree.

"A rock. I kicked into it with my right foot." She glanced at her ankle, then gasped as the antiseptic hit her hand.

"I'm sorry," Seth said, gently tightening his grasp around her wrist. "Just a little more. I didn't see a rock." Her story had been told in a simple and straightforward manner. There had been no embellishments that included her feelings or thoughts, just facts in a logical, orderly fashion. When she shivered slightly he wasn't sure for a moment if it was just reaction to the sting of the antiseptic, but this time when she spoke the fear was evident in her voice.

"My foot was caught under the rock. When I loosened it this morning the rock fell into the stream."

Seth looked up and then back at her hand. "Sounds like a pretty close call."

"Not really. I had managed to wrap my jacket around the tree."

"Hmm. All finished," he said, repacking the first aid kit. He let her sit quietly while he banked the fire and fixed the camp for the night. At last he turned. "Okay, into the tent."

The tent was small and just getting in proved to be a feat with her useless ankle, but at last she was inside, sitting on top of his sleeping bag. "I think I'll sleep through tomorrow," she sighed and then, looking first at the one-person bag and then at him she asked hesitantly, "How do we do this?"

Chapter Two

Slide in so I can get in there," he answered, his body half in, half out of the tent.

The adrenaline that had kept her going, the euphoria at being found and pulled out of the ravine and the attention required by details like washing and first aid had held her together, kept her functioning. Suddenly there was no need to keep going and Jessica felt herself losing control. She slipped into the sleeping bag, making herself as small as possible and then felt him sliding in, bare legs covered with crisp hair brushing her smooth ones. The sensation totally distracted her for a moment and then he settled next to her.

Jessica lay very still, trying not to shiver or fall apart. "If you hear me crying hysterically during the night, don't worry, okay?" Her back was to his chest, her legs against his.

He could feel the tension in her muscles as she tried not to tremble. "Turn over, please," he said gently.

It was awkward. She had so little room and she had to move her foot carefully, but at last she was facing him.

"That's better," he said, his voice quiet, gentle and soothing.

He unbuttoned his shirt and put her hands inside, against the warmth of his chest. Sore, bruised palms met soft, thick hair and instinctively she curled her fingers into it. His arms came around her back, pressing her closer as he lifted her head onto his shoulder. "Now, any time you want to let go is fine. I'm right here and you're safe. It's going to be okay."

The gentle reassurance in his voice, the strength and security of his body next to hers and the realization that it was all right to have a hysterical breakdown made the need to do so vanish. Instead she pressed herself closer to him, inhaling his masculine scent. She turned her head slightly and kissed his shoulder. "Thank you." She began to relax under his gentle stroking of her back and shoulders, and slowly she felt heat creeping into the depths of her legs and arms. Heat taken from him. Heat given by him. She sighed against the shoulder beneath her cheek.

"Is that it? All the hysteria over?"

"I think so. I feel too good to bother with hysteria at the moment." And she did. She was wrapped in a soft cocoon of comfort.

Seth felt her relax and the fine tremors that had been shuddering through her body begin to stop. "I like you," he whispered.

Jessica smiled, already more than half-asleep. "I think I'm falling in love," she whispered teasingly.

* * *

The feel of a definitely male body against hers jolted
Jessica fully awake. For a moment she couldn't remember how she had ended up where she was and then the
events of the previous evening came flooding back. She
still lay pressed against him, her head on his shoulder, his
arm around her, holding her securely. Carefully, she tilted
her head back to look at the man sleeping beside her. His
forehead was high, his nose was maybe a little too long and
the bridge was pronounced, giving the impression of deep-
set eyes. His strong and angular jaw was dusted liberally
with the stubble of a dark, thick beard. She realized he had
more body hair than any man she had ever known. His
eyes were closed, hiding the honeyed warmth she remembered. Or had that been her imagination? It had been
nearly dark when he found her. Her eyes wandered to his
mouth. It was almost too firm, the lips a straight line
across his face, decisive even in sleep. She realized he was
watching her and looked up again. His eyes *were* a warm
golden brown. Curious. She hadn't imagined it. They were
clear and deep and fascinating. He moved and her attention shifted to the play of muscles beneath her fingers.

"Interesting way to wake up," he murmured, suddenly
holding his body very still.

"Yes, it is," Jessica agreed, feeling only curiosity at the
situation. Briefly she searched for the fear or shyness that
should have been there, but couldn't find it. It had been a
long time since she had awakened lying beside a man, any
man. After her divorce there had been no one in her life.
It had been, and still was, the way she wanted it.

But it was such a warm, comfortable feeling to wake in
the circle of strong arms, inhaling the scent of a male body.
She wanted to reach up and touch his beard, to test how
scratchy it was and to compare it with the tanned skin of
his cheeks. Her fingers still rested against the warmth of his

chest, caught in the thick tangle of hair. She could feel his heart beating beneath her palm and realized with a start that its rhythm had increased in tempo. "I think I'd better—"

"Don't move," he said quietly, gazing down into her wide green eyes. They were shadowed with fatigue and pain, yet clear and open. They weren't eyes that would hide thoughts easily. Her smooth, oval face was pale, the scratches angry red lines across her cheeks. The tangled hair that spilled across his arm was light brown, not as dark as he had thought last night. In the summer it would be filled with sunlight.

Jessica had frozen at his quiet words and then had felt her face redden. The sleeping bag was too small to allow much space between them and there was no doubt why he had asked her to be still. She dropped her eyes to the column of his neck, seeing instantly the pulse pounding in time to the beat beneath her fingers. Again she searched for little warning signals and couldn't find them. Instead of the tension that should have been there keeping her at a distance, she found a warm response deep inside herself, a strong desire to relax against him rather than back away. But she knew the situation could get out of hand very easily. "One of us has to make the first move."

"I was just trying to decide which move to make," he said.

She looked up again, her eyes colliding with his. The honey brown had changed to a golden heat that took her breath away and caused her pulse to begin its own erratic race. "I meant the first move to get out of the tent." She wasn't sure she sounded very convincing, nor was she sure that was what she had really meant.

"Did I tell you last night how beautiful you are?"

Jessica smiled. "No, but then last night I was kind of hysterical." Then again, maybe she was still hysterical. Why wasn't she pushing this man from her?

She tried to ease away from his body, away from the seductive warmth of his skin and the heady smell of him, but she couldn't avoid the golden demand in his eyes. Though his eyes spoke volumes, he had made no move to do more and his voice was light and teasing.

"I like you when you're hysterical."

She knew she had to stop this somehow before she completely forgot herself. "What day is it?"

He lifted his left arm, forcing her head into the curve of his neck. "Friday, why?"

Her temple came into contact with the angle of his jaw. The beard was scratchy, but not the least irritating. It was rather enticing, she thought, bemused as her lips rested against the warm pulse point. "I'm supposed to call a friend tomorrow. If I don't get out she'll have the National Guard looking for me." Why did it feel so right to be in his arms? It was insanity to continue to lie curled in the false haven he offered, but she had no desire to leave it.

"Mmm, back to basics." He slowly moved her hands from his chest and buttoned his shirt, then turned away from her as much as he could and began to extricate himself from the confines of the sleeping bag.

Jessica felt suddenly bereft. Her body chilled as if a cloud had covered the sun. She closed her eyes to give him time to pull on his jeans and shoes without her eyes devouring him. "I'll get your clothes," he said, and she felt the cold morning air swirl into the warm tent.

Moments later her jeans and shirt were tossed inside and she was left alone. The process of getting out of the sleeping bag wasn't much easier than getting in had been the night before. After the first two movements sent pains traveling up her leg she moved with caution, trying to avoid any further sharp reminders of what lay ahead today. Gritting her teeth, she got her pants on. They were stiff with dirt but relatively dry. Then she pulled on her shirt and jacket, and over that she put his shirt, not yet ready to part with that last bit of him.

Scooting to the tent opening, she looked out at the fire he had burning. He was heating water and readying things for breakfast. She watched him straighten and move to his pack, his movements smooth and lithe. The brown plaid flannel shirt stretched across broad shoulders as he lifted, the pack down. He must be at least six-something, she thought, but from her position she couldn't be sure. She remembered the ease with which he had picked her up and carried her to the camp. "I'm afraid I have a problem," she said, keeping her voice as calm as she could.

"What?" he asked, turning.

"I still can't stand and I can't get my shoe on, either."

She saw the frown that passed quickly across his face, but his next words made her laugh. "Lady, if you think I'm going to carry you out you are hysterical."

"Well, it was worth a try," she retorted, grinning, and crawled from the tent to the fire. He knew she wasn't joking, but he wasn't going to panic. His light touch had kept her calm yesterday and had made his appearance at the top of the ravine even more wonderful than it otherwise would have been. He hadn't gotten angry or upset. He had just been there and she thought he was spectacular.

Slowly she looked up at his towering figure. It was just the situation. She was reacting to her own pain and fear and to her need for his help. When she got back to civilization it would be different. Then he would be just another man and she just another woman. He probably wouldn't give her a second glance, she thought, as he knelt beside her and looked at the swollen foot and ankle.

"Damned good try, too."

"I thought it was." She frowned at her foot. "I thought I kicked hard enough at that rock that was in my way. Guess I'll just have to try harder next time if I want you to carry me around," she said teasingly. She noted the doubt in his eyes and forced a smile she didn't feel. "Got any coffee, mister?"

Seth grinned and shook his head. "You're something else." He poured a cupful and handed it to her. "Any suggestions?"

"Three." She smiled again, though what she felt was much closer to tears. "You could carry me, which you've already ruled out. I could crawl, but that seems rather babyish, or you could cut me a nice strong crutch, even two maybe, and I'll jog out."

Seth returned to preparing breakfast. None of her ideas sounded very reasonable to him. "Let's start with your third suggestion and work backward."

"Okay." She sniffed appreciatively at the smell of food. "I'm so hungry I could eat turnip greens and I hate turnip greens. This smells delicious."

"It's a darn good thing you're hungry," he quipped. "I'm cooking turnip greens."

The oatmeal he had actually prepared was hot and filling, and Jessica ate two bowlsful, along with another cup of coffee. She sat contentedly by the fire while he went to look for suitable material for crutches. If she had to be rescued by anyone, he certainly was her choice for the perfect person. She was sure if he had said anything serious she would have burst into tears. She was almost afraid to ask how far it was going to be to get out of the woods, but she would have to find out and ration her strength accordingly.

He returned with two fairly straight saplings and sat down. Jessica watched him shape and smooth the wood, then fix handholds. He had rolled the sleeves of his shirt back several turns, revealing strong forearms and corded wrists covered with dark, crisp hair. His hands were strong and competent with long fingers. Jessica watched him dreamily, but finally she forced her attention back to the day ahead. "How far is it to civilization?"

Seth had been aware of her quiet observation. For a moment he debated the wisdom of answering her question truthfully, but then replied, "Not far. Maybe eight miles." He heard her gasp, but kept his eyes on the crutches.

"Downhill all the way, I'm sure." She wasn't certain her voice sounded as light as she wanted it to. Normally she did only five or six miles a day. And this was eight miles with crutches.

"Definitely." He smiled encouragement. "I only make downhill crutches."

Neither of them spoke while he finished his job and broke camp. At the last minute he knelt in front of her. "I'm going to splint your ankle." He braced her ankle with two smaller sticks he had smoothed, using a bandage to bind the foot and ankle. Then he slipped two of his wool socks over her foot.

Jessica did her best to hide the pain his actions caused, but Seth noted the tears spiking the edges of her lashes as he helped her up. Her lower lip had deep indentations where she had bitten down while he worked. For just a moment he wanted to take her in his arms. Again he hesitated, wondering if it was reasonable to let her try this, but then he shrugged and helped her get the crutches settled.

The lady had a lot of determination and courage. He wasn't sure he would even try what she was attempting.

It was awkward. Jessica felt clumsy and at first was afraid she was going to fall with each step. Gradually, however, she found a rhythm and relaxed her body into the new movements. The crutches were miserably uncomfortable, and the cuts on her hands throbbed with each step. After what seemed like hours he paused and sat down on a rock, leaving room for her. She sank down beside him and closed her eyes, breathing deeply. The most burning question was how far they had gone, but she was afraid to know the answer.

"Want some water?"

"No, thanks."

"You shouldn't get dehydrated." She was perspiring from the effort, despite the chill in the air.

"I know, but I have the definite feeling certain activities are just too impossible right now." It hadn't been easy this morning to go behind the tree while he was out looking for her crutches. Doing a deep knee bend balanced on one foot and holding the other off the ground was not her forte. She had decided then it would be better to be thirsty than to have to have his assistance with that.

He looked away a moment. "It could be difficult." His hand covered hers a moment. "Don't be embarrassed if you need help."

"Well, I'll let you know if I do," Jessica murmured.

"Ready then?"

His hand was still on hers, warm and encouraging. "Yes. I'm sure this is fun, I just haven't quite figured out how."

"Well, let's spend a little more time working on it and maybe you'll find the answer," he encouraged.

Seth walked behind, letting her set the pace. He watched as she placed the sticks in front of her, her shoulders hunched as her arms took her weight and she swung her body forward and then put her good foot firmly on the ground. She was going to have some very sore muscles later.

There were at least two other suggestions she hadn't mentioned in her list of solutions. One was his leaving her alone and hiking out to get help. He had sensed she didn't want to wait by herself, and more than that, she wanted to face this challenge. It was as if she were forcing herself to find a way out of a mess rather than take help. If she became exhausted he could always make a travois with the crutches and sleeping bag and tow her out. Until then he was going to admire her spunk and determination.

He smiled as he remembered her statement last night. "If you hear me crying hysterically, don't worry." She hadn't shed one tear, not yet. She had been on the verge of crying when he had finished splinting her ankle, but she hadn't allowed the tears to fall. He liked that. He admired strength and determination. He liked someone who wouldn't give in easily.

They reached the trail. The going was easier most of the time, the well-worn path smooth from many feet. Seth moved up closer to her. "You should make good time now. No more of that meandering around you've been doing back there."

"What? Are you timing me? I didn't realize I was in training." She glanced apprehensively at the sun. She was using time, lots of precious time. He might not have enough food to feed both of them tonight. And he probably didn't want to have to sleep cramped in the sleeping bag with her again. Her hair was a hopeless mess of tangles and filled with dirt. Her nails were dirty and broken.

It would be weeks before her hands looked decent again. She felt grimy and unkempt and very unattractive.

"Yup, and you are falling behind schedule. At this rate you won't qualify for the Peachtree Road Race, not even the handicapped division."

"Oh," she groaned in mock disappointment. "I thought I was training for the Boston Marathon. I can handle the Peachtree." She had run it several times.

"Why set your sights so low?" he teased. "Go for the Olympics."

"I'm impatient. That takes years and I like my rewards now." She paused in midswing, almost losing her balance.

Seth caught her as she swayed precariously between the two sticks. "Are you okay?"

She glanced up into concerned brown eyes. He must be at least six-three for her to have to look up so sharply. Suddenly she was very aware of him as a man, the warmth of his body so close to hers, the strength of the arm that encircled her with gentle assurance. She straightened slowly. "Fine. Sorry. Just thinking." She began to move again, falling back into the awkward rhythm. She was impatient with herself. She had always set firm goals and strove hard to achieve them. There was nothing wrong with that, was there?

She knew she had faults. She didn't like being told she needed more experience and time. She pushed herself hard. She had high ambitions, maybe ones that weren't realistic, at least in terms of the amount of time she had given herself to achieve them. Just like this bit of insanity. The most sensible thing would have been to let him hike out and get help. But no. She had insisted on doing it herself. What was she trying to prove?

That was silly. She wasn't trying to prove anything. If she could make it out this way it made a lot more sense than sitting alone on the mountain waiting for someone to carry her. And as far as her goals in life went, well, there was nothing wrong with having big ones. The higher you reached the better your chances were of succeeding with something at least. If you didn't strive for the best you could only expect to get the leftovers.

Seth didn't try to keep any conversation going. It was obviously taking all her energy to make each step. For a moment he doubted the wisdom of having let her even try this. Where had his judgment been this morning? She was probably in shock and dehydrated. She was definitely in pain and he was letting her try to hike out as if they were in the middle of the wilderness somewhere. Glancing at the setting sun, he made his decision. "We're going to have to stop. We're not going to make it."

"Oh, please," she said sharply, and leaned against a tree. "I'm sorry," she said more softly. "I'm tired." She didn't add that the pain was getting to be more than she could handle. It was so constantly there and in so many places. Her arms quivered with fatigue with each step now. The palms of her hands throbbed incessantly. "How much farther?"

"About three miles."

Jessica quietly admitted defeat. She couldn't make it another three miles. She looked up. "What should we do? The most sane solution?"

"Can you handle being alone for a couple of hours? Maybe as many as three?"

"Of course." It was the right thing to do. She looked at the deepening shadows and silent trees. Three hours she could handle alone, but not all night. "Won't it be too dark for you to come back tonight?"

"No." He shrugged the pack off and set it next to the tree. "Do you need anything, embarrassing or otherwise, before I go?"

"No." She smiled. It was a tired look that didn't reach her eyes. "I don't think I like your choice of motels. I prefer a first-class place. Nice big beds, a hot bath and maybe a steak and some wine. Raisins and pine trees don't make it."

"You'll get it." He grinned. "Hang in there, beautiful." He kissed his fingers and laid them gently on her lips. "I won't be long."

Jessica watched him stride away. Long steps that quickly, too quickly, took him out of her sight. Lightly, she placed her fingers on her lips, exactly where his had been. "Beautiful," she muttered as she slipped wearily to the ground. He certainly had a knack for overstatement.

It was distinctly different sitting alone in the woods with a game leg than when both legs were in good working order. There was nothing she could do but wait. Ordinarily she would have been putting up her tent, building a fire, cooking food and washing up. Now, as she watched the sun set and the sky slowly fade to black, she felt alone and even frightened. She had never felt frightened before. It was the fatigue and the pain in her ankle and her hands, her shoulders and her back.

She never questioned the fact that he would return. She knew that when the rescuers came with their stretcher he would be with them. And she hoped he would say something wonderfully crazy like he had last night, because if he didn't she might really cry and she didn't want to, not now. Not after all this. She heard a twig snap and she stiffened. Then came the rustle of a leaf, followed by voices and footsteps. And then he was there.

"Here she is, just like I said." His voice sounded light and teasing. "I knew she'd wait. She can't resist me. She would have waited all night if she had to."

Jessica smiled happily as the other men laughed. "Don't push your luck," she retorted. "All night may be asking too much. You aren't that irresistible."

"Impatient, impatient." He sighed in mock despair. "Here I rush around and do the impossible in two-and-a-half hours and she complains."

Amid good-humored banter she was lifted onto a stretcher. Warm blankets were tucked around her, and then she was strapped in. The men hoisted their burden and started back along the trail. "I feel like I'm doing some B-grade war movie," Jessica remarked. She turned her head and looked back at him. "Aren't you supposed to be walking beside me, holding the cigarette?"

"Sorry, you have the roles reversed. That's what you do if I'm on the stretcher."

Everyone laughed again. He must be exhausted. He had walked out and back after taking care of her all day. She glanced back and saw he had his pack on and was moving easily. "Why aren't you tired?"

"I took your advice and stopped off at a motel. Amazing what a hot bath and steak did."

She must have fallen asleep because the next thing she knew she was in a moving vehicle. She started to sit up, but again he was there. "Lie down, beautiful. We're almost at the hospital."

"Hospital? What happened to the motel, for heaven's sake?" She was frightened. She didn't want to know her ankle was broken.

He chuckled. "I promise you the best place I can find, the longest, hottest bath and the biggest steak. *After* you have your ankle checked. Anything else?"

"Yes. Do you always keep your promises?" Her fear was showing in her voice.

"Yes. Always."

His hand, warm and secure, had found hers beneath the blankets. "Yes, but that's because I'm beautiful and you know I can't resist you."

He laughed and squeezed her fingers. "I think you're pretty irresistible, too."

"That's good," she murmured. "I think I'm crazy about you."

"Save it, beautiful. We're here. X rays, casts and all the delights of modern civilization."

Jessica fell apart. Not in front of him, but in the emergency room while lying on a stretcher. When the nurse asked for identification and an insurance card she started crying. Her purse holding all her money and credit cards was locked in the trunk of her car, and her car keys were at the bottom of the ravine in her pack. She couldn't call anyone because she didn't have a quarter. She didn't even know where she was.

She fell apart again when the doctor told her the ankle was broken and he would have to put on a cast. All she wanted was a long, hot bath.

"Miss Buchanan," the elderly man said with marked impatience, "putting a cast on isn't going to hurt."

"I'm not afraid of it hurting." She blew her nose in the tissue the nurse handed her. "It's just all I want is a hot bath." She lifted herself up on her elbows and looked at her ankle. "What if I come back tomorrow after I have my bath and you can put the cast on then?"

The elderly man scowled. "It's gone untreated too long already," he snapped. Jessica sighed and watched as her leg was encased in sticky plaster. She wished *he* were with her. He would think of something delightfully funny to say. He would make it all seem less important than it suddenly was. She listened to the doctor's instructions, took the prescription form he handed her and eased herself on to the wheelchair with the nurse's help.

"B movie is right," Seth said, shaking his head at her as the nurse wheeled her into the waiting room. "Did you really have to go that far?" he asked teasingly, looking at the cast. She had obviously been crying, but from which of the many possible causes he didn't know.

"I just thought all the trouble you had gone to deserved some kind of recognition. This was the best I could do." Thank heavens he hadn't asked if it hurt or how bad it was. He was absolutely the most wonderful man to have around in a crisis. "Well, there went a hot bath, I guess."

The nurse walked up, smiling. "Honey, just don't get the cast wet. If you can get in and out of the tub, just prop your leg on the side and you can soak as long as you want."

Seth grinned wickedly. "Oh, she'll have all the help she needs for that."

Jessica grinned back. "Don't count on something that hasn't happened. You aren't that irresistible." Though she couldn't help but wonder if that was really true.

"No," he agreed, laughing, "but I'll bet a hot bath is."

Jessica sat tiredly on one of the double beds in the motel room, a half-eaten steak in front of her. "I think I just reached it," she said as much to herself as him.

"What?"

He was busy devouring his steak and fries as if he hadn't eaten in a week. "The end." She pushed the tray away and tucked the sheet around her. "Did you really have to take all my clothes to wash? Couldn't you have left me something to put on?" When she had finished her hot bath she had discovered he'd taken all her clothes and put them in the washer, including the shirt he had loaned her. And she was left to huddle as best she could under the sheet.

Seth looked up, startled. He had come to expect her to have no limits. She had kept going for so long that he'd forgotten how totally exhausted she must be, not to mention how uncomfortable. Her face was drawn with fatigue, her eyes dark and shadowed. "Does it hurt much?"

"Not the ankle. Just my back and shoulders and arms." She tried to recapture the lighter mood. "Guess I need to lose some weight. I had no idea I was so heavy."

"Don't lose an ounce. You're beautiful just as you are." It was time to stop joking. And she *was* beautiful.

Jessica leaned back against the pillow, tears filling her eyes. "How do you feel about a few hysterics?"

"Fine." She certainly deserved them. "Just give me a two-minute warning."

"Why? Going to clear the area?" she asked with a shaky laugh.

"No, get some extra towels."

She giggled and settled back. "The doctor didn't appreciate them at all."

"What do doctors know? Anyway, why would you have hysterics for him?"

"They asked for my insurance and ID and my purse is locked in my car and my keys are at the bottom of that ravine. I don't even have a quarter to make a phone call or a brush to fix my hair. It's a mess."

Seth moved the tray from the bed with a smile. She *was* close to losing it. He sat down beside her on the bed. "We worry about keys and phones tomorrow. Now you get your third wish."

He sounded so sure and calm. Didn't anything ever ruffle this man? She wanted to ask him to hold her like he had last night. She wanted him to take her in his arms and keep her against the warmth of his body. "What wish was that?"

"A big bed," he answered, chuckling. "Now, turn over and let me rub your back."

His fingers worked magic over the sore muscles as they gently but firmly kneaded the stiffness and helped her to relax. She slowly sank into the comfort of the mattress and gave herself up to the fatigue at last. Half-asleep, his fingers still easing away the tension, she turned her head toward him. "I don't even know your name."

"I don't know yours, either."

"Jessica."

"Seth."

He wouldn't be around much longer, and she was going to miss him. He was the perfect rescuer. So cool and calm and relaxed about it all. "I just want to know: Are you ever serious?"

"All too often," he said softly. "Go to sleep, beautiful." She felt the brush of his lips against her hair, and the warmth of his breath whispered across her cheek. "I'm going to steal your tub."

"I didn't leave any hot water."

"Greedy. You better have or you won't get your clothes back."

Seth watched her a moment and then moved from the bed. Later, still damp from the shower, he stood for a long time watching her sleep. After toweling his hair one last time he pulled a pair of briefs from the pack and put them on. In the morning she would probably raise hell and read him the riot act, but that still left hours of being near her. All day he had thought about what had happened this morning. Waking with her eyes on him, clear green eyes that gazed with such openness into his. Even dirty and bruised she had been lovely. The warm fragrance of her delightfully female body had been combined with wood smoke and antiseptic, but it hadn't thrown his body off track. He had wanted her, wanted her badly. All night she had lain pressed against him. He had felt her breasts pushing against his chest with each breath she took. The warmth of her soft breathing had heated his shoulder.

He eased himself into bed beside her. He just wanted to touch her. No. He wanted more, a lot more, but he would settle for just having her rest in his arms. The feel of her soft warmth against his body and her fingers curled along his chest would have to be enough. She had put so much open trust in him without question. He couldn't betray her now.

He pulled her gently against him and she moved into the same position she had slept in the night before. Only the presence of his briefs and her cast separated them. She smelled wonderfully fresh now. Her body was so soft and delicate against his. He moved his hand along her back, feeling the smoothness of her skin, the shape of her ribs, the slope of her waist. She moved closer, settling more firmly against him. He rested his cheek against her hair and slept.

Chapter Three

Seth watched her wake up. For a long time he had just been holding her, enjoying the warmth of her next to him, the silky feel of her skin and the delicate fragrance of her body. Now he watched with interest as she became aware of their position, she with no clothes on and he with next to none. She didn't open her eyes at first and he smiled. He could tell she was awake by the increased tension in her muscles and the slight alteration in her breathing.

Jessica lay without moving. They both had on far less than they had had yesterday in the sleeping bag. And what was he doing in her bed when there was another one in the room? With a mixture of regret and relief she realized he was wearing his underwear at least. She forced her hands to be still when what she wanted to do was run them over his chest and feel the hard muscles beneath the taut skin. After several minutes he broke the silence.

"Are you going to play possum all day?"

"Possibly. At least until I figure out what to do about this."

"About what?"

She opened her eyes at the innocent question and saw the teasing in his. "I've got this big, hairy creature in my bed and I'm not sure what to do with it." She knew what she wanted to do with it and that didn't include pushing it away.

"Big, hairy creature," he protested. "Thanks a lot. You make me sound like Big Foot."

Jessica laughed. "No, I'm Big Foot." She moved her leg with the cast just enough to indicate why, but even that small movement caused her thigh to brush against his, sending ripples of warmth through her. "You're a Yeti."

"I still object to the description. I thought you found me irresistible."

She smiled, reveling in the feel of his hard body pressed against her. "I never said I didn't find big, hairy creatures irresistible, I just said I don't know what to do with them."

"Need some suggestions?"

There was a slight huskiness to his voice that sent a shiver through her. "Oh, so much help all of a sudden. My first thought was to scream."

Seth laughed softly. "Yeties are terrified as little bunnies when beautiful women scream."

She loved the way he went along with her teasing—his pretense at being insulted, his insistence that he would run away frightened. "I could go back to sleep and imagine it isn't there. A bad dream that will be gone when I wake up." But if this was a bad dream she wanted to spend the rest of her life in a nightmare. Unconsciously she rubbed her cheek against his shoulder.

"Wouldn't work," he assured her. His hand stroked along her back to her waist. "Not a chance."

She felt so relaxed. Being next to him seemed natural and right, just as it had yesterday. Though yesterday there had been logical reasons for his long, muscular legs to be against hers the effect was the same: a warm, languid feeling that suffused her with contentment. "This is really strange, you know. I should be in an absolute panic and I'm not." But with the contentment was a tingling awareness, an expectancy. She realized she had to put an end to this quickly before she did something or they did something she'd regret.

"Does that mean I get to stay?" Seth asked, wondering if she was always this trusting and open.

She looked up again, but couldn't read the expression in his eyes. They were warm, glinting with golden highlights, but the question had been teasing. She pictured for one wild moment what would happen if she said yes. She was aware of every sensation—the hard length of his body, the thick mat of hair beneath her fingers. There was tension in his hand where it rested against her waist, yet he had not made one move to touch her more intimately. "Certainly not."

"So what's left?"

"I'll give the big, hairy creature one kiss, then he's going to go find my clothes and retrieve them from wherever he so rudely left them last night, which I hope was in the drier and not the washer."

"Now I sound like a St. Bernard," he complained.

"I like dogs, too," she said, turning her face up to him.

It was a sweet, gentle touch, certainly not the usual kiss of two people lying in bed together. His arm tightened around her for a moment, his lips brushed lightly across hers and then he pulled away. The tenderness was more seductive than if he had kissed her deeply,

Seth sat up and looked back, feeling nothing but long-ing to be back next to her. "You could be addictive," he said gruffly, and then pulled on his jeans. "Back in a minute. Order breakfast, I'm starved." He was asking too much of both of them. Many more seconds next to her and he wouldn't be responsible for his actions. He pulled his shirt on, keeping his back to her, needing to break both the physical and visual contact.

Jessica's heart was pounding crazily against her ribs. Her toes still tingled from the kiss. She watched his quick exit, wondering if he felt the same way, only not sure exactly what she felt, other than overwhelmed. "I must have hit my head in that fall and not known it," she muttered when the door closed. She sat up and carefully wrapped the sheet around her, toga-style, until she was well covered.

Maybe she should have screamed or gotten mad about his being in her bed. She had been so out of it yesterday she hadn't realized half the time what a powerfully attractive man he was. She caught sight of the phone and grimaced. She distinctly remembered babbling about not having a quarter to make a phone call last night. She must have really been in a daze. However, she wasn't this morning and what might have been excusable yesterday certainly wasn't today. Resolutely she turned to the phone to call her roommate.

"What I need are my spare car keys, some clothes and a driver for my car." The door opened and closed softly behind her.

"How badly are you hurt? Tell me, Jessica." Emily's voice came across the wires filled with a mixture of impa-tience and concern. "Don't just say you were in an acci-dent and you need a driver. What happened?"

Jessica smiled at Emily's excited tone. Her roommate liked emotion and drama, and Jessica's normal factual simplicity drove her crazy. "Calm down, Em. I fell on the trail and broke my ankle." Seth moved into her line of vision and her breath caught in her throat as he smiled and laid her clothes on the bed. He had to be the best-looking thing she had seen in ages. "You wouldn't believe the cast they put on it. It's nothing serious, though. I just can't drive my car." She listened to Emily's excited chatter for a minute.

"No, I'm not in the hosptial, I'm at a motel." Again Emily asked a couple of excited questions. "It's just my ankle, Emily, I'm fine. There's no rush." Seth turned with a teasing smile and she wondered if maybe there was a rush, after all. "Oh, there's room service with breakfast. Hey, Em, do me one more favor. Call Neil and ask him to call me. I want to know if I still have a job."

Seth looked back when he heard the sudden tension in her voice. She was serious. He frowned, then shrugged as he went to let room service in. She would be leaving as soon as her friends came. There was nothing he could do about it and no reason for him to care. But he did care, he realized as he poured a cup of coffee and handed it to her.

Her fingers tingled where they touched his when she took the cup. She rested it on her knee to hide the sudden trembling. "Yeah, I know, Em, I know how you feel about it, but I really messed up this time. In lots of ways. Just have Neil call. He'll have the best handle on the situation."

Seth watched her withdraw into herself after she hung up. He was surprised by the resentment he felt at the intrusion of all the things he didn't know about her life. "Hey, try screaming. Maybe reality will run away like a frightened bunny."

Jessica smiled wistfully. Calling the real world had broken the spell. Now she was in a motel room with a man she didn't know, not sure if she had a job or if she wanted it if she did. "I'm sorry. I left a bad situation behind me and I don't know if I want to straighten it out. But if I don't, I'm not sure what I'll do instead." She was still wrapped in the sheet. Really, she should get dressed. "Life gets crazy sometimes, doesn't it?"

"It can. Want to talk about it?"

She looked up. Who was this man who had so easily pulled her out of that ravine, then treated the whole incident as if it were an everyday experience, keeping her spirits up and not letting her fall apart? She knew nothing about him. Not where he lived or what he did for a living or even if he was married or seriously involved with anyone. She felt closer and more comfortable with him than she could ever remember feeling with any person. "When do you need to leave?"

"I don't have to be anywhere until a week from Monday. I'm being transferred by my company. The time between is to relax and get settled. But I settle easily, there's just me." He glanced at her left hand. It lacked any signs that she belonged to someone. No wedding ring, no diamond and no band of pale skin to indicate she had removed the ring while hiking. And, after all, she had called a woman for help.

Jessica felt a strange sense of relief at hearing that he wasn't married. "You don't have to stay if you don't want to. My friends will be here later. You've done so much already." She smiled, trying to release him while wanting him to stay.

"I don't have anywhere to go except another motel and I've grown very comfortable here." He settled back in the chair, his long legs stretched out and crossed at the ankles, his fingers entwined and his hands resting on his flat stomach. "The scenery is very appealing." He smiled as she absently touched her tangled hair and then the sheet. But her mind was obviously on other things. "So why do you think you may not have a job?" He wanted to know everything about this woman.

"I got mad and walked out. I was supposed to be on vacation, but I had agreed not to take it because we were shorthanded. Then when I got mad I just left. Pretty dumb."

He shrugged. "Depends. Why did you get so mad?"

"Because I didn't get a promotion. For three weeks I've been doing my job *and* the other one and I really thought I had a chance." She shrugged. "When I found out I didn't I just lost my cool." That wasn't quite the whole truth, but she didn't want to get into the more personal aspects of the problem.

Seth chuckled, his eyes sparkling with laughter. "I find that difficult to picture. You have to be one of the coolest ladies I've ever met." What other woman would have lain there in bed this morning without making a scene? And he didn't know anyone who had been through what she had the last few days who would have remained calm and not let herself go to pieces.

Jessica ignored the implied compliment. The last thing she felt was in control. "I told off the big boss and got so stupidly upset I wandered off the trail and ended up at the bottom of a ravine. That's cool?" She sighed and shook her head. "Right now I don't like myself very much at all."

"Hey, hold on a minute." She looked up again. "You're being too hard on yourself. We all make mistakes. Some are just bigger than others."

"I'm trying for the Nobel Prize in errors."

"You need to learn to forgive yourself," he said gently.

The phone rang and she snatched it from the cradle. She listened a moment and then laughed. "It's nothing really, a simple broken ankle and a long story. How are things at work?"

Seth listened to her end of the conversation. She kept her voice light and cheerful, but he could see the tension in her shoulders and back and in the way her hand tightened on the phone. She was holding too much in. Beneath that layer of calm was fear. Fear of what, he wondered and poured her another cup of coffee. It seemed the only thing he could do at the moment. "Do you have a job?" he asked as she hung up.

"I guess so. There's no indication otherwise. Neil thinks that if the big boss wants to get rid of me he'll let the new guy do it." She looked down at the coffee. "Anyway, I've got a couple of weeks. They haven't even made any announcements yet that anyone's been hired for the position."

"And what are you going to do?"

"Evaluate things and try to figure out if I should stay or quit." Seth sat down on the bed next to her, and she was aware of every breath he took. "Back to the ravine," she said. "Lord, that tree wasn't very comfortable."

"Don't worry, you won't be there long. Someone will throw you a rope."

"I don't think anyone could be that lucky twice in a row." She lightly touched his face. He hadn't shaved yet and his beard was stiff and scratchy against her fingers, his cheeks firm and smooth above. He was probably about thirty-five. "I'm going to miss you."

"I'm still right here." He held her gaze a long moment. "However, I don't think I'll hang around to receive all the praise and plaudits."

He didn't want involvement. She had known that it was just a coincidence, an accident, but her heart felt torn by the words. She smiled, trying for the lighter touch again.

"I didn't think you were the hero type. The role doesn't suit you at all."

"You are hard on a man's ego," he groaned. "First you question my taste in women and now you tell me I'm not a hero."

"Heroes always carry the damsel in distress," she teased. "I walked."

"I'm just smarter than the average hero," he retorted. "My back still works."

Jessica's eyes narrowed with challenge. "Compliments? You want compliments?" She almost laughed, but fought to keep a straight face. "You think I'm hard on your ego?" She ran a hand down her side. "So, I guess that means you think I'm fat."

His eyes ran over her sheet-wrapped figure. Her breath caught at the intimate look. She really should have gotten dressed and kept her mouth shut.

"Never that." He took the cup from her hand and pushed her back against the pillow, hovering over her with his hand on her waist. "You need to work on your self-image." His eyes traveled slowly over her breasts and stomach to her legs. "To be honest, so far you are perfect, except for your opinions, of course."

"And I'm sure you think you can change those." Her heart was pounding wildly again, and he had to feel it.

"Definitely," he murmured and bent to kiss her. It was a light whisper of a touch. "It's just a matter of saying the right things often enough and soon you'll have changed your mind." He kissed her ear. "You're very beautiful."

"Brainwashing," she groaned, but didn't pull away.

"Mmm, gorgeous." His mouth was warm against her neck, sending sparks to her brain. At first the kiss was as gentle as earlier, a soft brush of his lips against hers. Jessica turned toward him. Instantly he pulled her closer, his mouth claiming hers firmly. She felt herself being drawn irresistibly toward him, losing herself in the warmth that suddenly consumed her. His fingers tangled into her hair, tilting her head back as he deepened the kiss.

Her entire being was centered in the taste of his mouth and the heat of the body next to hers. All her senses were heightened, and even the smooth touch of the sheet against her skin was a caress. His warmth was like the spring sun after a long winter. The clean smell of his cheek was as heady as any wine. Her hands found his hair. The thick dark strands had a life of their own, curling over her fingers, claiming her hands. Slowly his hand moved from her waist, sliding upward to her breast. The light touch sent rivers of fire coursing through her body.

The phone rang. Once. Twice. His hand left her breast and for a moment she felt the pleasant weight of his body on hers. "Answer it," he whispered against her ear.

Jessica took the phone and spoke. His eyes held hers as she listened to the sound coming from another world, a world that seemed unimportant and unrelated to her. "What?" She had been listening to sounds, not words. "Tomorrow? Why not today?"

"Jess, what's wrong with you?" Emily demanded. "I just explained everything. You are all right, aren't you?"

No, she wasn't, but she couldn't tell Emily that. "I'm fine Emily, really. I was, uh, half-asleep when the phone rang." She listened as her roommate explained again.

"Are you sure you'll be okay?" Emily asked.

"Of course I will be." Seth moved, his hand tightening slightly at her waist. She wasn't at all sure she was going to be okay if he stayed and she *knew* she wouldn't be if he left. She didn't understand what was happening to her. Nothing she was doing was like herself. "I'll call if I can't handle it."

Seth was grinning wickedly as he leaned across her to replace the receiver in the cradle. "Does that mean I have another day and night to spend with you?"

She looked up at the man who held her pinned lightly to the bed with his body. Did he want that, to spend time with her? Or did he just want to take her to bed, a process he wasn't having much trouble with at all. "If that's what you want." She should have told him to leave. Suddenly nervous, she pulled away and sat up. "I think if you're going to stay we should go out for a while. I'll get dressed." Dressed and away from these beds.

"I love undressing, too," he announced teasingly, lying back against the pillow.

"And you're counting on something that hasn't happened." And wouldn't happen. She had enough problems in her life without adding a weekend fling with a man she didn't know.

"Not counting," he said quietly, his eyes holding hers for a long, burning moment. "Just hoping and wishing."

Jessica looked away from his demanding gaze. She didn't know what to do with him, or worse, with herself. She quickly picked up her clothes and practically dived for the bathroom, only to return seconds later. "I hate to ask, but would you get me a brush and comb? How could you possibly sit across from me and eat when I look like this?" She pushed her hands into the mass of light brown hair that framed her face.

"You may ask for anything your heart desires." Again he looked at her with that strangely seductive gaze. "And it wasn't hard at all, enjoying all that beauty over my coffee." He got up and started for the door. "Is there anything else you want?"

"No." She watched him leave. Nothing important, she thought. Just him. Just him for the rest of her life. She shook the thought away as quickly as it came. If there was one thing she knew she didn't need it was an emotional involvement. She had to put her own personal life in order, not complicate it further.

"Never send a man to do woman's work," Seth said as he dropped the bag onto the bed. "Do you know how many different kinds of hair brushes there are? There are round ones and flat ones and twisted ones. There are some with holes in them. There are natural bristles and nylon bristles and wire bristles. How do you ever decide which one to use?"

Jessica laughed at the mock tirade and then continued for him. "And there are pocket combs and regular combs and picks and teasing combs and combs just to hold your hair back. How did you ever manage?" Not only had he managed, he had done very well. He had bought a plain comb, a good brush, several barrettes to hold her hair back and even some ribbon.

"Lucky guess and a sweet old saleslady. Are they okay?"

There was doubt in his voice, as if it really mattered. Jessica smiled. "They're perfect. Thank you." She should offer to pay for them, but that would mean she would have to send him money and would also mean he would have to give her his address. And there was the motel room and all the food. She was costing him a fortune.

"Why the sudden frown, kitten?"

Kitten? She liked that. She liked everything he did and said, she thought with a sigh. "I just realized how much I'm costing you. The motel and food and now all this." Why was he doing it? His job had been finished last night when the rangers came.

"What you're costing me in money doesn't count. Now my willpower, on the other hand, may be drained for a year. I never knew my clothes could look so good." She had tied his flannel shirt at her waist. The knot pulled the fullness of the oversized shirt taut across her breasts, enhancing her slender waist.

"I'm afraid mine is too torn to be decent." Add one shirt to the list of expenses. Anyway, she wanted some part of him to take back with her, something she could touch and feel and remember. Not that she was ever going to forget this man, but she still wanted a tangible piece.

"While you fix your hair I'll shave," he said. "Any idea what you want to do today?" Seth watched her a moment. She seemed completely unaware of her own beauty or of how overwhelmingly feminine she was. Totally devoid of guile, she hadn't done anything designed to be enticing, yet every move she made was seductive.

Jessica noticed the hungry look he was giving her. "Work on your willpower." And mine, she added to herself.

Seth laughed and headed for the bathroom. "You do like challenges, don't you?" he teased and closed the door.

Jessica realized her heart was beating erratically against her ribs again, but she was smiling, too.

Maneuvering on real crutches with a cast wasn't easy, but it was a lot better than the day before. Her shoulders were sore and her hands hurt, but they spent most of the time in the car, driving down small side roads into pretty valleys and then up to enjoy another view of the mountains. They stopped for lunch at a small diner and enjoyed steaming bowls of homemade vegetable soup.

Jessica had the feeling of being detached from the world. Whatever was happening between them was more fantasy than reality. She knew that, had they been in their real lives, this would never have happened. They talked easily and even their silences were comfortable. Frequently he picked up her hand and held it, sometimes resting his on the gearshift with hers enclosed in it, at others laying her hand on his thigh and covering it with his own.

They stopped again for coffee and sat talking for a long time. He kept questioning her about her job and the problems that had made her walk out. She felt pleased that he really seemed interested, but his conclusions upset her. He had taken her hand again, a habit she was falling in love with, but one which seemed to sap her willpower with surprising speed. He looked at her a long moment. "I don't know what field you're in, kitten, but you aren't happy with it. You've told me you have goals and plans to get up the ladder, even though you didn't make it this time. You've talked about the stress and tension. But you've left out one very important part."

"What?"

"How much you love it."

She stared at him a moment and then at her empty coffee cup. "At first it was fun, lots of fun. Every day was exciting and interesting." When had that feeling of excitement died? She shrugged. "I don't know, maybe it's just the routine that's made me forget how I feel or it could be the constant hassles." The waitress interrupted to refill their cups and give them a curious look.

"Many things are fun and exciting, kitten, especially at first. What I'm talking about is love, an avocation. If you really care about what you're doing it doesn't die with age or stress, anymore than love between two people does. I guess what I'm trying to say is that if you really like your work the stress and tension don't wear you down, they're simply invigorating."

Jessica couldn't imagine stress and tension being invigorating. They were simply exhausting. Nor could she quite compare a job with marriage. Yet a career *was* a relationship of sorts. If that was the case she could easily have made a big mistake in her work, just as she had in her marriage. "The job wasn't my first choice," she admitted after a long moment.

"What made you choose it?"

"I changed fields to try to save my marriage."

"And?"

She grimaced and picked up the cup. "It didn't work. In fact, it made it worse." She took a long drink of coffee, avoiding his eyes.

"Made it worse how?"

Jessica shrugged slightly. "I'm very competitive, I guess. Chad, my husband, always resented the fact I got ahead before he did. The competition in our careers spilled over into our marriage. I thought it was because we were in the same field. So I changed." She shifted restlessly in the booth. "It backfired. I did even better in my new job, at least until now."

"Did your first choice have a lot of competition, too?"

"Yes. I'm not sure it was as cutthroat as it is now, but I didn't go as far as I have here, either." She didn't mind fighting her way up as long as the games were played fairly and the results were dependent on what you did, not who you were or who you knew.

Seth covered her hand with his, lightly stroking his thumb across the back, the scratches on her knuckles a subtle reminder of all she had been through the last few days. "Then maybe what's missing isn't in the job, kitten. You need to think about your whole life before you make a decision."

"I know." Only her job was her life. But that was an issue she would have to explore another time.

"Promise?"

He was so serious, as if it really mattered to him. "I promise." The man had so many facets. Yesterday he had been strong, protective and supportive. This morning he had been totally provocative and now he was being serious and seemed truly concerned about her career and her happiness. "Doesn't your job have stress and tension?"

"God, yes," he said with a laugh. "Tons of it. The same as yours. You get that in any highly competitive field, along with the politics. But I love it. I thrive on it. I think if it wasn't there, I'd be miserable." His look was almost apologetic. "I'm afraid I'm one of those corporate wonder boys who got your job."

He was a wonder, all right, she thought. Tilting her head to one side, she smiled. "And are you really?"

"What? A wonder boy?" She nodded and he grinned. "That depends on who I'm with." He laughed as her face turned pink. "I just do my best, kitten."

Jessica's heart pounded at the provocative promise. What would his best be like? *Get the conversation back on track, Jessica.* Avoiding his eyes, she stirred her coffee a moment. "What's it like from your side, coming in to work miracles?"

"It's not easy." She looked up, surprised at the doubt in his voice, but his eyes had taken on a faraway look. "Management expects overnight miracles and the staff expects some egomaniac who's going to fire them and bring in all his old friends. It usually takes about three months for everyone to start feeling comfortable. By then you've weeded out the really bad employees, hopefully added a touch of spice and have gotten things cooking. It's a rough few months."

He was telling her to give it time and to remember that the new man would have his own set of problems to deal with. "Do you come in with a fixed goal?"

"Only in the sense that I want it to be a success. But each situation is different. There are different problems and different personalities. I don't set precise goals until I have a sense of the operation."

Jessica listened, asking questions and liking the answers. He cared about people. He cared about the staff who would be under him, but the fine line he had to tread seemed undesirable. "It sounds like a case of damned if you do and damned if you don't."

"Enough of this," he said, pushing his cup away. "Let's go next door to the drugstore and drive *them* crazy. I think that waitress is about to have us evicted for loitering."

Jessica laughed. "It's probably my appearance." She knew she looked like something the cat had dragged in and forgotten. Even though she had brushed her hair and caught it back with two combs its natural body and curl made it look rather wild. Without her blow dryer there was no hope of styling it. Her jeans were ragged and stained and with his shirt she knew she must look like a castaway.

Seth laughed and laid some money on the table. "I'd love to see you all dressed up if you think you look bad now."

"Thank you, kind sir." She smiled. "But maybe the problem is that you need glasses." Jessica had never thought of herself as especially pretty. Attractive but not beautiful. Nor had anyone ever used that word to describe her before, either.

"Or maybe you need another lesson to work on your self-image," he teased.

Jessica couldn't look at him as she remembered the warmth of his body and the melting heat of his kisses. "I believe. I believe."

Seth laughed softly as he held the door for her. "Not yet, but you will," he whispered as she maneuvered past him.

They browsed through the paperbacks and talked about books they had read, comparing impressions. Jessica was beginning to feel very tired and the pain in her ankle was increasing. "How's your willpower?"

Seth looked down at the half-joking question and frowned. She looked exhausted. He should have been paying more attention. "All restored. Need to borrow some?"

Jessica tried to smile but couldn't. Her shoulders ached more than her ankle and standing here talking about books was just making the pain worse by the second. "Could we just go back?" She shifted her hand slightly, feeling the sharp sting as the crutch touched her cuts. She must be tired, or all this wouldn't be bothering her so much.

"You should have said something sooner, kitten," he said, holding the door for her.

In moments they were back at the motel. Jessica hadn't realized he had been steadily working his way homeward after lunch. She had been paying more attention to him and what he said than what went on around her.

"Stay in the car until I get the door open."

She looked at his retreating back for a moment and smiled. Opening the car door, she turned and got both feet out, positioned the crutches and started to stand. The right crutch slipped and she shifted quickly to keep from falling. A searing pain shot through her hand and up the nerves of her arm. Biting down on her lip to keep from crying, she closed her eyes.

"I told you to wait," he said from beside her. "Here, give me those." He took the crutches and lifted her into his arms.

Jessica couldn't say anything. She knew she had broken one of the deeper cuts on her hand open and she clenched her fingers tightly shut.

Seth glanced down as she laid her head against his shoulder. Quickly he carried her into the room, kicking the door closed behind him. For a moment he just held her, then laid her on the bed. "You need to learn to stop before you reach the end." He kissed her forehead gently.

Chapter Four

Jessica opened her eyes and tried to smile. "The crutch slipped and it hurt my cuts." She hadn't meant to tell him. "It's nothing."

Seth frowned and picked up her hand, gently prising the fingers open. "Nothing?" he demanded in a near growl. "You should have had stitches in that. Damn it, kitten."

He was up again, going into the bathroom, getting things from his backpack. Jessica turned away as he started cleaning the cut, hiding the tears that filled her eyes. Tears caused by the stinging pain, the fatigue and all the turmoil of emotions she had gone through in the last few days. The run-in with Daniels, the fall, the fear. So many emotions and events. One on top of another with no time to assimilate them and put them in order.

And this man gently tending her hand. This man who was kind, gentle, caring, strong, protective, funny. He was everything any woman could ever hope to find in a man.

She felt confused by her reactions to him as well. When had she stopped trying to tell herself the things she felt were because she had needed him in desperate circumstances? She knew she wouldn't see him again after tomorrow. He had given her no information about his identity.

"Kitten," he said softly, turning her face to his. She tried to hide the tears, but he saw them. "Don't cry, love. Don't cry." He lifted her into his arms, holding her and gently stroking her hair. "Does it hurt that much?"

"No." It wasn't the pain or any of the other things. "I just . . ." *think I've fallen in love with you and don't know what to do about it.*

"It's okay, love," he whispered, pulling her closer. "It's okay."

Jessica looked up. Love. Did he mean that or was he just treating her the same way you would treat an injured child? He held her cradled against his shoulder and gently brushed her hair back, tenderly wiping the errant tears with his thumb.

The soft caresses that were meant to be soothing were having a totally different effect. She trembled as he wiped a drop from her cheek. He looked so concerned. She reached up and smoothed the frown from his brow. "I'm fine."

He captured her hand in his and kissed the palm. Jessica trailed her fingers across his lips. How could a mouth that looked so hard be so soft? His eyes held hers for a long moment, golden suns burning her face, taking away her breath. He shifted slightly, turning her in his arms so her breasts pushed against the hard wall of his chest. She couldn't seem to tear her eyes from the heated message in his.

Slowly, he lowered his head until his lips barely touched hers. "So sweet," he murmured against her mouth. "So sweet."

Jessica touched his face again, letting her fingers trail over the varied surfaces. She traced the tiny lines at the corners of his eyes, moving across the taut smooth skin of his cheek down to the slightly rough texture of his jaw, then exploring the hard line around to the center of his chin.

He laid her back on the bed until her head was on the pillow. He gazed at her, propped on one elbow, his hand resting on her waist as it had that morning. Jessica told herself to move, but there was no answering response from her muscles except for a fine tremor as he gently cupped her face. She thought she told herself to speak, but any words were lost as his mouth claimed hers, draining away the last vestige of resistance in her mind. She floated in a timeless world of taste and touch. His tongue teased across her mouth, asking. She gave permission with the slight parting of her lips, and he took possession. Taking and giving, searching and seeking, finding all those hidden places of passion until she was breathless and limp beneath the sensual demand.

He left a string of hot kisses across her face to her ear, pausing to nibble the lobe. The heat of his breath sent tremors down her spine. The hand that had cupped her face only a moment ago slid slowly over the column of her neck until finally he covered her breast.

Jessica realized in some part of her mind that he was still giving her a chance to say no. She couldn't. She needed this man. She pulled his mouth back to hers, seeking the warmth and tenderness he held for her. He lightly stroked across her breast until the nipple was tense under the cloth.

He raised up and stripped off his shirt, tossing it aside. Jessica ran her fingers over his shoulders and down his arms, amazed to see him tremble under her touch. She stroked her fingers across his chest, grazing her nails over his flat nipples. With a groan, he crushed her beneath his weight as his mouth recaptured hers in a demanding kiss. Then he trailed kisses down her throat, pausing to explore the erratic pulse. Lifting himself up again, he helped her take off her shirt. For a long moment he just gazed at her, the golden heat in his eyes as real as any touch. Slowly he reached out and lightly stroked the side of her breast. "You are so beautiful." His voice was ragged, his breath as unsteady as hers.

The light touch sent heat racing through her to settle between her legs. He unsnapped her jeans, then released the zipper. She raised her hips, allowing him to remove the rest of her clothing. He stood, stripping off his own jeans and briefs before lying down next to her, taking her in his arms and pulling her against the heated length of his body.

There was only him. The weight of his leg on hers. The feverish caresses. The searching, seeking heat of his mouth on her breasts, her stomach, her shoulders. The crisp feel of his body hair against smooth skin. The taste of his shoulder on her lips. The movement of the muscles across his back and shoulders beneath her searching fingers.

He took her slowly and gently, his eyes never leaving hers as he parted her thighs and claimed her.

Jessica clung to him desperately. Fear and curiosity mingled with a myriad of sensations. Questions loomed, then burst like a shiny bubble as he pulled her higher and higher until she was teetering on the edge of a precipice high above the world.

For a moment she struggled not to fall. His rhythm shifted, plunging deeper, faster, pushing her over the edge.

She felt the stiffening of his body, the slight convulsive movements. His arm tightened around her, holding her, taking her with him. She clung to him as her body took control away from her, shuddering beneath him. It wasn't fear now, it was ecstasy and wonder that floated her back to the safe harbor of his arms.

Jessica lay still under the weight of his body. She felt limp. Even her fingers and toes were useless. Her breathing gradually steadied and her heart slowed. He moved, exposing her damp skin to the air. She shivered and he covered her, pulling her back into the circle of his arms, cradling her head on his shoulder.

"You are fantastic," he said softly and kissed her temple.

"That never happened before," Jessica said with awe in her voice.

"What never happened before?" he asked, lightly touching her face.

"Like that." She sighed and smiled at him. "It was…" There were no words to use to tell him that at the age of twenty-nine she had never before experienced what she just had. Sex with her former husband had been pleasant sometimes, but mostly disappointing.

"For me, too," he murmured.

Jessica relaxed against him, knowing he didn't understand what she had wanted to say. It wasn't important now. In the morning they would both be gone. He to his new job and she to her own world. That thought filled her with an aching sadness. Not wanting to think about it, she turned, slipping her arm around him, wanting to cling, yet knowing she shouldn't. His arm, firm and strong, tightened around her in response, holding her close.

Later Seth woke and lay holding her, listening to her soft, rhythmic breathing. At last he eased himself from the bed and dressed. He turned the television on, keeping the sound low.

His mouth tightened into a thin line as he looked back to be sure he hadn't disturbed her. She looked so tired. There were shadows beneath the thick, light brown lashes and her mouth, those sweet, soft lips, was compressed. How much pain was she in? Why hadn't the doctor given her a prescription? He didn't like the care she had received. They had never suggested admitting her to the hospital as he had expected. No one had bothered to treat the cuts on her hands. When they got back he would...

Seth felt a weight settle on his shoulders. She'd be gone in the morning. Her friends would arrive and she would leave. Other than last night when she'd been past the point of thinking rationally, she hadn't asked anything about him. He sat down, watching her sleep. He could tell her his name. He could make arrangements to see her, but she hadn't said anything to indicate she wanted that.

At last he turned his eyes to the television screen. His thoughts drifted back to his first marriage. The mistakes hadn't all been his. In fact, they hadn't really been mistakes at all. He and Marion had just been wrong together—two people who had been in love, but hadn't understood each other's needs and hadn't been able to bridge that gap.

That wasn't quite true. They had been too young. And he had been impatient. Not with Marion, but with himself and life. He had been too anxious to climb the ladder and be successful. In his eagerness he hadn't given much thought to what his wife wanted and needed. The constant moves he had found exciting had frightened Marion. She had needed stability and permanence, but in his drive to succeed he hadn't seen that.

She was happy now. She had met a man who worked regular hours. Her life was steady and sure. She had a child as well as her home in the suburbs. And it had been right for them to separate. Though he was alone, he didn't have to feel worried each time he came home late. He didn't feel guilty when his profession demanded that he pull up roots and move two thousand miles. No, it was a lot easier now, without the burden of responsibility for another person's life.

He no longer felt guilty, but he did feel lonely. He hadn't realized until this afternoon how lonely. Sitting and talking with Jessica, he had suddenly noticed how hollow his life had become. There had been many friendships, both male and female, but his encounters with women had all been casual, consisting of dinner, movies, the theater or sports activities. There had only been one serious relationship. That had lasted less than two years before he had transferred again and it hadn't been serious enough for him to suggest she move with him. He was ready for something more, something full and loving, something giving and sharing.

He had shared with Jessica this afternoon. When he had talked about his career he had expressed thoughts and feelings he had never spoken of before. And she had understood.

Seth turned, watching her sleep. She had come so close, given so much of herself and put so much trust in him. He sighed and turned back to the flickering screen. Trust. It had been lacking in his marriage. There had been no trust and no open communication. He glanced again at the woman lying on the bed. Had he broken her confidence in him by yielding to his desires? There was a wariness in her green eyes that told him she had been hurt in the past. He didn't want to hurt her again.

Jessica looked at him through half-open eyes. He was far away somewhere. He sat in the chair, his feet propped on the corner of her bed, eyes staring blankly at the television, but he wasn't focusing.

What would it be like to share every day with him? To wake each morning next to him and see those warm, brown eyes looking at her. To begin each day wrapped in the scent of his body. It was funny, but she couldn't remember Chad having a special smell. His after-shave, maybe, not him.

But then nothing that had happened earlier could be related to any past personal experiences. She had heard of chemical reactions, but never believed in them. She had read about relationships filled with fireworks, but hers hadn't been. Even now, just watching him, her body warmed with the memories.

What she was feeling was mixed up in too many crazy emotions: fear, need, pain, dependency. In ordinary circumstances when she wasn't afraid and wasn't desperate for help would it be the same?

Jessica had realized long ago that her marriage had been torn apart by the demands of separate careers. She or Chad had always been working or attending some job-related function. There had never been time to talk. And when they were together, they were too tired to respond to each other's emotional needs.

There had never been weekends like this, when they could touch each other without the outside world intruding. Even if there had been would they have done more than bicker? Would they have gotten past the point of his accusing her of not understanding? Somehow she doubted it. She had made Chad feel threatened, though she hadn't meant to. And that threat had spilled over into their personal lives.

Chad had never made love to her as Seth had. He had never held her. He had never touched her, caressing each inch of her body as if she were beautiful and desirable. And she had never experienced the level of passion she had with Seth. When she got home she was going to have to do a lot of thinking about a number of things.

She looked at him through her lashes. "Are you watching that—" she pointed to the wrestling match on the television "—or is it just background for your thoughts?" Sometimes when she got home in the evenings she couldn't relax without the dull drone of the television. There were always monitors on at work, always noise. Chad had claimed it was a way to cut him off.

"Just background, want me to turn it off?" He remembered that his habit of watching had driven Marion crazy.

"No, it doesn't bother me." She looked at him for a moment. "Are you wishing you'd left?"

"No." He smiled and stretched. "Just wishing... It wasn't important." He stood and looked down at her. "So, do you want to go out dancing or shall we dine in tonight?"

Jessica looked down at the cast sticking from under the blanket. "Definitely dancing. The Ritz, I think."

"I don't think they'll let me in without a tie and I didn't pack one." He picked up the menu and looked at it a moment. "You didn't make it through that steak last night. Do you want to try again?"

He was spending so much money. "Are you a multi-millionaire?"

"Many times over." He moved to the bed and sat beside her. "Kitten, I can afford it, really. I make a very good salary and there's just me. I'm not in debt except for my car. Buying you a steak isn't going to break me."

"I'm sorry," she said, feeling embarrassed. "I don't usually ask such tactless questions."

"It's forgivable and under the circumstances, quite proper. I'm glad you care enough to ask." He smiled at her. "So, now that you've found out my financial status, what else would you like to know?"

"Everything." Everything that was possible to know about a person. What foods he liked and didn't like. If he liked his shirts starched. What his favorite color was.

"That, kitten, would take a lifetime." He turned to pick up the phone.

A lifetime is what I need, Jessica thought, turning away when she saw him withdraw, his eyes losing their sunny warmth. A lifetime of waking up next to him and talking with him every day. I only have one night left of that life.

"Now that you know all my personal data, it's your turn."

Jessica smiled. "I make a good salary and I'm not in debt, not even for my car. And there's just me." Pushing herself up, she wrapped the blanket around her and looked at her jeans, shirt and underwear, which had been tossed haphazardly to the floor. "Would you, please?" She gestured toward the floor.

Seth gathered the clothes and laid them on the bed. She looked awkward and unsure. She probably needed a little space. "I'll step out and let you get dressed."

Jessica watched the door close, sudden tears pricking her eyes. Neither of them had been embarrassed earlier. Neither of them had been embarrassed when he had helped her in and out of the tub, or the morning before when they had lain together in the sleeping bag. Slowly she pulled on her clothes, knotting the shirt at her waist.

When Seth returned there was a tension in the air, an uneasiness, that hadn't been there earlier. Neither seemed to have anything to say to the other, where only a couple of hours earlier conversation had flowed steadily. He changed the channel to look at the news.

Jessica watched too, noting several mistakes, a badly read introduction and the wrong tape run twice. That crew could make a mess of the best story. She would have to spend the next few weekends working or when the new news director saw that mess they would all be out on their ears.

They ate in silence. Jessica couldn't look at him. The air felt heavy and weighted. Was it embarrassment? Maybe, but she wasn't ashamed. But then again—regret? Did he wish he hadn't? Maybe she shouldn't have done it. Only time and distance would really put things in perspective. She sipped the milk he had ordered, feeling nervous and unsure. Perhaps she should have demanded that Emily come today. She shouldn't have stayed and let this happen. She shouldn't be here like this.

They finished eating and he stacked the dishes and put them outside the door. Why was he here? Was he afraid she was so helpless she couldn't have ordered a meal for herself? Or had he simply stayed to get again what he had gotten before? She didn't want to think thoughts like that. Jessica looked around the room, searching for something to occupy them. Finally she picked up the television guide and scanned the lists. "Do you like silly old horror films?"

"Love them. Is one on?"

"Yes." She changed the channel and then loosened the knot in the shirt and lay down on the bed, her head at the foot. She didn't look at him when he eased down beside her, a little space between them. Still that strange tension hung in the air.

Briefly she regretted her inexperience, wishing she knew what the protocol for such a situation was. Surely there was some standard way of handling casual sexual encounters in this day and age. Only for her this hadn't been casual. Yet she knew she couldn't tell him how she felt. That much she didn't need experience to understand. Instead, she forced her attention to the film, laughing at the story and the jokes Seth made. When the heroine opened a box that turned out to be full of rats, Jessica yelped and dived under Seth's arm, laughing at herself even as she did.

"I don't believe it," he said, chuckling. "You're scared."

She smiled sheepishly. "Afraid so. I love these things, but I get frightened every time."

"This could be fun." He tightened his arm around her, pulling her close to the warmth of his body. "I hope this film is just full of scary things." He kissed her hair.

"I've seen it before," she confessed, "but I just can't seem to help it." At that moment one of the rats ran across the screen and Jessica shuddered, dropping her head forward.

Seth looked at the exposed neck so close to him and bent to lightly kiss her nape. "Watching a horror film with you is delightful."

Jessica turned slightly and looked up, her spine tingling from the brief touch of his lips. "You're getting hysterical again," she teased. And so was she. His kiss had just been a light touch, but it had sent shivers all the way down to her toes.

"I know. You have a habit of doing that to me."

Her gaze collided with his. His honey-brown eyes were burning now with the heat of a tropical sun. They were golden pools of light enticing her, luring her deeper into their depths. Pools burning with desire. Desire for her. She couldn't remember any man ever looking at her with such open passion, such demanding hunger.

For a long moment neither of them moved. His eyes held hers. She needed this man, whoever he was, and this was the only time she would have with him. She turned, relaxing against the arm that held her. His hand slid beneath her shirt, flattening her stomach, his eyes never leaving her face.

The world receded. There was only him. The touch of his lips on hers, the searing heat of his fingers where they rested against her skin. With a small sigh, her lips parted. He answered with a low groan as his tongue instantly took possession, delving deeply, exploring and caressing, until she was breathless and dizzy with the impact.

Seth lifted his head and gazed down at her flushed face. Her lips were slightly parted and swollen from his kisses. His stomach tightened at the invitation he read in the green eyes that met his so openly. "I can't remember wanting someone as much as I want you."

The words took her breath away and made her heart trip. Jessica didn't know what to say. He slipped his hand from under her shirt and lightly traced the planes of her face.

She was so special. A brave, valiant lady who lay by him, unafraid and willing. "Kitten, are you going to regret this?"

The question she had asked herself an hour ago with no answer now had an answer with no doubt. "No. I'll never regret this time with you." She reached out and slowly unbuttoned his shirt, letting herself explore his chest, the smooth hard muscles, the thick dark hair that curled crisply beneath her fingers. "No, I'm not sorry," she said softly, pushing the shirt off his shoulders.

"I don't want you to be." Still he waited. He combed his fingers through the thick waves of her hair, brushing it back from her face. He cared about her. "I know I shouldn't be taking advantage of you, but ever since yesterday morning... You're a very special lady, kitten. I want to make love to you."

"Love me," she whispered. "Please love me."

She never knew when or how her clothes came off, only that they were gone, as were his. The hard, heated length of him was pressed against her. She felt the roughness of his thigh next to hers, the brush of his chest against her breasts and stomach. The firmness of his back beneath her searching fingers. The taste of his shoulder and neck and mouth on her lips.

She wondered at her hands. Hands that seemed to possess an innate knowledge of how and where to touch him. She had the power to make him respond to her, just as she was responding to him, trembling under his touch. She gave herself up to instinct, letting her fingers tangle in his hair. Her body arched to meet him, aching with a need only he could satisfy. She clung to him fiercely as he gently opened her thighs to take final possession. He thrust slowly into her, filling her with the power of his body.

It was a heated branding that claimed her for his, a branding she willingly accepted. They moved, meeting and parting to meet again in an elemental rhythm belonging to the timeless world they now shared. A world where man and woman were one, where bodies and minds fused into a single entity for the space of an eternal moment.

When their hearts had slowed and their breathing returned to normal they lay talking in the flickering light cast by the forgotten television screen. The talk slowed, turning to soft touches, sweetly murmured words. They made love again.

Jessica turned as Seth moved away from her a little later. He kissed her lips lightly, gently stroking the hair back from her cheek.

"Go back to sleep. I'm just going to turn off the lights."

Though she missed the heat of his body next to hers, Jessica was content to stay in the warmth of the bed as Seth walked around the room. A teaser for the upcoming newscast penetrated her dreamy thoughts. The world seemed far away and unimportant and not quite real. All that mattered was what had occurred this afternoon.

Not only the intimate moments, but everything that had happened between them, from their conversations earlier to the silences they had shared. A warning voice inside her told her it wasn't real. How could something that was an accident be the real thing? She knew nothing about him. Her heart insisted she knew everything she needed to know, but her thoughts continued to waver. It was a fantasy and a mistake. Not a mistake she would regret, but still a mistake to have let this happen. She shook her head. No, she would never regret these moments—this time and this feeling they had shared—but it just wasn't reality.

Jessica opened her eyes drowsily and glanced up at the television, then at the man who had been holding her only moments ago. Seth was sprawled in a chair, his attention fully on the broadcast. He sat much as he had earlier this afternoon, feet propped on the end of the bed, head tipped back to watch the screen.

Something teased at the back of her mind, something uncomfortable that disturbed her drifting state of half sleep. Uneasiness began to replace the lassitude in her limbs. Earlier the TV had obviously been background noise—just as she was used to. After hearing monitors eight or ten hours a day it was hard to think in silence, almost unnatural. It could mean nothing, but then he had been so attuned to her this afternoon, so understanding of the problems she had at work, at least those she had mentioned. And she had understood him just as well. Again she glanced over at him, remembering how he had turned to the news earlier. Hadn't he said he was a corporate wonder boy?

Jessica's eyes widened as everything fell into place. He had even told her he was being transferred. It had to be. There couldn't be that much coincidence. Heart pounding, she curled her fingers tightly in the blanket. "Seth?"

He glanced over at the tense sound of her voice and immediately moved to the bed, sitting down next to her and smoothing her hair back from her face. "Go to sleep, kitten. I didn't mean to wake you."

She wished she could rest again, but she had to know. She wished she could lay her head on his shoulder and go to sleep without thinking, but her fears couldn't be ignored. "You said you were being transferred?"

"Yes, I am."

"To where?"

"Atlanta."

He hadn't been at the station. She would have recognized him had he ever been there. An even worse thought crossed her mind. If he was who she thought, then Gerald Daniels had known the position was filled before he had even suggested they talk about the promotion. He had known this man was going to be the news director before he had suggested dinner to Jessica. If she had had any doubts about Daniels' intentions she had none now.

Seth felt her muscles tighten against him. He had no idea what had made her so upset. He slipped under the covers, taking her in his arms and gently stroking her back, holding her close. "What's wrong, kitten? Is your ankle hurting? Your hand?"

Jessica shook her head. Why hadn't she put it together this afternoon before they had made love? Why hadn't she figured out everything then? "Are you in television?" she demanded abruptly.

"Yes. Why?" She lay still as his hand gently cupped her face. "Kitten?" The wariness was back in her eyes.

"At Channel 9?"

Seth looked down at her as he suddenly realized what she meant. "You applied for the position at 9?"

Jessica didn't bother to remind him she had said she was already there. She didn't bother to remind him she had said she was doing both jobs. She simply nodded.

"My God. I'm sorry, kitten."

"Me, too," she murmured and started to turn away, but he tightened his grip, stopping her. "I'm sorry this happened."

Seth looked down at her, but she turned her face away. He had only meant he was sorry he had the job she had obviously wanted so badly. He certainly had no regrets about anything else, but her response told him she meant something more. "You're sorry what happened?"

Again she tried to move and again he tightened his hold. "Us. This." She tugged futilely at the sheet. She felt trapped. Her life, which had already been complicated, was now an impossible mess. "Why didn't you tell me who you were?" she demanded.

"What was I supposed to do, pull you out of the ravine and give you my life history?" Seth regretted the sharp answer as soon as it was out of his mouth, but she had hurt him by saying she felt regrets.

"Maybe not then," Jessica retorted, stressing the last word.

"It wouldn't have changed anything, kitten."

"It would have changed everything." She looked at him, her heart breaking. She would rather have had an intact dream to cherish than lose again. She would rather have taken home the memory of these two days than face the reality of watching it wither and dry. She had needed a fantasy more than she needed reality. "It does change everything."

Seth reached for her again, wanting to ease the pain and fear. "Kitten—"

"No." Jessica tried again to move away, but the cast and the fact she had no clothes on kept her in the bed and easily within his reach.

"I'm sorry you didn't get the job, kitten." Seth pulled her back into the circle of his arms. "I'm not sorry about the rest." He didn't understand her reaction, yet he didn't doubt that he had found someone very special. She was brave and courageous, spirited and strong. She was open and trusting. She had given him so much of herself in the last two days, not only physically but emotionally as well.

He knew she was someone he could relate to on all levels. Hadn't they already proved that? Their long talks about their jobs, the way they had worked together to get her out, and then tonight they had shared something that went deeper than a casual physical encounter. Holding her, loving her, had opened something within him, something he didn't want to lose.

"Jessica."

"I don't want to talk."

She didn't know what to do or say. She had walked out on her job in anger because of harassment and into the arms of the man who would be her direct supervisor.

"Kitten, I know you wanted the job. I—"

"It's not the job," Jessica muttered.

"Then what?"

"I don't want to talk now." She didn't want to tell him again she regretted what had happened. She didn't want to, but she would.

Jessica lay rigidly on her side of the bed remembering the jealousy and bitterness over the last months of her marriage. She had been working hard and putting in long hours. Chad had made it more difficult with petty demands and derisive comments. She had been hurt and confused, but she hadn't slowed down. She had kept trying, both at work and at home. And she had finally gotten the promotion. Excited and happy, she had rushed home to fix a special dinner. She had even bought champagne to celebrate.

She had rushed to Chad when he came in, wanting to share her happiness. Chad had leaned back and crossed his arms, his look one of disgust. "You must be better in bed when there's a reward."

She had jerked back as if he had slapped her. "What?"

"Don't play the innocent with me," Chad sneered. "There's only one way a woman makes it. In bed."

Since then she had never let her business and personal life overlap except with one or two female friends. Until now.

Seth watched Jessica push the eggs around on her plate. He didn't understand what had happened. Other than insisting it wasn't because he had the news director position she had told him nothing. Nor had she let him touch her again. He had refused to leave the bed so they had slept together, yet they couldn't have been farther apart if they had been in different cities.

He had tried repeatedly to talk with her this morning, but she had erected a wall around herself. "Jessica, I think you at least owe me an explanation as to why you're so upset." He had suggested he wait until her friends arrived and she had adamantly refused, requesting that he go. "I'm not leaving until I understand what's going on here."

Jessica looked at him a moment. Where before she had been able to read his thoughts through the sunny windows of his eyes, now she couldn't. The eyes that had laughed with her, warmed her and made love to her were dark and shuttered. There was no teasing demand for a smile. There was no passion demanding a response, only a blank she couldn't begin to decipher.

She did owe him an explanation. What had happened was no more his fault than hers. "I've made it a practice never to combine my personal and professional life," she answered at last. "We didn't know, but I wish this weekend had never happened."

Seth would have laughed with relief had she not looked so serious. "Is that all? The fact that you and I know each other and will be working together?"

"Is that all?" Jessica demanded. "That's enough. It changes everything."

"Jessica, I've dated people I work with before. It's no problem." Mature adults were easily able to keep one part of their life from spilling over into another.

"I was married to someone in the same field and it was a problem."

She was serious, he realized, and he thought about all she had been through in the last few days. Her face was drawn, her eyes shadowed. He rounded the table and pulled her to her feet. "Kitten, it really doesn't have to be that way."

"Please go. Emily will be here soon."

Each time he tried she withdrew further and became more upset. "Okay, kitten," he said with a sigh. He tipped her face up and kissed her, drinking in the scent of her hair and skin, delving into the sweet warmth of her mouth. Finally he released her. "I don't understand, but for me nothing has changed."

"Everything has changed," Jessica muttered, fighting back the tears. "I want you to go. Now."

It was wrong to leave her this way, but as much as he wanted to stay he had no right to push. Seth bent and picked up his pack. At the door he turned. "What are you going to do?"

"I don't know."

Chapter Five

Jessica's eyes roamed restlessly over the room, not seeing the gray sectional sofa or the chrome and glass tables and lamps, or the colorful pop art posters. She moved her leg restlessly, readjusted the pillow and settled back into the corner of the sofa. It had been a week today and she still didn't know what she was going to do.

She had cried that morning until her eyes were red and sore. Emily and her boyfriend, Jeff, had thought she was either in terrible pain or that something much worse than a fall had happened. She hadn't told them the truth. She wouldn't have been able to explain. She had just said it had all caught up to her at once.

Now it was the constant feeling of emptiness and loss that wore on her. She knew what had happened. It was logical, reasonable and not something about which she felt shame or guilt. She had been hurt, alone and yes, even frightened. She had been in pain and tired to the point of exhaustion. Yet she didn't feel used. She hadn't been manipulated or forced in any way. It had been her choice to respond. Seth had been the most attractive man she had ever met and what had developed was . . . understandable. She had rationalized those hours spent with him, explained them. She even accepted them without regret.

But what she hadn't been able to comprehend was what was happening now. She didn't understand the emptiness that plagued her constantly. It was a hollow feeling that nothing sated. It wasn't hunger for a certain food or activity. It was a relentless hunger for a certain person. "It's ridiculous," she muttered irritably, "absolutely ridiculous." Jessica Buchanan did not believe in love at first sight. She didn't really believe in love at all, and she definitely didn't think she could have fallen in love with a man she didn't know. She could hardly believe she had slept with him and at moments she seriously doubted the ecstasy she had found in his arms.

Only in the dreams that haunted her restless nights did she not doubt. Only in the dreams of a kiss, a touch, a whispered word, a golden-eyed glance did she believe with her unguarded heart. But those same dreams woke her each night. No, not the dreams. Her hands that reached to touch and hold, only to come away cold and empty, woke her. And in those first moments of waking, when reality was a mist, the emptiness was a pain that constricted her chest and tightened her throat. And she had so many wishes, too. She wished one of them wasn't involved in television. She wished it could have remained a platonic relationship.

"You certainly have been very quiet all weekend," Emily said, interrupting her aimless thoughts.

"Just thinking."

Emily flopped down on the opposite end of the sofa. Jessica and Emily had been best friends since the seventh grade. As teenagers, they had shared everything about their lives, even though they had chosen to go to different colleges. The fat letters and long phone calls had kept them in touch and informed. Now there were things Jessica didn't talk about, and she was sure Emily hadn't told her everything, either. But they still turned to each other for advice and support.

"Is your ankle bothering you?" Emily asked.

"No." The break had been much worse than the first doctor had said. Jessica had been ordered to stay completely off her feet for the entire week, but after two days of sitting at home she had rebelled and gone to work. Emily had protested vehemently and Jessica wasn't about to admit that it hurt now.

"Work?"

Jessica shook her head. "It's nothing, really."

Emily twisted around on the sofa, watching her. "You aren't having more problems with Daniels, are you?"

Jessica smiled ruefully. "No." She wasn't having any problems with Gerald Daniels because he had refused to acknowledge she was still an employee. He wouldn't talk with her and when she had returned to work he'd informed her there would be no more evening meetings to critique the newscast until the news director started. Even then he didn't think it would be necessary for her to attend.

"Em, I've been doing a lot of thinking." It had been a circular type of thinking with no answers, but she had to open some escape hatches. She had no idea what would happen tomorrow or next week. "I've decided to get out of television." That much she was fairly certain about, just not when or what she would do when she did.

"Jessica! That's absolutely wonderful."

"It's absolutely frightening," she countered.

"Why? You've been miserable for a long time. It can't do anything but make your life better."

"I've got years of my life tied up in television. It's a lot of time to throw away. I'm going to be starting over, you know. I think it's scary."

"All that time you spent won't be lost, Jessica. You've learned a lot, both good and bad. You've advanced into a management level position where you're directing people and you're responsible for their actions. All that's good, no matter what you decide to do. It's not a loss at all."

"I know." Jessica sighed and shifted on the sofa. "I've told myself all that too, but I'm still going to be starting over." She was throwing away five years of her life, five years of hard work. But when she thought of staying another five years she knew she couldn't do it. Somehow she had to get back to that other woman, the happy one that used to live inside her, the happy one she had found last weekend.

She had tried to decide how much of a part the past weekend was playing in her decision. She had thought she would come back and just quit. But she couldn't. She dreaded next week, but she had already made several major mistakes because she had reacted emotionally. She was trying not to make any more decisions like that.

She wouldn't have walked out and she wouldn't have let Daniels get to her so much if she had really loved the job. It would have just been a problem to put up with and ignore because the rest of the job was so exciting. That, however, was the key. She could find no satisfaction in anything dealing with news anymore.

"The best thing that has happened to me in years is probably what Daniels did." But she knew it wasn't Gerald Daniels that had changed. It was herself. Her life had lost its balance. She needed to put things in perspective again.

"If it's had this result, I agree." Emily smiled. "So, when are you going to do it?"

"I guess I should stay for a while yet," Jessica said at last. "It wouldn't really be fair to walk out now. Not during the transition."

"You don't owe them a thing," Emily declared vehemently.

"Maybe I don't. But I do need a recommendation. After all, my only job before this was at the newspaper. And I was there for just a year. Besides, staying a while will give me time to look around."

They sat talking for a long time, discussing the options. When Emily said again she thought Jessica should just quit, Jessica smiled and shook her head. "I really want to leave on good terms, Em. If I stay I might be able to do it. If not I'll at least know I gave it my best try."

Emily sighed. "You're crazy. You'll just get sucked deeper and deeper into that morass. You should resign tomorrow."

"No, I won't get in any deeper. But my conscience demands that I stay. If I see things are getting worse I'll go ahead and quit."

Jessica lay in the warm cocoon of her bed and watched the minutes blink past. 5:30. The blue digital numbers were the only light in the dark room. 5:31. She should be sleeping, not staring at the clock, but the nervous knot in her stomach told her she wouldn't sleep any more. 5:32. It was going to be a very long day. Seth was starting as news director. 5:33. She needed to be ready for anything. Anything from not being introduced to him by Gerald Daniels to being expected to go to dinner with him immediately after work. 5:34. The odds—and her hopes—were much greater for the first than the second. She didn't want to have to face him today. 5:35. She didn't want to have to face today at all.

Crawling from the warmth of the bed, she struggled to the bathroom. Nothing was simple with a cast weighting down one leg. In order to keep the cast dry she soaked half the bathroom as she showered. After mopping the floor and cleaning up the mess, she hobbled into the kitchen and started the coffee. It was too much trouble to even sit down so she propped herself against the counter and stared sightlessly out the small window as the coffee brewed.

At last the coffee was ready and she worked her way back to the bedroom, wondering how the handicapped survived. Sitting on the bed, she drank the coffee slowly. But at last it was gone and this morning it didn't seem worth the effort to get another cup. She certainly didn't need the caffeine to wake her up.

"What's wrong?" Emily's dark head appeared in the doorway.

Jessica glanced at the clock. "Nothing. I'm sorry I woke you."

Emily yawned and stretched. "Having second thoughts about quitting?"

"No." She was having second thoughts about her decision to stay and face Seth again. Jessica glanced at the empty coffee cup. "Would you mind?" She hated asking. It was bad enough having to ask at any time, but when it was something she really could manage, even if just barely, she hated to do it.

"Ah, coffee," Emily sighed. "It's going to be a good day."

For you, Jessica thought sadly. For me it's another story altogether.

After a long moment Emily spoke again. "Jess, I know the promotion thing pushed you over the edge, but what really made you decide to quit?"

"He, I—" The question had caught her off guard. "I had a lot of time to think." She sat her cup on the nightstand, keeping her face turned from Emily. "There's not much else to do in a ravine."

"And?" Emily prompted, obviously very awake.

"And I realized I don't love what I'm doing." Seth had said the words and she had agreed. More importantly, though, she had promised to think about what he said and Jessica always kept her promises.

She remembered the excitement in his voice as he talked about his job, the eagerness to face a challenge that had sparkled in his warm, brown eyes. He had had doubts. He had known that what he was facing was difficult, but beneath his concern had been the joy of doing something he loved, a love that couldn't be killed by a few hard days or a few rotten people.

"No, you don't," Emily agreed after a thoughtful silence. "You did love what you were doing at the newspaper." Bouncing off the bed, she laughed. "You even loved it when you were writing obituaries."

Yes, she had, she thought as Emily picked up her cup and left the room. That happiness had been marred by Chad's jealousy, but she had loved her job then and even if it meant starting over, she would find something she loved again.

"I'm going to go shower." Emily stood up, smiling. "The world awaits."

The anticipation she saw in Emily's face was the feeling Jessica wanted to find again. She sighed, sat down in front of the mirror and picked up the blow dryer.

"You aren't dressed?" Emily asked from behind her as Jessica stared at the closet. Last night she had decided on a suit, but this morning she wasn't so sure. "Do you think a suit—or maybe a dress?"

"Oh Jess, I'd forgotten. The corporate wonder boy starts today, doesn't he?"

"Yes." Jessica grimaced and decided on the suit. It wouldn't really matter what she wore, anyway. The look of any outfit was destroyed by the crutches and flat loafer she had on her left foot. "I know I should feel privileged to have the opportunity to work with 'God'." The memos that had been circulated about Seth's arrival had made it sound like an angel personified was arriving.

"Come on, Jess, you know it's all hype."

"Yeah, I know." She glanced at Emily as she buttoned the cream-colored silk blouse. "It's just that..." She fell silent. She couldn't explain, not even to Emily.

Jessica felt as if something disastrous were about to happen. She told herself that the worst thing would be being fired and, though it would make life difficult, it wouldn't be a disaster. But the feeling of impending doom persisted.

Channel 9, WAKQ, was located on a back street of midtown Atlanta. It was an old two-story building, boxy and unattractive. From the outside it looked more like a factory than a television station, but once inside there was no doubt this was the world of glamour the public imagined.

The lobby was huge. Large, thickly padded modular furniture was grouped in several conversational settings, all of them managing to face the large screen television that dominated the wall opposite the door. The set was never turned off and it was always tuned to Channel 9. The floor of the lobby was covered with a thick, plush, dark blue carpet. The two outside walls of the area were solid glass. They overlooked the street, parking lot and choked expressway system beyond. Above and to either side of the television screen were ten-by-twelve glossy photographs of all the anchor people and celebrities of Channel 9.

Once inside the main part of the television station Jessica could feel the tension. The main floor was dominated by the news department with all its editing rooms, work areas for the reporters, weather forecasting offices and studios.

With each step she took she could feel the tension rise and as she entered the maze of her world she tried to readjust her thinking. The last time they had changed news directors she had been a young reporter. Three years ago she had been nervous and tense, not knowing what to expect. This time she was on the front line. Working her way through the maze of cubicles, she wished for a moment she was just a reporter again.

It wasn't uncommon in other fields for there to be general firings when new management took over. It was easier to start with your own people than to wait for an old crew, used to different techniques, to adjust. And a few strong-arm tactics always forced those who hadn't been fired to keep protests to themselves or face the same consequences. Jessica paused at the door to her office and looked around the slowly waking newsroom, then, consciously pushing her own fears aside, she turned her attention to the work that needed to be done.

"Busy? Want to go get some lunch?"
Jessica turned from the monitors and shook her head.

The noon show had looked awful. Everything had gone wrong, and Neil, an experienced reporter, was clearly trying to take her mind off the situation. "No, thanks, Neil."

"It's not going to help to starve to death," Neil scolded gently.

"Did you see the noon show?"

He nodded. "Everyone is jumpy. It won't change anything to sit here and fret about it."

Jessica smiled. Neil could play a good bluff. He was worried, too. "If I am fretting it's because nothing I can do will help." She straightened some papers on her desk and looked up again. "Has he made an appearance yet?"

"He's in the building. He came in about ten and he's been upstairs ever since."

"After the memos last week I would have thought his arrival would have been accompanied by a clap of thunder at the very least."

Neil laughed. "Good girl. Don't let it get to you."

"I'm not worried about me." What was bothering her at the moment was that her overreaction and walking out a week ago meant she was valueless on the front line. What news director, even Seth, was going to trust her after that type of hysterical behavior? It wasn't her job she was worried about as much as the way she had let her co-workers down.

"Then what is it?" Neil pushed the door shut and sat in the chair next to her desk.

"It's that I can't help anyone here." Neil started to speak but she shook her head. "I don't mean with their nerves but later on. I just know Cameron isn't going to listen to me about anything after that crazy stunt I pulled."

"Jess, you're jumping to conclusions. We all have days and situations we can't handle. You came up against one. If he's worth the title he won't base his opinions about you on what Daniels says."

Jessica shrugged. "And while he's busy making up his mind about me he'll be busy making up his mind about a few others. What if he comes to the wrong decision because they're having a bad day and he still doesn't believe I'm reliable?"

"You aren't responsible for everyone in this department, Jess. And you are allowed a few mistakes yourself." Neil glanced around the office. "You need to get some fresh air and clear that mind of yours."

"My mind is very clear today," she assured him. "Clearer than it has been in a good while, in fact."

"Why today of all days?" Neil asked.

Neil had been with the station for fifteen years. He was an excellent reporter who could handle any assignment. He had acted as her mentor and guide from the day she had been assigned to work with him during her internship. When she had been hired full-time she had turned to him for advice and help, and he had pulled her out of a few near disasters. Neil had never wanted to climb the ladder. He said he wasn't cut out for it and was happy doing exactly what he was doing. "Because I'm going to quit."

"Why?"

The question was asked calmly. It was another thing about Neil she liked. He rarely, if ever, got excited, and he always wanted the facts before he started offering advice and judgment. "I'm not happy. I'm just tired of it all. Like today. You know and I know and everyone out there knows I'm on shaky ground. If I wasn't I would have already been upstairs to meet Cameron." Jessica knew her reactions were ambivalent. She was not ready to face Seth.

Nor did she like admitting she had failed at a job, which is what not being introduced to Seth meant.

"Jess, I know things have been rough recently," Neil said, "but you're good at the job. You're damned good. Don't let one setback do this to you."

"Being good doesn't mean I'm happy. It's not just today or last week. It's the whole thing. I don't find my job satisfying anymore. If it was it would be like it was at first when I learned to deal with the aspects I didn't like and to put them in perspective. I can't. I just can't find any rewards in the work anymore."

"What are you going to do?"

"I'm not sure. I think I'd like to go back into print. I'm still in the thinking stages." Neil looked discouraged. "I'm not going to make any big announcements around here yet," she assured the older man. "I don't want to leave things like they are. When I walk out it's going to be because I want to."

"You had me worried for a minute." Neil smiled. "Don't make any rash decisions, kid. Things have been rough around here. You've been doing your job and acting as news director, too. That's not an easy load to carry. Maybe if you get a few nights of sleep the world will look better."

"Maybe it will." The tension around Neil's blue eyes eased a little with her agreement. Neil would think about it, ask her a few questions and, she felt sure, eventually understand and support whatever decision she made.

The tension within the news department increased with each minute. Jessica forced her attention to the six o'clock news. That was her baby. She was the one who decided which stories to run, in what order and how they would be covered. She also made sure the producers of the other shows followed her lead.

At three the expected announcement of a general staff meeting was finally made. It was standard for it to be held when new executives were hired, but no mention had been made until late afternoon, and then it had also been announced that attendance was mandatory. There had been more than a few grumbles and complaints at that.

Shortly after the announcement Trish Larkin, a reporter, rushed into Jessica's office, saying she couldn't possibly stay for the meeting. Jessica's brief reminder that attendance was mandatory was met with a flurry of childish excuses. "It has to be your decision, Trish," she said at last, bringing the younger woman's stream of words to a halt.

Jessica watched as Trish hurried from the office. The younger woman didn't have what it took to be a reporter. She had been with the station for a little less than a year and still hadn't learned to cover a story. Trish would definitely be one of the first to go.

With a sigh, Jessica finished checking the newscast, cleared her desk and sat back to watch the monitors, one for her station and one for each of the competitors. She only half paid attention, her mind drifting back to that weekend.

Seth hadn't seen this as a problem. He saw no conflict in having a relationship with an employee. He had even admitted he had dated more than one woman he had worked with and it had been fine. For him maybe, but what about for the woman?

Had anyone ever accused his girlfriends of sleeping their way up? Had anyone ever accused them of only holding their job because they were having an affair with the boss? It had happened to her once at a time when there was no possible justification for the remark. It had made her doubly aware of how easily relationships could be misconstrued.

"You ready for this?" Neil asked from the doorway.

"As ready as I'll ever be." She stood and turned off the monitors.

"Never got the big call to meet him?"

"No."

The second studio had been filled with folding chairs, and a table had been placed at one end. The staff was pouring into the room now, speculation and supposition rampant in the low-toned voices around her. Jessica chose a chair to one side where the cast and crutches wouldn't be in everyone's way.

The door opened and Gerald Daniels stepped through, followed by the man of the hour.

She had thought she was ready for this moment. She had thought she was prepared to see him this way. But she wasn't. Her body, sensing her confused response, reacted with its own discomfiture. Her heart slowed, then pounded frantically, sending a dizzying rush of blood to her face. Daniels moved to the center of the table and smiled benevolently at everyone. Seth Cameron looked slowly around the room with a gaze that expressed confidence and control. Before his eyes reached her corner Jessica looked down, concentrating on her tightly folded hands.

Daniels began speaking, extolling the virtues of the man on his right. After the first few words, Jessica paid no attention to what was said, but she knew when Seth started speaking. His voice had a resonant timbre that set up a harmonic vibration within her own body. She was drawn like a magnet to the sound and slowly looked up, peeking through her lashes. He was looking at her!

It had been seven days, seven years, seven decades since he had left her, closing the door on her life. Slowly she opened her right hand and stared at the thin red scar there. Gently she traced the line with the index finger of her left hand. She had walked out of the newsroom because of implied sexual harassment and had ended up sleeping with her new boss. Her stomach churned at the thought, and Jessica closed her eyes tightly.

Another part of her scorned the idea. He knew she hadn't known the true situation. She was as innocent as he had been. He understood that what had happened between them was something totally separate and apart.

A feeling of total despair settled over her. Then it had been separate and apart. It never could be again. Why couldn't he have been an accountant or a salesman? Her first marriage had been broken up by jealousy and competition. She couldn't go through it again, not with him.

"Jess, are you all right?"

Neil's whispered question broke into her confusion. "What?"

"Are you all right?"

"Yes," she murmured, her quick nod more the answer than the whisper of sound.

Slowly she looked up again. He was looking at another part of the room. For a moment she allowed herself to study the angular planes of his face, the hard angle of his jaw, the dark eyes and the firm, straight line of his mouth as he listened to a comment being made by Daniels. He had had his hair cut. The soft, teasing curls at his nape were gone. But his suit fit his broad shoulders with the same ease that the flannel shirts had.

He had asked her if she would regret what had happened. Never. No, she would never regret those beautiful hours spent with him. But she would agonize over every encounter from now on.

She had wanted to pretend it hadn't really happened, but it had. For the last week she had tried to convince herself she could approach the situation calmly and rationally. She couldn't. As much as she had tried to persuade herself otherwise, it hadn't just been something casual and meaningless. At least not for her.

Everyone was getting up and moving toward the front of the room. Jessica forced her frozen muscles to function and stood, positioning the crutches under her arms before turning toward the door. Neil was facing the center table, and Jessica felt a surge of panic streak red-hot through her veins. "Neil, can we go now?" It was a desperate whisper, the fear barely suppressed.

Neil paused and glanced at her. "Don't you think you should at least say hello? That's the point of these things."

She wasn't a newcomer to television. She knew the point. To see and be seen and she had been seen. "No." She knew she wouldn't be able to explain to Neil, but he knew her well enough to know she was upset and simply nodded. It took endless minutes to work her way to the door. Everyone else was moving in Seth's direction.

"You should probably at least say hello," Neil advised as she reached the doorway. "It might help."

She could not pretend to meet him for the first time now, while Gerald Daniels and everyone in the room were watching. She couldn't calmly introduce herself and she certainly wasn't going to let anyone know they knew each other.

"No. I can't now. I'll meet him soon enough." She saw Neil's surprise and paused, leaning heavily on the crutches. "I'm sorry, Neil. You stay if you like." She wasn't being fair to Neil, who still wanted a future in television.

"Are you all right, kid?"

"It's just a headache. Guess I should have eaten some lunch." It was a lame excuse and they both knew it.

"Why don't you come home with me? You know Beth always loves to have you." Neil helped her into her coat, obviously worried. "It would give us a chance to talk, Jess."

Talk was the one thing she wanted to avoid tonight. She needed time to make plans, to decide—she just needed some time. "No. Please, just take me home." Again she saw the puzzlement in his eyes as the panic she was feeling showed through plainly. She turned away.

Jessica knew her behavior made no sense to Neil and she couldn't begin to explain why she was refusing to meet Seth Cameron. She was aware of Neil's occasional bewildered glances as he patiently walked with her through the nearly deserted newsroom and down the steps to the parking lot.

Neil started the car and eased it out of the crowded parking lot onto the street. "What happened in there, Jessica?"

Jessica glanced at Neil and then stared out the window. "Nothing." Silence followed the answer and she glanced nervously at Neil again. He was a reporter. He was used to putting facts together, seeing what people didn't want to be seen and drawing conclusions.

"Do you know Cameron?"

"No!" Jessica realized she had to do something to defuse the situation. "Has he been here before?"

"No, not that I know of," Neil said after a moment.

"Then why would you ask that?"

"The way he was staring at you," Neil responded.

Jessica wanted to disappear into the seat. "Staring at me?" He had been looking at her when she glanced up once, but he hadn't been staring at her later.

"Like you were a ghost from his past or something. But then you were so pale, maybe he thought you were a ghost."

She was from his past all right. And that was what she needed to remember. It was past. It had only been a weekend. She had known it then and so had he, despite any pretense otherwise. "Did you eat any lunch?" Jessica finally managed, desperate to turn the conversation into less serious channels. Luckily Neil went along.

"Or maybe it was a case of love at first sight," Neil teased as he turned off Peachtree Road onto West Paces Ferry.

"Neil, please." It wasn't unusual for him to tease her about her single status, but tonight just wasn't a good time and Seth Cameron wasn't a good subject to choose. "He's probably married and has six kids or something."

"Nope. Divorced. No attachments of any kind. Eligible and from the looks he was giving you, I'd say definitely interested."

How did pertinent information get around so fast? "I'd love to know who your sources are," she said, laughing weakly. "What else?" She may as well ask because he would tell her whether she wanted to know or not.

"Last worked at our station in Denver. Not into the swinging singles scene. Leads a fairly quiet life aside from work. Not apt to be a big socializer with Daniels." Neil glanced at her. "Word is he's in line for a corporate promotion, possibly vice-president of news."

"How did you find all this out?" Jessica asked, momentarily sidetracked by her own curiosity.

Neil laughed. "I do have a few sources. Interested?"

"In your sources?"

"No, in Cameron."

Interested wasn't quite the word to use to describe what she felt about Seth or the situation. In fact, she wasn't sure which word to choose, worried, scared, curious. But no matter how much she might be interested it had all ended that weekend. "Not a chance," she sighed.

Chapter Six

Jessica said a small prayer of thanks as she entered the dark apartment. She didn't have to face Emily tonight. The strain of trying not to show her feelings had left her shaking and unable to move for several long minutes, but at last she forced herself through her evening routine. Like an automaton she washed her face, brushed her hair and teeth and changed into a nightgown and robe.

She dropped a tape in the cassette player and sat down in the Boston rocker by the bedroom window. The fact that she hadn't been able to convince herself she didn't love Seth really had nothing to do with what was going on now. She was the executive producer and he was the news director. She would have to act as if she didn't know him. She would have to treat him as if he were just any person who had come in to assume that position.

But how could she do that? How did she pretend not to know a man she loved? No. She couldn't. But that didn't mean she had a future with him. She had simply had an affair with a very gentle, extremely sexy man. She had been frightened and hurt. He had been lonely. They had simply responded to each other's needs, openly and without reservation. They hadn't lied to each other or pretended it was more than that. It was her problem if she thought she loved him.

She had hoped she could ignore her feelings, ignore the past. Now, after spending only a few minutes in a crowded meeting, she knew she couldn't.

"Why?" It was a strangled whisper in the dark room. Why hadn't she recognized the qualities of his voice or the way he understood when she had talked about her job? Why hadn't she realized before things had become so complicated? She threw herself across the bed and cried for all the secret hopes and dreams that could never be.

"Mr. Cameron."

Seth looked up at the young woman he had inherited as his secretary. "Please, Amy, call me Seth. I prefer to work informally." She nodded, obviously not quite comfortable with the idea.

"Jessica Buchanan, our executive producer, asked me to be sure you got this," Amy said, laying a sealed envelope on his desk. "She seemed upset about something."

Last night and this morning Seth had been immensely thankful that no one here knew him well enough to recognize his own emotional turmoil. He looked at the plain white legal-sized envelope. "Did she say anything?" She wouldn't. She would hold it inside, he was sure of that.

"No, sir, she hardly spoke. She usually stops by in the morning and talks for a few minutes. She's been..."

Amy's voice trailed off hesitantly, and Seth forced himself to look up. "She's been what, Amy?"

"Well, I guess you know she's been the acting director since Mr. Smith left."

No, he hadn't known, though he should have. Jessica had told him she had been doing both jobs, but Daniels had spoken as if no one had been taking care of the everyday tasks, at least no one person in particular. "I'm glad to know someone has been handling it," he said with an encouraging smile. "And I'm glad to know there is someone I can ask questions if I need to."

"Oh, you'll like Jessica," Amy said happily. "She'll do anything to help." Amy's face clouded again. "She was so upset, though. I told her you were free for a few minutes, but that seemed to upset her even more. She looked almost frightened when I said that."

Seth glanced at the plain white envelope again. He understood Jessica's discomfort, but he didn't like the word frightened. Was she afraid of him or was it something else? There were obviously problems here, though he didn't understand them all yet. "What time is the budget meeting?"

"At ten, and you're to have lunch upstairs with Mr. Daniels and the others afterward." Amy turned toward the door and paused. "Can I get you some coffee? I'm going down for some."

"No, thank you, Amy." Seth glanced at his watch. "Just buzz me about ten minutes before the meeting. Until then I have some things I need to go over."

"Yes, sir."

Less than thirty minutes. That wasn't enough time. He didn't know what was in the envelope, but he knew after last night that his first meeting with Jessica Buchanan was going to take longer than thirty minutes. He hated the first few days on a new job. It was all table talk. Budgets. Ratings. He wanted to get his fingers in the operation, to meet his staff and start dealing with the people.

He waited until the door was closed before opening Jessica's letter. He read the terse paragraph slowly. She was resigning. But why now? Why this morning and not yesterday or last week? What could he say to stop her? What arguments could he use to keep her at the job until they had a chance to talk? Sighing, he closed his eyes and leaned back in the chair. What a mess!

He read the short paragraph again. This situation shouldn't even exist and the fact that it did was all his fault. He should have known from what she said that the job she had been talking about was in television. He should have realized from the intense way she watched the news that evening. How could he have been so blind?

He raked his fingers through his hair. She had disappeared so quickly last night. And then he had made the mistake of calling Daniels's attention to her. When the crowd had finally thinned out he had asked who the woman on crutches was.

"That's your executive producer," Daniels had sneered. "You can see her attitude is as bad as I said earlier. She didn't even bother to stay."

He had overreacted to the remark. It had been a long day that had accomplished nothing. Gerald Daniels had spent most of it dwelling on his own accomplishments. During the few minutes Seth had managed to steer the conversation to the news operation he had gotten little information. Daniels had implied that most of the staff were incompetent. Seth had asked about either an assistant director or executive producer, and Daniels had quickly informed him they had no assistant director and that the executive producer was worthless.

"She probably left because she was tired," Seth had said to Daniels as they started to leave the room after the staff meeting.

"Some people always have an excuse," Daniels had replied.

"She's on crutches," Seth had protested, wondering how her ankle was doing. Had her hands healed yet? "How did she break her leg?" What had she said when she got back?

"Mighty interested in her, aren't you?"

He had glanced at Gerald Daniels, feeling a wave of repulsion. "Just curious."

Daniels had given him a speculative look. "She isn't worth the trouble."

Jessica hadn't looked at him last night. She had kept her eyes down the entire meeting, never once glancing up. He had stared in her direction until he realized it was calling attention to her. After that he had carefully kept his eyes moving around the room. Not before Daniels had noticed his interest, though.

He wanted to know how she was. He wanted to look into those green eyes again. He didn't want to have to treat her as one of the staff. He wanted to treat her as the special woman she was to him. Seth grimaced as the intercom buzzed. And there wasn't time now. They needed more than ten or fifteen minutes squeezed between other meetings.

Jessica was barely functioning. Just knowing he was in the same building was having a devastating effect on her nervous system. She jumped at every sound, all too aware that at any moment she could look up into honey-brown eyes and be lost. Her heart skipped and stopped each time her name was spoken. At any moment it could be his warm voice caressing her.

And with every moment that passed she went through agonies. With each minute and hour that crept by she knew she had made the right decision. He must be glad that she had turned in her resignation. He didn't want to have to work with her, despite his claim that it wasn't a problem. He didn't want her to be there as a memory or a reminder. And that hurt, much more than she cared to admit.

The day was almost over. In another hour she could leave and maybe she wouldn't even bother to work out her notice. Maybe she would— She almost fell out of her chair as her name was spoken softly from the doorway. "Yes, Amy?"

"Mr. Cameron, Seth, wants to see you in his office immediately after the news."

Jessica could only nod. Why now, at the end of the day? If he had wanted to talk to her why not during the morning or afternoon? Why had he waited until she was tired? Did he realize she was more vulnerable now?

That wasn't fair, she chided herself. He wasn't the type of man to take advantage of someone. That weekend he wasn't, the voice that had haunted her all day whispered. Then he wasn't, but this is now and everything has changed.

As the news ended she realized her heart was pounding and her palms were sweaty. She might feel vulnerable, but she didn't have to show him how much all of this was upsetting her. She could and would be cool and professional, just as if he were the stranger he should have been. She dried her hands on a tissue and, taking several deep, steadying breaths, moved slowly across the newsroom to his office.

The outer area was empty, Amy's desk clear and neat. Jessica went toward the half-open inner door and tapped. The light was on, but Seth wasn't there. Of course. She hadn't thought about the fact he would be upstairs with Daniels critiquing the newscast.

She glanced curiously about the office. The only furniture was the large desk, a few chairs and the usual bank of monitors and videotape decks. She glanced at the desk, but it, too, was nearly bare except for a stack of computer printouts and the envelope she had given Amy that morning.

After a moment's hesitation, Jessica entered the room and crossed to stand by the window, looking out at the street below. It was dark and poorly lit, the curbs lined with cars parked bumper to bumper. If her car had been there she would just— Neil. She had forgotten to tell him not to wait. She turned to leave and what she had feared all day happened.

Her eyes collided with a broad chest covered with a cream-colored silky shirt. She would have known that chest even if she hadn't been standing in his office. Her eyes moved upward over the neatly knotted tie to the angle of his jaw. It was shadowed with late-day beard. Her glance moved steadily over the taut planes of his cheeks to his eyes. All thoughts of Neil or going home vanished as the warm brown pools held her.

"I hadn't forgotten, kitten."

Forgotten? Jessica's blood warmed with the memories. Her heart fluttered against her ribs like a wild bird.

"I'm sorry you had to wait. I know it's been a long day for you."

Mentally she shook herself. He was talking about their meeting and she was thinking of the past. He had thought she was leaving the office while she was remembering another time and place. "No, I—it's..." He looked so tired. The lines of his face were too sharply drawn. His hair was mussed, as if he had pushed his fingers through it repeatedly. Her fingers burned to touch him, to smooth the lines creasing his brow and ease those bracketing his mouth.

"Would you like to get something to eat?"

Eat? How could he possibly think about food? But the commonplace question snapped her back to reality. She curled her fingers tightly about the crutches. "No, thank you." No, whatever happened now had to be strictly business and she was afraid that away from the four walls of the television station she would totally forget that this man was now her supervisor. Why didn't he just say whatever he wanted to say?

"Sit down, please." Seth gestured to the chairs. He hadn't known what would be the best approach. Now, seeing her, seeing the confusion in her eyes, he knew. He had to tackle this head on, laying everything on the table.

Seth watched her go to sit down. Her movements were stiff, almost awkward. Last night there had been a moment when he hadn't been sure if the woman he was seeing was her. She had changed her hair from the shoulder-length, blunt style she had had before to a soft cut that swept back, exposing her face and enhancing the wide green eyes. But it hadn't been her hair that had caused his uncertainty.

It was her clothes. Yesterday and today she had been dressed in suits. They were perfectly appropriate for the job, but what confused him was the way she wore them, their style. They hid the curves of her body and denied the warmth and passion he knew lived within the woman.

Jessica sank gratefully onto the chair, her knees weak. She watched as he reached for the envelope and opened it. Then he sat down on the front of the desk, one leg bent. She swallowed as his slacks tightened across a taut thigh and forced her attention to the bare wall behind him. Now was not the time to deal with memories.

"Jessica."

She started at the sound. It was almost a whisper, a murmur, as if he were thinking to himself just as she had last night.

"Why are you resigning?"

What else could she do? What other choice was there? She looked at him, knowing she had to give him an answer. She wondered what he would do if she said she was leaving because of him. She could tell him it was something she had been considering, but he wouldn't believe it, she hadn't mentioned it last weekend. She had said too much then and at the same time, not enough. All her reasons suddenly sounded like excuses.

When she didn't answer Seth studied the tersely written paragraph again. It said nothing other than she was resigning. At least she was giving him two weeks. He laid the paper aside. During the dry business meetings his mind hadn't been on ratings or advertising sales. He had been trying to remember everything she had said, searching his memory for clues.

"Jessica." She looked up and her eyes focused on a spot just over his shoulder. "I can understand you're disappointed about not getting the job, but I don't think resigning is the answer. Do you?"

Jessica stared at him as he finished speaking. "I'm not leaving for that reason."

"Good. In that case we'll just forget about this."

"No." She didn't know whether to be relieved or disappointed that he had misunderstood her reasons. But she wasn't going to change her mind.

"Then would you please explain why you're going?" Seth demanded.

Jessica searched for some safe words to use. She hadn't expected him to question her. She couldn't tell him she wasn't happy as she had told Neil. She couldn't explain about Daniels as she had to Emily.

"Are you doing this because of us?" he asked gently.

"No," she denied quickly.

"Aren't you?" He looked down at her, his eyes questioning.

"No." She caught the panic in her voice and forced herself to be calm. "No, I'm not leaving because of . . . us. There is no 'us'. We had an interlude, a moment in time, but there wasn't and never will be an 'us'."

"Jessica, I won't accept that. You're resigning because of our relationship."

"No." She took a deep breath, forcing herself to speak calmly around the rising hysteria. She hadn't expected a protest. He was supposed to be glad, relieved. He wasn't supposed to object. "No, I'm not," she said firmly, daring at last to look up. Didn't he understand? Something would be said about their relationship. One of them would make a slip and then it would be known. She could feel the currents between them even now, an electricity, waiting for some small move or word to breathe life into the spark and turn it into a consuming fire. "And I won't withdraw it."

He hadn't been sure until she looked up, but then he was positive. He remembered her remark about the jealousy and competition in her first marriage. What had happened to make her so sure people couldn't be friends and work together? And what had happened with Gerald Daniels that had made her walk out? He needed some straight answers. "Kitten, those lovely green eyes of yours can't lie."

A tremor raced through her at the use of the name and the soft caress of his voice. She needed space and distance between them. Pushing herself from the chair, she moved around the corner of the desk to the window. "All right," she admitted at last. "It is because of what happened."

Seth studied the tense line of her shoulders, searching for answers. "Then why now? Why not last week?" She could easily have turned in her resignation before he arrived.

Jessica swallowed. "I thought about it. But I had a job to do. I couldn't just walk out."

Jessica wasn't a quitter. That much Seth knew from personal experience. She didn't give in easily, at least not to physical challenges. "Do you always run from your problems, Jessica?" he asked gently. "Is that the way you handle all of them, just run and pretend they don't exist?"

She stiffened against the accusation. "I don't run from problems."

"You ran out when you didn't get the promotion and now you're trying to run again," he persisted. "You left the room so fast last night I couldn't have spoken to you without making a scene. I want you to stay this time and see if we can work this out." And not just with the job, but with their relationship as well.

There was some truth in what he said. She had run when she didn't get the promotion, she had run from sexual harassment and now she was running from a sexual history. Yes, she had done that, but he only knew part of the story. It was the half he didn't know that had her leaving now. That half she hoped he never knew.

Jessica straightened her shoulders slightly and tried to put things on a professional level again. "Mr. Cameron, what happened between us was an—accident. And what happened has nothing to do with now."

Seth crossed the short distance between them and turned her to him. "An accident, kitten? No." He would never consider finding this woman an accident. "And what happened does have everything to do with now."

Jessica fought the urge to melt into the protective gentleness of his arms. She fought the need to trust his words. She couldn't allow herself to believe that meeting him or being with him had been anything other than a mistake.

"I am not going to let you quit, Jessica."

She could see the pain in his eyes and opened her mouth to say she wouldn't go. But how could she stay when all she wanted to do was throw herself in his arms and be held against the strong wall of his chest? How could she stay when all she could think of was the heat of his lips against hers?

Slowly Jessica moved back. Seth let his hands drop to his sides, and she was both grateful and sorry. "What happened is history."

He settled against the edge of the desk. What they had couldn't be called history. It wasn't history when you ached to take a woman in your arms. It wasn't history when the misery in her eyes tore at your heart. "I told you, I don't see our relationship as a problem. And I'm not going to let you go until we've had a chance together." Did she think he saw their weekend as a one-night stand, just a situation he had taken advantage of? "Jessica, we shared something beautiful."

She shook her head. "This is . . ." Her voice trailed off as he rose and moved closer again.

"This is what?"

"Another mistake," Jessica retorted. She straightened, looking him in the eye, daring him to deny it was anything else.

"It's fate," he said softly. "It was fate before."

"What happened before is past. Over."

"Over?" His arms came around her, gently but firmly. His lips brushed hers lightly, tentatively. "Is what we had really over?" His lips touched hers again, gently at first, then more persuasively, drawing out the response she couldn't pretend wasn't there. Seth felt the capitulation, the softening of her body yielding to his as her mouth parted in invitation. "Can you call this a mistake?"

"Yes," she whispered, even as the crutches fell with a clatter to the floor. Yes, she thought as her hands lifted to his shoulders and then moved to encircle his neck. His hands had found their way beneath her suit jacket to leave a burning path on her back as he pulled her to him. His tongue teased across her lower lip before delving into the secret recesses of her mouth. She met the incursion eagerly, willingly losing the battle.

"Jessica, I need your help now," Seth said, lifting his mouth from hers slowly. "I need your support for the next few weeks." He traced the shape of her cheek. The scratches had healed completely, except for a faint line, and there was no sign of a bruise. "Don't walk out on me now, kitten. I need you."

"You walked out on me." For a long moment she stared at him, not believing she had said the words. She turned, staring out the window, her heart pounding painfully against her ribs. "I'm sorry. I didn't mean that."

"Yes, you did." Gently he turned her back to face him. "I did walk out on you and it was wrong. For both of us. Don't make the same mistake now, kitten."

Jessica couldn't stop the tremor that coursed through her body or the way she swayed toward him. "That's not fair. You're twisting everything."

"No, I'm not. I'm asking you to give yourself some time, kitten," he said, and lightly brushed her hair back. "And me."

Jessica was fighting a turmoil of emotions and his light touch on her hair didn't help. Could she be positive this decision was one made strictly on the basis of what was best and not because of her feelings for him? If she stayed and worked for a month, made plans, then both she and the world would know it was because it was her choice. Maybe she needed to stay.

Seth watched her a moment. He hated being the cause of so much pain in her life. "If you don't stop biting that lip, kitten, there won't be anything left to kiss." He lightly touched her with his thumb, gently easing it from between her teeth. "It's a bad habit for such a pretty mouth." A mouth he was aching to taste again.

Jessica felt her heart stop and then plunge downward. She was acquiescing because of a kiss, a touch, a need in his eyes she understood only too well. "This won't work. You can't ask me to stay and then call me that name. I won't stay under those conditions."

"Around any of the other staff I'll be very careful to use only Jessica," he assured her, letting his hand drop to his side. "When we're alone, I reserve the right to call you whatever I wish."

Jessica looked up to meet his gaze. It was only a brief glance, but the golden flames burning beneath the surface of his eyes served as a warning this time. "In that case I can't stay," she declared, stepping back and bumping into the windowsill. "It would never work."

Seth didn't understand why, but he knew he had suddenly lost ground. Where a moment before she had been open, she was now closed. An invisible wall had been erected between them. "Stay and prove we can do it," he challenged. "Don't you believe we can work together as two professionals?"

"The resignation has nothing to do with my ability or inability to work with you," she lied. If each time she talked with him she was left this shaken she would never be able to stay at the station. If each time she was with him he touched her as he just had it couldn't even be called work.

Seth sensed he had nearly lost the battle, but he was determined to keep her on any terms, use anything he had to make her stay. They needed time. "I'm asking you to stay, Jessica, to work with me as a professional with this news department."

Jessica felt totally confused. Was that all he wanted, a professional relationship? If that was true, then why had he taken her in his arms, why had he brought up all the reminders of that weekend?

"I'm asking you to reconsider this. If, in a few weeks, you still wish to resign, we'll talk again. Now I'd rather not have to replace key people on my staff." He saw the confusion in her eyes, the doubt. She had lost her balance by his sudden change of tactics. One part of him felt guilty and another part pushed ahead for victory. "You know how I feel about replacing staff. We talked about it. It's not fair to yourself, Jessica. Or to me."

She would hate to be the cause of him getting off on the wrong foot with the staff. And she knew no one would believe she was quitting by choice. She wasn't conceited enough to think her leaving would be the cause of unrest and disgruntled remarks. It was just that whoever was first to go would cause that problem and the higher up that person was the stronger the reaction would be. Could she do that to him? Could she set the staff against him without his having an opportunity to prove himself?

"If you resign, no one here will believe you weren't fired, especially after the problems you've had recently.

They'll think I did exactly what Daniels wants and fired you." He didn't know what had happened, but he knew Daniels had wanted her out. And she knew it, too. Hadn't she said that her friend thought he would wait for the "new man" to fire her?

Seth was afraid for a moment that he had pushed too hard, that he had stepped across the line she had drawn. He forced himself to stay still and wait for her answer.

How much did he know about the problems she had had? Jessica felt she was being shoved into a corner with no escape. "I'll stay." Even as she said the words she realized the decision was based on emotions and not on sound judgment. He had trapped her. "At least for a few weeks. A month."

"That's all I need, kitten," he said, brushing her lips with a light kiss. "That's all I need."

Jessica stiffened, refusing to allow the heat of his touch to melt her knees. She wasn't going to play games with him. He had asked her to stay and work with him as a professional and that was what she would do. "Mr. Cameron, I'm staying as the executive producer. Nothing more."

His eyes danced with golden light as he looked down at her. "I don't suppose I can ask for more than that tonight," he agreed teasingly.

"I don't suppose you can ask for more than that any night," Jessica said firmly.

Seth laughed softly. "I can ask. And you can always say no." He bent and picked up the crutches.

Seth knew he hadn't been wrong about her motive for resigning, but he was more than a little curious as to the causes behind her reaction. Rather than pursue it immediately, he turned to the desk and glanced at his calendar. "I'd like to set up a meeting to go over the operation of the department and get your opinion about our weak and strong points." He flipped a couple of pages. "Unfortunately, my days are tied up this week with budget and planning meetings upstairs. Would tomorrow at seven-thirty be okay with you? There just isn't any time free during the day."

"That's okay. Seven-thirty is fine."

"Great." He made a note on the calendar. "You pick the restaurant."

Jessica stiffened slightly. It was normal to have the type of meeting he'd described away from the station, but the thought of being alone with him was frightening. Could she, and would he, remain "professional" under those conditions? "I'd rather stay here."

"I'd rather the walls didn't hear what we have to say to each other," he said with a teasing glint in his eyes.

"Okay," she conceded, feeling her heart beat erratically. It was true that the walls did seem to have ears and she couldn't help but wonder what they had heard tonight.

Seth smiled. "See. We can work together with no problems."

"I don't think agreeing on one meeting means we can work together," she protested. "And I've only agreed to stay for a month. I *will* resubmit my resignation."

Seth glanced up. "We'll talk about it then if that's what you decide," he agreed without hesitation. A month. A lot could happen in a month and he would make sure that it did.

Chapter Seven

Where have you been, kid? I was getting worried."

Jessica started guiltily as Neil spoke. "I'm sorry. You shouldn't have waited." He had a wife and a life outside this building. "Seth—" that sounded too personal "—Cameron wanted to see me after the news."

"Hey, that's good."

Jessica used the excuse of getting her purse and coat to keep her back toward her friend. "Why?"

Neil sounded hesitant as he spoke again. "I assume it was good. He didn't fire you, did he? I'll go in there and—"

Jessica started laughing. She knew it was a way of releasing tension, but Neil sounded so righteous. "You'll what?" She laughed. "No, he didn't fire me. He just wanted to set up a meeting to discuss the department."

"Then it was good," Neil said firmly. "It means he isn't going to take Daniels's word on the subject and it means you have a chance to stay here."

"I don't really care about a chance," she said softly. "I'm still going to quit." She saw the protest forming on Neil's craggy face and hurried on. "But you're right. He isn't the type of man to take anyone's word without investigating first." *Not even mine.* "He'll make his own decisions."

"We need that around here," Neil said as they started across the newsroom.

"I know," Jessica agreed. Alex Smith had been nice enough, but he had been too much of a yes-man to Daniels. "And by the way, you can get out of here tomorrow evening. I'll let you off for one night at least."

Neil smiled as he held the heavy glass door. "My heart will be broken. What will I do with all that time?"

Jessica laughed. "Oh, I imagine you'll think of something."

Seth stood just inside the door of his office. It was good even just to hear her voice. He glanced through the doorway at the older man with her. He was much too old for her, in his forties at least.

He studied the pair as they walked down the hall. She had said there was no one in her life. So what was this relationship and who was this man? Seth was startled at the jealousy he felt. Well, tomorrow he would find out who the man was and tomorrow night it would be him who was walking her out of the building and occupying her evening.

Jessica was as nervous as a mouse cornered by a large cat by the time seven o'clock rolled around. She had mentally gone over and over their meeting last night and she still didn't know how she had been talked into staying. Things had swung back and forth too rapidly. One moment there had been sparks flying between them and the next they had been just employer and employee. One moment his eyes had touched her like golden suns and the next they'd been unreadable blanks. The worst had been her own behavior, as she had responded to his kiss with unguarded abandon and then claimed she only wanted a professional relationship.

She clicked the monitors off and went to the ladies' room to check her hair and make-up. She couldn't help but wonder what Seth would have done with her resignation had she been anyone else. If she hadn't spent that weekend with him would he have insisted she stay, or would he have just ignored her presence like Daniels wanted?

Daniels wanted her out. What Seth hadn't done, though, was to give any clue as to what Gerald Daniels had said or implied about her. If Daniels had said much, Jessica had already discredited herself with that kiss last night.

She had been the one who wavered, the one who first insisted on resigning and then responded to him. She could have refused to kiss him back, but she hadn't, she had clung to him with a hunger and need that was all too evident.

"Big date tonight?"

Jessica glanced up with a start and grimaced as she realized she was looking dreamily at the mirror, absently brushing her hair. She hadn't heard the door open or Diane Howell, one of the anchors, come in. "No, big meeting with the new boss." She watched a moment as Diane opened a cosmetic case, then turned back to her own reflection.

"I don't know why I bother to take this off," Diane said, applying cream to her face. "I just have to put it back on for the evening broadcast. Cameron sure is a hunk, isn't he?"

"Is he?" Jessica had never thought of him as a hunk. Sexy. Dynamic. There was something about his expression that was alert and alive, so vital. And yes, that all added up to being a hunk.

"Come on, Jessica," Diane laughed. "No one's that blind. The man is gorgeous."

"Well, this meeting is strictly business," Jessica said, as much for her own benefit as Diane's. And it would stay strictly business, unlike last night.

"What's he like?" Diane asked.

Jessica ran the brush through her hair one last time, remembering the morning he had bought it for her. She paused, looking down. Seth Cameron was warm, kind, funny and provocative. He was also her Yeti—tender, gentle, caring and sensual. But now she was dealing with the man on a professional level, as her supervisor.

"I don't really know." Jessica was hedging. "I just saw him for a few minutes late yesterday."

"Has he said anything about making any changes?" Diane asked with a quick look at Jessica in the mirror.

"No." Jessica tucked the brush back into her purse and straightened her jacket.

"Oh Lord, I hope the man can stand up to Daniels." She glanced sideways and shrugged. "For you too, Jessica, you know that."

"I know. Thanks, Diane." She looked at her watch and then at her reflection one last time. "I'd better get going or he'll think I forgot."

"Say something nice about us," Diane called after her.

That wouldn't be hard where most of the staff was concerned. Overall they had a very good group of reporters, editors and staff. Diane was a perfect example. She was excellent on camera; charming, intelligent and quick-witted. No, the hard part was simply being alone with Seth for a couple of hours.

Jessica started up the stairs, wondering, not for the first time, why she had never noticed that going anywhere required climbing stairs. She lived in a second-floor apartment, the lobby of the television station was reached by some really gruesome steps, the restrooms were downstairs. Until she had the cast and crutches she had never given any of it a thought. Now it was a constant struggle to go anywhere.

"There you are. I was afraid you'd left."

Jessica started and teetered precariously on the landing for a moment. A strong hand reached out and grasped her upper arm, steadying her. "No. I was just downstairs." She had her balance now and glanced pointedly at the fingers still curled gently about her arm.

Seth grinned and slowly dropped his hand. "Are you ready then?" He had been looking forward to this all day. Having dinner and a little time with her away from the frantic pace of the television station and all the inevitable interruptions was his reward for having survived another day of meetings and dry discussions.

Her arm burned where his fingers had touched it, even through the jacket and blouse she wore. "I have to get my coat and lock my office," she said, glancing ruefully at the second half of the stairs.

"You wait here," Seth said, catching her look. "I'll get your coat and lock the office."

"I can—"

"Do as you're told." His eyes focused briefly on her right hand. "You get in trouble when you don't."

He took the steps two at a time, making any further argument useless, not that she had any comeback for the unexpected reminder. She had barely had a chance to get her pulse rate under control when he was back again. Taking the crutches from her, he leaned them against the wall and helped her with her coat. Jessica shivered as his fingers unexpectedly brushed the nape of her neck.

"I like what you did with your hair," he murmured. "It's beautiful."

She touched her hair absently. "Thank you." Beautiful. For one weekend she had felt beautiful, desirable and totally feminine. He had given her that. It was a priceless gift to treasure.

"Your transportation, my lady."

Jessica pulled herself back to the present and realized he was waiting for her to take the crutches. She glanced around nervously to see if anyone could have heard his earlier words. Yes, what he had given her was a priceless gift, but it was also something that could play no part in her life now.

Holding the door for her, he waited while she stepped out onto the landing leading to the employee parking lot. "If I didn't think you'd yell, I'd offer to carry you down," he teased.

"You aren't the hero type. Remember your back?" she retorted.

He laughed softly. "I just wanted to be sure you remembered."

She would have to watch what she said. She couldn't keep falling into his verbal traps. She couldn't keep letting him throw her off balance like this. "I'm trying to forget. Please—" Her protest was cut off as he placed two fingers against her lips. The teasing glint that had been in his eyes a moment ago was gone.

"I know you're trying, I just don't know why." The only reason he had been able to come up with was that she saw their weekend as a one-night stand. He was going to make her see it was more.

"I want you to remember, kitten. I'm not going to let you forget." She just looked at him, her eyes filling with a hurt he could see even in the poorly lit parking lot. "Now, where did you decide we would go?" He gently urged her down the steps.

"There's a small restaurant on Northside Drive near West Paces Ferry. It's quiet and not usually inhabited by TV types. If that's okay with you?"

"It sounds perfect," he agreed. "I've definitely had enough of TV types today."

"You don't like them?"

"Only for eight or nine hours a day."

"What if I'm the TV type?" she asked, suddenly curious. He chuckled as he escorted her to the car, but didn't answer.

Seth looked around the restaurant, wondering what had made her choose it. It was decorated like an old English hunting lodge with lots of rich panelling. The atmosphere was quiet and reserved. They could obviously discuss business without being interrupted, but it struck him as having the atmosphere of a men's club. "What made you decide on this place?"

Jessica settled into her chair and glanced around. "It's quiet and the food is excellent." More importantly, the tables were larger than average, meaning they wouldn't be accidentally bumping knees or brushing hands. And it was also one that was more than halfway home. She could call Emily and not have to wait forever for her to arrive.

Seth ordered a drink, but Jessica declined, afraid to take a chance on not having a perfectly clear mind. It took her only a minute to decide on what to order and she folded the menu and laid it aside.

"What will you have?" he asked.

"Just a salad and coffee," she said.

"This goes on the expense account, you know. Besides, you don't need to worry about your weight," Seth said with a slow, teasing grin. "You're perfect."

Memories flooded through her. The taste of his kiss, the heat of his body next to hers, the warmth of his hand touching her. "Just a salad."

The waiter approached and she listened enviously as he ordered roast beef, a baked potato, and broccoli with hollandaise sauce as well as a salad and bread. "And for the lady a chef salad and milk."

"Coffee," she put in firmly.

"And coffee," he added.

"Milk?" the waiter questioned.

"She broke her ankle," Seth explained pleasantly. "If she insists on not eating protein and living on rabbit food, the least she can do is get some calcium. A glass of milk, please."

"Yes, sir." The waiter gave Seth the kind of smile men shared when they thought a woman was being irrational and unreasonable.

Jessica waited until the man was out of hearing. "I can drink milk at home."

"But are you?" he questioned.

Jessica bit back a retort and forced herself to be calm. "My broken bones fall under the category of personal and we agreed our relationship was to be strictly business." She could have told him she was drinking three glasses a day just as she had promised. But she stubbornly refused to give him even that much.

"How do you know I wouldn't treat another employee the same way?" he asked. "Are you so sure I wouldn't care if another of my staff was injured?"

"No," she admitted reluctantly. In fact, she felt fairly certain he would care.

"Then I think you might be jumping to conclusions."

Jessica stared down at the table in embarrassment. "I did and I'm sorry," she said softly.

"I'm not sorry," Seth assured her quickly. "And I did reserve the right to be personal when we were alone." His gaze traveled slowly around the room before coming back to linger on her face. "I certainly don't know anyone else here. Do you?"

Jessica barely suppressed a sigh of exasperation, yet she was curious about this new side of him. He was the same man, but there was a difference she couldn't quite define. "No, but as I told you, Mr. Cameron, our relationship will remain strictly professional and will continue only until the transition period is more stable. Then I will resubmit my resignation."

"I'll cross that bridge when we get to it," he said softly. "Why are you so adamant on this subject?"

"Why are you just as adamant against my quitting? You're only hurting yourself."

"It would hurt me much worse if you weren't here, kitten."

Jessica looked down at the table, toying absently with the handle of her fork. "Please be serious."

"I am being very serious. Losing you again would hurt." His hand covered hers. "Can you honestly tell me it wouldn't hurt you, too?"

So much for large tables, Jessica thought, as his hand settled over hers. She resisted the urge to turn her palm up, to wrap her fingers around the warm, firm flesh and tell him how much it would hurt, how much it had already hurt. Instead, she forced herself to speak calmly. "Not accepting my resignation will only make Daniels angry. You've just started. You need his support as well as the support of the news department."

"How much support would I have from the staff if I let you quit? I need their help, but I need you more." His hand tightened on hers, forcing her to look up. "I need you, kitten, not just at the television station, but as a part of my life."

She needed him, too. She needed his strength and wit and patience. She needed his teasing and the warm invitation in his eyes. "I've told you my marriage was torn apart because we were in the same field."

"Jessica, I don't want to compete with you. I want to share your life."

Slowly she pulled her hand from his and returned it to the safety of her lap. "I don't plan to be hurt that way again—or to hurt another person that way."

Seth sighed inwardly. Hadn't he told himself last night to be patient and give her time? Sitting alone in his motel room, he had thought about it for hours and knew that she needed to build some trust in him again before he could push things further. In the mountains she had been forced to accept his help. She had been dependent on him. Perhaps he had broken that trust or perhaps it was simply the new situation. She was still bitter about not getting the promotion and obviously whatever had occurred that had resulted in her walking out was still a bone of contention. Daniels, after all, was adamant that she needed to be replaced.

The waiter served their food and for a few minutes they ate in silence. Then, to Jessica's relief, Seth began to ask the questions about the news department and the staff she had expected. Before he had even half the picture of the operation he signaled the waiter for the check, paid and started to lead her out. There were some advantages to crutches, she thought wryly. At least he had to stay a couple of feet away.

"Tired?" he asked as he held the door for her.

"Yes," she admitted.

"I'm sorry. I didn't mean to keep you so long."

"You didn't ask very much," she said, glancing up.

"No." He grinned boyishly. "I've saved some for another evening." He had called a halt tonight when he'd realized he wasn't listening to a thing she said. Instead he had been watching her, dreaming of the sweet delight of her kiss.

"That's not fair," she protested. One or two meetings were to be expected, but if he stretched all the issues as an excuse to see her the staff would start talking and speculating.

"Maybe not," he agreed with a frown. He paused, his hand on the car door and looked down at her. "What happened between you and Daniels?"

"Nothing."

Seth slid the crutches behind the seat. "I might be able to help if I knew."

Jessica shrugged. "He's angry because I walked out."

Seth closed her door. It went much deeper than that. The problem clearly lay in the *reason* she had walked out, but he didn't press her further during the short drive to her apartment.

She had hoped he would just drop her off, but that thought barely formed before he had turned off the engine and was at her door, helping her from the car. Jessica glanced at the second floor, glad to see that Emily wasn't home.

Slowly she worked her way up the stairs, all too aware he was just behind her. At the top she paused and dug into her purse for her keys.

"How is your ankle, kitten?"

An aching mess she started to say, then stopped. Where was her independence? "It's fine."

"New cast, isn't it?" At least that would mean she had had it checked after she had returned. He was still worried about the care she had received.

"Yes." Her hand trembled as she tried to put the key into the lock. "After the initial swelling went down they put another one on." Seth's hand covered hers and gently guided the key into the lock. "There shouldn't be any problem. It's just a matter of time."

"Most things are," he said, his voice a soft whisper on the dark landing. "Good night, kitten."

It had been another long day. Seth had scheduled a second meeting and the hours of talking and trying to keep her mind on business had totally worn her out. Now, as he helped her from the car, a wave of dizziness made Jessica cling tightly to his wrists for a moment. She honestly couldn't have said if it was fatigue or his presence that made her feel this way. The touch of his hands as he helped her from the car, the nearness of his strong body were almost overwhelming.

"I'm so tired of this," she muttered as he slid the crutches from the back seat.

"Tired of what, kitten?"

"Please don't call me that."

"Why?"

"The name belongs to another person, another time, another place."

"Does it?" Seth asked softly. "Does it really?"

Jessica didn't answer as she climbed to the top of the steps and started fumbling with her key.

"Jessica?"

"Yes?"

"Can I come in, please?"

Why, she wondered, biting her lower lip.

"That's a very bad habit." Seth touched her mouth lightly. "I think we need to talk, kitten."

Her lip tingled, and she shivered. "No." She fought to control the war of sanity and insanity his touch had ignited. "It's been a long day."

"Jessica." The way he said her name was a caress. "We need to talk about us."

"Us?" She bit her lip again, this time to keep from crying. "There is no us. There never was."

"There was, kitten." He smoothed her hair, his fingers brushing against her cheek. "And there is."

The fatal tremor that raced through her body left her feeling exposed and open. "I have no wish to continue with that relationship. I knew then it was simply a one-night stand."

Seth heard her anger, but also sensed the fear and pain beneath the surface. A fear he didn't understand and a pain he hoped he wasn't responsible for. "One-night stand?" he asked with a teasing smile. "So, I'm just one of hundreds." He had no doubt he wasn't. She had been too vulnerable, too shy and hesitant.

"That's none of your business." She recognized the teasing, but couldn't respond to it. He was too close to breaking down all her defenses.

"And you don't want to try again?"

"No." She did. Oh she did, but she wouldn't admit it. She couldn't admit it. They had to work together. "What do you want from me?"

What did he want from her? He gently caressed the satin smoothness of her cheek. He wished he could see into those vivid green eyes, but the night that surrounded them guarded her. "A lot," he assured her softly. "I want a lot from you, Jessica Buchanan."

"I can't," she whispered and hurried inside before he could say more, leaving him standing alone outside. It was several minutes before she heard his steps retreating down the stairs.

Jessica didn't turn on a light or take off her coat. She simply headed for the sofa and sat down. Emily found her there a few moments later, sitting in the dark, staring at nothing.

"Jessica?" Emily questioned from the doorway, then hurried into the room. "Jessica? What's wrong?"

Until that instant Jessica hadn't realized she was crying. "I'm just tired." Tired of the unexplainable but undeniable need to be in Seth's arms, to simply be with him. Her emotions went much deeper than physical desire, though that was there, too. Belatedly Jessica realized that Jeff, Emily's boyfriend, was standing in the doorway.

"Another late meeting?" he asked as he closed the door.

"Yes."

"Doesn't the man realize you've already worked nine or ten hours by the time he wants to play director?" Emily demanded angrily.

"So has he," Jessica said defensively.

"Well, maybe, but he isn't hobbling around in a cast and on crutches, either," Emily declared, propping Jessica's leg on a pillow. "Have you had supper?"

"Yes." Jessica smiled weakly. "I'm fine, really, just tired."

Emily sat down by her. "Jess, go ahead and quit. You're killing yourself for nothing."

"I can't."

"Why?" Jeff asked. "I didn't think you were under contract."

"I'm not, but I can't quit now."

"Jessica—"

"No, Em!"

Jessica started to stand, but Jeff placed his hand on her shoulder. "Emily, why don't you pour us all a glass of wine? What Jessica needs is to unwind."

Unwinding was something she had been unable to do all week. She didn't believe a glass of wine was the answer now, but she took her coat off and accepted the drink.

"Why can't you quit?" Jeff asked after a few minutes of silence.

Jessica sighed and rubbed her neck. "I promised him I wouldn't."

"Promised who?"

She knew if it had been Emily demanding answers in her loving but brash way she wouldn't have answered. But Jeff was asking as Neil would, just trying to understand. "Seth Cameron. I started to quit Tuesday, but he wanted me to stay for at least a month."

"And you agreed?"

"Yes." She accepted a second glass of wine, hardly aware of what she was doing. "He said it would make it difficult for him if I quit and that he needed time before he made any big staff changes. So I agreed to stay." She glanced up, wanting them to understand. "He's going to be a really good person for the job and I didn't want to hurt him. My reasons for leaving, after all, are strictly personal. It didn't seem fair to jeopardize his position that way." She missed Jeff's quizzical expression as she continued talking about how good Seth would be for the job.

When she got in bed later she wasn't sure if it was the wine or the talking she had done, but she knew she would sleep.

Jessica still dreamed about her Yeti, but she steadfastly refused to make any move in his direction. She was happy when she heard one of the staff say something complimentary about Seth, but she was glad he was keeping his distance as promised. Still, beneath her surface calm, there was a deep sadness and sense of loss. There were moments when she watched him, remembering dreams that could never come to pass now.

When the second week went by, her tension began to abate somewhat. There were no more after-hour dinner meetings and no private conversation. As the third week started Jessica decided she could last out the month, after all. Seth was around the department more, but the end result was that his presence made her job easier. He was taking over the day-to-day responsibilities she had handled before he arrived.

One evening the lineup had been approved rather late for the six o'clock show and the reporters and editors were scrambling in a last minute dash to get tapes edited and stories written. Jessica glanced around the hectic news department, listening to the strange, high-pitched sound of tape being run at fast speed, the noise of typewriters rattling, phones ringing and the more than occasional curse. It was chaotic, but things were normal. At least this much of her life was stable.

"Jess, you'd better take a look at this," Ben called.

Jessica turned, registering the note of panic in the assistant producer's voice. Panic this close to the deadline bordered on disaster. "What?"

"Our lead is unusable." Ben threw a sheaf of papers down and ran a hand through his thinning hair. "Three minutes shot to hell. Down the tube."

Jessica quickly scanned the story and watched the accompanying piece of tape on a monitor. One of the many road reconstruction plans underway in Atlanta had developed into a major controversy between those who wanted the road and the homeowners in the areas that would be directly affected. A neighborhood coalition had been organized and members were going as far as chaining themselves to trees to prevent construction. Jessica bit down on her lip and looked at the story in her hand. The report was so emotional and biased in favor of the local residents there was no way to salvage it. "Any chance of making it into two parts?" she asked when she'd looked over the material. "One for the neighborhoods tonight and then tomorrow night we do the other side, equal time, et cetera?"

Ben shook his head. "Look at this section in the middle." He advanced the tape. "It just blows us out of the water."

Jessica bit down on her lip and looked at the story in her hand. It was a mess and three minutes had been given to it. They had no choice but to dump it and use a different lead. As she made suggestions, looked at the available choices and checked over the new lineup every muscle in her body was tight as a drawn wire.

"Jessica, Cameron wants to see you in his office now."

She looked up at Amy with disbelief. He knew it was the most pressure-filled time of the day and that their key program went on the air in less than ten minutes. Less than ten minutes and the entire newscast had to be salvaged. She turned away. "Tell him I'll be there soon," she muttered, her mind on the changes still to be made.

With less than one minute to spare, the control room had been notified, the videos rearranged, copy pulled and the prompter changed. There was nothing more she could do. Once in her office again she turned on the three monitors. Her teeth tightened on her lower lip when both the other stations led with the story about the roadway. "Damn, damn, damn," she muttered under her breath.

"You wanted to see me, Jessica?"

She looked up. Jed Brown, the assignment editor, stood in the open doorway. "Yes. Come in and shut the door." She waited until the noise from the department had been shut out. "I want to know why Trish Larkin was assigned to that story. We blew it today."

Jed sat down in the chair. "I didn't have anyone else to send."

Jessica's eyes narrowed, turning dark. "With a staff the size of ours you had no one else to send? Come on, Jed, I'm not buying that."

"She wanted a chance, Jessica. She deserved a chance. She's been here eight months and all she ever gets are the fillers. She's never gotten a good story."

Jessica sat back in her chair. According to the rumors, Trish and Jed had been seeing each other. In fact, if gossip was to be believed, they were living together. This was the result of mixing professional and personal lives, Jessica thought to herself. It was the opposite side of the coin from her marriage, but nevertheless it was a lesson she should heed as well. "Jed, how you feel about Trish after six is your business. But just remember this. Trish hasn't been assigned to any major stories for the very reason that she hasn't learned to be impartial or to dig for facts."

Jessica studied Jed a moment. He was usually good at his job. His judgment in selecting stories and juggling and arranging news crews was always sound. Until today.

"Jed, don't let your personal involvement cloud your judgment. Trish can't be sent on stories like that."

"It won't happen again," Jed assured her.

She nodded, knowing it wouldn't. "Send her in on your way out, please."

When Trish walked in minutes later Jessica knew she had to be sterner. "Did you see the reports on 7 and 4?"

"No."

Any reporter worth the name always watched the competition. "That's really too bad. You might have learned something." She stared at the younger woman a moment. "Are you even aware that we didn't run your story tonight?" Trish's mouth dropped open, but she didn't say anything.

Jessica picked up the copy and tore the story apart point by point. Her questions were hard, driving and relentless. Trish was in tears long before she had finished.

"Am I fired?" Trish asked, hands fluttering nervously in her lap.

Jessica considered a moment. "I don't know, Trish. That will be up to Mr. Cameron."

Trish stood to leave, her blue eyes filled with shimmering drops. Jessica stopped her as she reached the door. "Do you realize Jed could lose his job because of today?"

At that moment the intercom buzzed and she reached irritably for the switch. Trish had messed up too many times and really deserved— "What?" she snapped.

"Exactly my question."

Seth's voice grated from the speaker. She had forgotten he wanted to see her. "Oh, I—"

"My office, Buchanan. Now."

"Yes, sir."

"And I want an explanation about the parkway story."

"Yes, sir." The intercom went dead. Jessica slowly released the button and looked up. Trish still stood in the doorway, her expression one of stunned disbelief. "We all have to answer to someone," she said with a shrug as she stood up.

Chapter Eight

When Jessica arrived at Seth's office he motioned her in with an impatient movement of his hand. "Shut the door."

She had never seen him angry. It was going to be a new experience. And from the hard look he gave her, it was one she wasn't sure she was anxious to try. She sat down without invitation and pushed the tape and copy for the story Trish had turned in across his desk. She had to just meet him head on. After all, she was the producer and he was the director, and this was strictly business. "We covered the story. The reporter brought back something that wasn't usable and we didn't have time to salvage it."

It might be business, but she couldn't help the small flicker in her abdomen as she looked at him. He had taken off his jacket, loosened his tie and released the top button of his shirt. The thick mat of dark hair curled teasingly at the edge of the shirt and unconsciously her fingers curled, aching to feel the crisp warmth. He had also rolled up his shirt sleeves, and she had to force her eyes away from his wrists and corded forearms to the wall behind him.

There was no safe way to look at Seth Cameron. If she looked into his eyes she remembered golden suns. If she looked at his face she found herself studying the tightly drawn mouth and remembering the devastating tenderness of which it was capable. If she looked at his hands she remembered—

"How long has Trish been working here?"

The question jerked her back to the present, unprepared. "Uh, about, oh, eight months, maybe nine."

"She won't make it."

His words were so blunt and cold. She had been saying the same thing to herself all evening but he didn't leave any hope for Trish and surely everyone deserved that at least. "She gets involved with the stories. She hasn't learned to distance herself from the issues yet. I think with time she'll do all right."

"Why are you protecting her?" Seth demanded coldly.

"I'm not protecting her, I'm protecting what we put on the air, the lineup and the newscast."

"What did you tell her?" he demanded.

Jessica knew the problem tonight could be the end of her job. Instead of finding the thought disconcerting it was almost a relief. With any luck he would fire her and it would be over. "I told her what happened next would have to be your decision."

"What do you recommend?"

She took a steadying breath and met his cold gaze levelly. "Put her back on less important things until she learns."

"No. We don't keep reporters who can't cut it. Assign her to some stories with some meat to them."

"That's setting her up to be fired," Jessica gasped.

"It's showing her she has a job to do. I don't want a staff that we have to baby-sit. I don't want the assignment editor trying to decide if a reporter is qualified to cover a story every morning. I want him concentrating on the stories and I want a staff that is good, across the board. Assign her to some stories with issues."

"I can't do that."

"Can't or won't?" he demanded. His voice was like steel in the otherwise silent room.

She hadn't meant to say won't aloud, but the room was so silent that even her thoughts seemed to be audible. It was as if there was no one in the world but them. "Both," she snapped. "We'll lose stories."

"So we lose a couple of stories," he said with a shrug.

"That's cruel. How can you be that uncaring?"

"It would be cruel to let her continue to believe she has a future here."

He pushed the tape and story aside as if putting an end to the conversation, but Jessica wasn't ready to let it drop. "You're being so hard."

Didn't she realize this was difficult for him? What did she want from him? But this was their job and she had to understand that. He hated upsetting her, but she had to learn to separate the two parts of their lives. Seth got up and came around the desk, sitting on the edge. "Are you going to deal with Trish?" he asked.

"Of course I am," she snapped. "I just hate doing something like that."

"I'm not asking you to fire her, that's my job. Just make it plain this is her last chance."

"It feels like the same thing."

Seth understood all too well. "If you really can't do it, I'll talk to her, but it would be more appropriate if it came from you."

"No, I'll take care of it. Doesn't it bother you at all?"

"Of course it bothers me. Kitten, it's never easy. If you need to talk about it, I'll be here." He shrugged. "It's something you have to learn. It's necessary to be hard sometimes."

"I am hard," she said defensively.

"I don't remember a thing about you that was hard."

Jessica caught her breath at the soft words and the teasing glint in his eyes. The part of her that knew this man from another time and another world realized he was trying to ease the tension, but that remark was too personal. "Was there anything else you wished to discuss?"

Seth straightened and glanced at his watch. "Yes. But over dinner. It's been a long day for both of us."

Jessica shook her head. "That's fine if it's business; otherwise, I'd like to go home." His face hardened to an uncompromising expression and when he said he would meet her in the lobby in five minutes, she only nodded agreement.

Seated at a small corner table in a quiet restaurant, Seth studied her a moment. They were both pushing too hard. They couldn't continue like this for much longer. The strain was beginning to show. He had tried to give her time and space, a chance to adjust to his presence. After their last dinner meeting early last week he had pointedly kept their contact to a bare minimum. He had hoped she would relax, but she hadn't.

Seth studied the menu a moment. What he wanted, no, needed, was just to talk. It was one of the things that had drawn him to her in the first place. She had listened to him, asked questions and understood. Tonight he was angry and frustrated and he needed to talk. It was always hard at first, the loneliness of a new town, the weeks earning the trust and respect of the staff.

And he had started to earn their respect. He had met and talked with all the staff now. Some he had liked and respected instantly, like Neil Patrick. Neil worked closely with Jessica and clearly liked her and relied on her judgment.

He almost smiled as he remembered his first meeting with Neil. The man obviously cared about Jessica, but Seth had found out quickly that Neil had a wife he adored, who was also a friend of Jessica's.

"Would you like a drink before we order?" Seth asked.

"No, thank you." Remembering the other nights they had been out for business, she added, "And if you don't mind, I'll drink my milk at home."

"Would it matter if I did mind?" Seth dropped his eyes to his menu. If he couldn't do better than that he had better try to keep this evening strictly business as well.

Jessica started at the sharp tone and looked up, but he was studying his menu intently. Could whether or not she drank milk really matter that much to him? Yes, it could, she admitted to herself. For one weekend she had thought of him as a very caring person, and so far nothing he had done had changed her impressions from that weekend. Even tonight what he had done wasn't out of character, though she had accused him of being hard and unfeeling. But, in fact, he was giving Trish a chance when he could just as easily have fired her without asking questions. And Jessica knew Trish wouldn't make it as a reporter.

She wanted to talk to him. She wanted to explain everything, but the reality of their situation loomed before her each time. Seth asked what she'd like to eat and, as usual, she requested a salad. But all she really wanted was to sit someplace quiet and just be with him.

For one lovely afternoon and evening she had done that. They had talked and shared ideas and dreams. They had shared so much and she wanted that again.

Seth placed their orders, then turned to her, all business. "The reason I needed to talk to you earlier was to let you know about some changes that are going to be made. Diane Howell will be taken off the six o'clock and moved to the noon."

"You can't do that. We need her on the six." Stay calm, she reminded herself. This was just business. "She's our only female anchor now. Our demographics show we don't attract a very good percentage of the female viewers, and she should give us a boost."

"Females watch good-looking guys. We'll find a dreamboat sportscaster for them."

She stared at him a moment. "Are you serious?"

"Very."

He couldn't be that crass. "What about women's rights and equal time and FCC regulations?" He only shrugged. "That's ridiculous," Jessica cried.

"It works. We have to bring the ratings up. Don't be stubborn, Jessica. The station makes its money from ratings. You get paid by those ratings."

So that was how it was going to be. Never mind about news and journalism, they were going to do an entertainment show, something to attract the viewers and entertain them. It didn't matter if the world was coming to an end, the ratings would be all-important.

A part of her felt like it was dying. This wasn't the man she had talked to one timeless afternoon. That man had cared. That man had principles and values. She tried to appeal to the Seth she remembered. "Diane is a competent, qualified and extremely valuable asset to our news department. Our ratings went up three points after she was put on as co-anchor for the six and eleven. The viewing audience appreciates her intellect and ability.''

"The ratings dropped one-and-a-quarter points for the last period."

"I don't believe that drop is related to the way Diane does her job. She's gotten better, not worse."

"You apparently have a very high opinion of her."

"I do, but undoubtedly my opinion won't influence the outcome."

"No, it won't," Seth said bluntly.

The waiter approached with their food. Neither spoke as Jessica was served her salad and Seth his full meal, this time chicken on a bed of wild rice.

"Who's going to replace Diane?" she asked at last, breaking the tense silence.

"We've hired John Jacobs from 4."

Jacobs had been with Channel 4 many years. Jessica could see the reasons for his being hired. He would hopefully bring a number of viewers with him, people who were loyal to the personality rather than to the station. "And I suppose you'll look at 7 for a new sports personality," she said sarcastically.

"Not a a bad idea at all," Seth mused. "I'll pass it along."

"Do that," she retorted. This calculating coldness didn't agree with her perception of him. Jessica frowned. She was doing it again, trying to tie together pieces that shouldn't and wouldn't unite into a whole. She did it every time they were together, every time an issue was discussed.

She sighed and pushed her salad away. Didn't anything ever get to him? No matter what happened his appetite stayed intact, and one would never know they had snapped and snarled like two children earlier. It was an impossible situation. "Can I order that drink now, please?"

Seth nodded and signaled the waiter. "You didn't eat anything. Was the salad not to your liking?"

"No, it was fine. I'm just sick of lettuce," Jessica admitted.

"What would you like?"

Jessica smiled ruefully. What she wanted most of all was a very thick, very large pizza, covered with everything and dripping with cheese. But, until her ankle was removed from the cast and she could get some exercise, large meals were out. "I'm really not hungry. Please, go ahead with your meal." The waiter returned and set her drink on the table. Jessica stirred it a moment before taking a sip of the creamy mixture, savoring the kahlua. "When do we make the changes?"

"Jacobs starts next Monday."

Jessica stared at Seth, but his expression revealed nothing. She didn't need a script to understand, however. None of this was his idea. Jacobs was very popular with the viewers and it would have taken more than the two weeks Seth had been at the station to break his contract. It must have taken several months to accomplish this.

A feeling of total frustration and helplessness washed over her. His anger earlier and the sharp tones he had been using weren't for her. She knew he hated what was being done. But she also knew he wouldn't express those opinions to her. He couldn't say anything, not while she was his executive producer. No matter how much he might deny it, there were lines that had to be drawn and not crossed.

"Seth, this isn't going to work."

"What?"

"Me staying. It's not working."

He couldn't have agreed with her more, but he had the definite feeling her reasons were going to be diametrically opposed to his. "Why do you say that?"

She took another sip of the drink before trying to answer. Was he refusing to accept her resignation because that weekend had meant nothing to him? Or was he keeping her at the station because he expected it to happen again? She didn't want to think thoughts like that. She wanted to believe that the two weren't mixed, but his actions weren't supporting her hopes.

"You said earlier you didn't believe in babysitting staff. You can't fire Trish on those grounds and yet keep me. I'm not carrying out all my duties, either. I'm not upstairs in the evenings like I ought to be."

"I think it's a different situation entirely. You're not a handicap to the department, even if you aren't fulfilling all your duties. Trish is a handicap. Your situation arises from a difference of opinion involving management. It'll work out, Jessica, if you give it time."

She knew it was a different situation. He had no history with Trish. But she didn't want more time. She wanted out. "You are protecting me—protecting my job. If I was anyone else you wouldn't be doing this," she accused. "You aren't behaving fairly, and it's going to show."

"To some extent, maybe, I'm not being impartial. But I don't like to replace staff this quickly. I like time to evaluate each individual before I make a decision."

"You've been able to make that decision about Trish and Diane this quickly," she challenged. "How can you evaluate me if I'm not doing all of my job?"

Seth smiled, despite the seriousness of what she was saying. "I think you know as well as I do that Trish won't make it. Sometimes the evaluations are easy. I'm giving her an opportunity to prove I'm wrong."

She couldn't refute that. Trish wouldn't make it as a reporter and he had given her another opportunity. "But Diane?" she challenged.

"Diane is not open for discussion."

"If I were fulfilling my job, Diane would be open for discussion." *If I weren't working for you, Diane and this entire situation would be open for discussion.*

"No, Jessica. It has nothing to do with whether you're handling all aspects of your job or not. The subject is not up for debate."

Jessica studied her drink a moment, absently twisting the glass around. "Okay, but it's still not working for me to be there."

"Why?" Seth fought the urge to reach across the table and stop her as she bit down on her lower lip. It was a nervous habit, but he hated to see such a sweet mouth abused so carelessly. To keep his hands busy, he slowly buttered a second roll.

"It just isn't." Jessica shifted restlessly in her seat. She should have known he would gnaw at her statement like a dog worrying a bone. "I'm sorry for the things I said in your office. Those remarks were inexcusable."

Seth smiled and laid down his fork. "I'm sorry too, kitten. We were both out of line."

"It's not you, it's me. I really think it would be best if I quit." Jessica finished her drink in one swallow and sat the glass down, wondering if she dared order another. Deciding it wouldn't be wise she turned the empty glass, restlessly waiting for his reply.

"It's not just you, kitten. I didn't have to respond to the remarks." Seth reached across the table and took her hand, stilling the restless movements. "The tension and stress are caused by us trying to pretend business is our only relationship. Tonight was pure and simple sexual frustration—for both of us."

Jessica couldn't believe he would say something that blatant. Anger and embarrassment fused as she snatched her hand from his. "And I suppose your solution would be to jump in bed and cure it." Her face flamed at her own words. She wasn't sure which embarrassed her more: his bold statement or her own.

"It's a solution that has crossed my mind more than once," he admitted with a chuckle. Seth was surprised that she would suggest it herself, but not the least surprised when he saw her face reddened. "But I don't think it's the cure."

"It's not," she assured him. "The cure is to let me quit."

"No, the solution is to admit that our relationship is more than a professional one and allow ourselves to let the walls down."

Letting the walls down would only lead to exactly what she had just suggested. "Mixing a personal and professional life doesn't work," Jessica insisted.

"Denying either part of yourself doesn't work, either, kitten. We've proved that."

"Then accept my resignation." She hadn't meant to beg, but her voice was pleading as she said the words.

"No," Seth said firmly. "Accept the fact that we have a relationship that goes deeper than work. Go out with me Friday. Try it my way."

"It won't work, Seth."

"Two weeks."

"What?"

"We've tried it your way for two weeks and it hasn't worked, now try it mine for two. If it doesn't work I'll accept your resignation. What do we have to lose?"

"I've been down that road, Seth. I know what can happen."

Seth reached for her hand again. "I'm only asking for time. Time to talk, to be together, to get to know each other again. Will you at least think about it?"

She knew she should say no, but if she did, he would pursue the argument endlessly. "Yes, I'll think about it."

Seth didn't push further, but he wondered why she couldn't trust him now. The first few days he had tried to understand. But two weeks had passed, and she still said nothing, gave him no answers. What happened to the woman who had been so open before?

Jessica hobbled up the steps to her apartment, aware of Seth behind her and wishing he would just drop her off and leave. But each time he had insisted on walking her to the door and waiting until she was inside before he would go.

"Kitten."

"Yes?" She paused and looked up into the shadowy planes of his face. Standing alone on the dark landing, it would be so easy to forget this man was her boss. It would be so easy to remember him as she had first known him. The air suddenly seemed filled with the warm, masculine scent of his body.

"I want to see you again, Jessica," he said, moving closer to her. "We shared something beautiful before."

His voice, low and caressing, was wrapping her in a seductive web. She wanted to move away, but there was nowhere to go. His hand cupped her chin, forcing her to look up.

"I need you, kitten, not just at the television station but as part of my life."

"What happened that weekend was a mistake," she whispered.

"If what happened between us was a mistake it was the right one. I didn't plan it, Jessica, it wasn't why I stayed, but it was beautiful and I wouldn't change it for anything in the world."

"There's no such thing as a right mistake," she protested.

"Yes, there is and now I want exactly what I said—time with you."

"That's all?"

He couldn't tell if she was disappointed or relieved or maybe a combination of both. "No, that's not all." He pulled her into his arms, cradling her head on his shoulder. "I want to make love to you again. I need you that way, too, but I won't rush you, Jessica." He set her back gently. "Good night, kitten."

He left before she could even say good-night.

Seth had told her about the changes Tuesday night. The news article announcing Jacobs' move from Channel 4 hit the paper three days later, as did word that Trish, who had managed to totally bungle two more stories, had been fired. That Friday she walked into the middle of a discussion of the events.

"Well, I said you had to watch the ones who were so unobtrusive at first. They always hit hardest."

"It doesn't matter if they come in quietly or like a tornado, the results are always the same."

"Can you imagine Jacobs taking over for Diane? Diane has brains. She was more than a face stumbling over lines of script. Jacobs' IQ must be all of ten."

"Yeah, and Cameron's must be five if he thinks bringing Jacobs over here will help."

"Ratings," spat out another voice. "I get sick of hearing the word."

"Did you see the figures listed in the paper?"

"I saw them."

Jessica had seen them, too. John Jacobs was being brought in at a salary nearly three times what she was making. She understood their feelings only too well.

"I really thought you would have walked out by now, Jessica," someone said from behind her. "You still aren't upstairs in the elite circle."

Jessica looked at the angry faces around her. In the five years she had been at the station she had passed most of them in rank, yet had managed to keep their friendship and support. "I don't think trying to be supportive of a new director is wrong."

"Not if he's trying to direct," Jed said. "I haven't figured out what he's trying to do. Explain why he set Trish up. That was the most deliberate move to get rid of someone I've ever seen."

Jessica leaned back against a counter, taking the weight off her cast. The walking heel had finally been put on that morning. "Was it? He could just as easily have let her go the night she destroyed the parkway story. Instead he gave her the opportunity to straighten out. She didn't."

"He could have put her on fillers again, worked her back up, but he didn't. He stuck her out on big stories with decisive issues. He gave her two days. He set her up. And now Diane."

"You guys aren't thinking," Jessica protested, looking at the circle of irate faces. "Jacobs has been with Channel 4 ten years. Look at your own contracts. You can't quit here and go to one of the other local stations right away. Talent clauses prohibit that. There's no way Cameron could have pulled that off in less than two weeks. That was something presented to him by Daniels."

"Getting the inside scoop now? All those late meetings paying off?" Jed asked derisively.

"No," she retorted angrily. "I'm just trying to look at the situation logically."

"Yeah, we know how a woman's logical mind works," someone snorted. "All you see is a good-looking guy. Logic tells you to be sweet and compliant. That way you'll have a chance."

Jessica straightened. "That's totally unfair. You know I try to do what I think is right. I just don't happen to believe Cameron had anything to do with Jacobs and I also don't think he had any choice where Trish was concerned."

"Or maybe you just haven't happened to think since he walked in," Jed needled angrily.

She knew Jed was reacting emotionally. "Did you ever try to see it from his side?" Jessica challenged. "He's sent in to work a few miracles with the ratings. He's got Daniels on one side pushing and all of us on the other side feeling hostile and threatened." She grimaced and turned away, knowing her remarks had been purely emotional. "I'm glad now I didn't get the job."

"If you had, Trish would still be here and Jacobs wouldn't," a voice said from the edge of the group.

Jessica shrugged. "I doubt whoever is sitting in that chair could change those two facts."

"I can see it now," another voice muttered. "All the women swooning over him. At least Diane had the courage of her convictions. She turned in her resignation this afternoon."

Diane had quit? Jessica felt sick at the thought and then angry. If it was common knowledge that Diane had quit, then Seth hadn't stood in her way as he had in Jessica's. "Some of you are the same ones who told me to give it time," Jessica said reasonably.

"Yeah, but that was before you tried to sleep your way up," a voice said from behind her back.

Jessica turned angrily and then stopped. Seth was standing several feet away and had obviously been listening to the entire discussion. Bill Jordan, who had just spoken, was leaning against a partition. He had been there the day Gerald Daniels had suggested they had become "close," and clearly had misunderstood the situation. But there was nothing to be gained by arguing. Keeping her head high and her shoulders back, she turned from the group and proudly crossed the newsroom to her small office. It wasn't until she was safely inside with the door shut that she let her shoulders slump in defeat.

Jessica leaned on the crutches and stared at the street, wishing the taxi would hurry. Seth had heard. He had been standing there and heard it all. Worse, he had not said one word. He believed. If he hadn't known before, he knew now and he had believed. Jessica leaned her head against the cool glass of the door. He had simply turned away.

"Jessica?"

"Oh, Diane, hi." Jessica straightened and stepped away from the door.

"I'm not leaving yet, but today is my last day and I just wanted to thank you."

"Thank me? For what?"

"For being on my side. Do you have a few minutes? I'd like to talk to you."

Jessica glanced at the empty street and nodded, then followed Diane to the far side of the lobby. "I'm sorry about what happened, Diane."

"I know." Diane smiled. "There wasn't anything you could do about it, but I did want to thank you for your support."

Jessica perched on the edge of one of the many sofas that were arranged throughout the large lobby. "My support?"

"With Seth." Diane sat down beside her, turning sideways on the sofa and tucking her legs up. She looked relaxed and happy, Jessica thought, as she continued. "He took me out to dinner last night to break the news. I can tell you, Jessica, at first I was furious." Diane grinned ruefully. "I accused him of selling out by hiring Jacobs. If it was a stranger or someone with ability it wouldn't bother me as much, but it's infuriating to be replaced by a man who can't even read."

"I know," Jessica sympathized.

"But Seth didn't have anything to do with it," Diane continued.

"Did he tell you that?"

"Not in so many words, but I've got a contract, too, and a few hints made it clear that he didn't like what he was doing. But let me tell you what happened. Here I was ranting and raving, and he started laughing." Diane's face lit with a smile. "I was screaming about everything from quality journalism to equal rights and he was laughing. I was so furious the man couldn't get a word in edgewise, and he kept laughing, which only made me angrier."

"He was laughing?" Jessica asked incredulously.

"Yes, but listen. When he finally managed to get a word in he said it was because he had gone through the same thing with you the night before. He wasn't laughing at what was happening, just at the similarity of our reactions."

"I should hope he wasn't at your situation."

"You must know him better than that," Diane chided. "I think it was just a way to release the tension. It was really hard for him."

Jessica started to speak, but Diane shook her head. "Let me tell you what he did. I still don't quite believe it myself. He spent all day yesterday going through my old tapes. None of us have been at our best the last couple of weeks, and he knew that so he pulled some older ones and watched. He told me which parts would make the best resume and he even offered to make some calls. I was so surprised that he had gone to all that effort I didn't know what to say. He took my silence as agreement and, Jessica, he's spent all day calling people and making contacts. I've got a fantastic interview set up in Chicago. I'll be flying up Sunday. I just didn't want to leave without thanking you."

"I don't think I'm the one you should be thanking," Jessica pointed out. "I didn't do anything."

"Yes, you did. You spoke up." Diane reached out and squeezed her hand. "He said you were the one who made him think. He also said he likes having you as his right hand because you aren't afraid to speak your mind."

"I wonder if he knows how often I do that," Jessica mumbled.

Diane laughed. "If he doesn't now he soon will. Oh, your ride's waiting. I won't keep you any longer."

"My ride?" Jessica turned to look out the window, but there was no taxi sitting on the curb.

"Diane, Jessica."

There was no mistaking that voice, Jessica thought with despair. Nor was there any mistaking her reaction to him. Why did his voice alone tighten everything inside her and make her mind leap from simple thoughts to dangerously complicated issues? Why did the sonorous timbre strike cords within her that changed her pulse, slowed her blood and heated her skin until speech was as difficult as movement?

Chapter Nine

Seth had come down the back stairs after the usual evening meeting feeling depressed. He had been at Channel 9 three weeks and he didn't feel he was making any progress. Three weeks and he had gotten nowhere with Daniels, the news department or with Jessica. And it was the situation with Jessica that bothered him the most.

The low tone of the conversation caught his attention as he entered the news department from the back hall. So the grumbles had started already. He stopped just inside the door and looked at the group of reporters, camera people and editors gathered near the center of the room. They were all clearly angry, hostile and upset.

It had to come sooner or later and this ridiculous business with Jacobs replacing Diane Howell must have been the catalyst. He listened to the gripes and remarks, sympathizing with some, recognizing others as simply a way of letting off steam. It wasn't as bad as some of the things he had heard at other stations.

Then Jessica stepped up to the group and was willingly accepted for a moment. At first he couldn't quite believe what she was doing. She didn't need to defend him. But if he doubted what he had heard he couldn't mistake the expressions on the faces surrounding her. The faces that a moment before had been open were now closed, the anger turning to a specific target.

He had stood, hands clenched into tight fists, aching to step in and stop what was happening, but knowing that if he did it would only make the situation worse in the long run. He knew the staff needed to vent their frustrations. He knew that, but his heart twisted each time a remark was aimed at Jessica. The employees were angry and unfortunately she had made herself a target by defending management's actions.

Seth didn't know whether to feel elated or sad. The fact that she was trying to defend him told him she cared. The same fact told him she really didn't know how to separate the compartments of her life.

"Yeah, but that was before you tried to sleep your way up," a voice said at that moment.

It was too much. He felt his muscles tense as he straightened, ready to do battle, but he forced himself to ignore the inner demand to step in and protect her. Anything he said or did at the moment would only fix the idea in everyone's minds.

Seth watched her limp toward her office before going on to his own and dropping into his chair. He was a man of action, used to following his instincts. If a situation demanded a response, he moved. But not tonight. Tonight he had fought against those feelings. Why? Jessica was a woman he dreamed of nightly, and his body ached to feel

ers beneath him, soft and pliant and responsive. But the
physical need was transcended by something stronger. She
had tapped a part of him that he hadn't known existed before.

That weekend he had responded to something within
her. He had sensed it in her eyes, in her touch, a vulnerability that had made him feel protective and needed. And
had been more than his physical strength that she had
leaned on. And that emotional vulnerability in her was
that had kept him from stepping in to stop the remarks.

The newsroom had gradually grown quiet. Seth started
through the lobby, but paused at the door when he saw
Diane and Jessica talking, one exuberant and happy, the
other quiet and reserved. Diane looked up, saw him
watching and gave him a welcoming smile. Seth knew Jessica wasn't going to be pleased, but he would have to speak
to her now.

"Diane, Jessica."

"Hi, Seth," Diane said with a warm smile. "I was just
telling Jessica everything that's happened and about the
interview in Chicago." Diane glanced at her watch. "I'd
better grab a bite to eat before things start jumping again."

"Would you like to go with us?" Seth asked Diane, ig-
noring Jessica's icy stare. He had heard Diane's earlier as-
sumption that Jessica had been waiting for him and he
planned to take advantage of it.

"No, thanks anyhow. I'm just going to grab a quick
salad," Diane replied.

"I'm beginning to think women in Atlanta are half rabbit," Seth groaned. "Doesn't anyone ever eat anything but
salads?"

"Jessica doesn't eat salads," Diane said.

"She has ever since I've been here."

"I guess it must be her foot then," Diane laughed. "Sh used to run a lot. Whenever we went out she'd order th largest, thickest pizza stuffed with about five differe things and so covered with cheese it was unreal. Then she' eat three-fourths of it."

Diane's innocent chatter explained a lot of things fo Seth. "Pizza, huh?" Not only was Jessica denying the relationship, but she had also temporarily lost the activi she normally used to ease tension and stress. As a runn himself he knew how caged and irritable he got when h didn't exercise.

"Yes and lasagna. She loves Italian food, though ho she can eat it and stay so thin is beyond me." Dia glanced at her watch again. "I've got to go. I'll call yo and let you know what happens, Seth." Suddenly sh hugged Jessica tightly. "I'm going to miss you. We'll kee in touch, okay?"

Jessica returned the hug. "Yes, please do." As Diane le the lobby with a quick wave she felt tears threatening spill over and she turned again to the window. "I'll mi her," she said after a moment.

"She'll be fine," Seth assured her, placing his hand her shoulder. "She's talented and, in the long run, th might be a good thing for her career."

Jessica looked up with a weak smile. "I'm glad you we to all that trouble for her."

"It was no trouble and I wanted to do it." Seth glance out the window and then back at Jessica. "Were yo waiting for someone?"

"A taxi," she admitted after a moment.

"Nonsense." Seth smiled. "I'll take you."

Jessica hesitated a moment before taking his hand ar standing. With one last glance at the street, she nodded. A the door he took the crutches from her and slipped his ar around her waist, supporting her as she went down the steps. Jessica was hardly aware of her awkward gait. The cold night was filled with the warmth of the man next to her. She struggled against the urge to lean into him.

"Could I tempt you with that pizza?" Seth asked as they reached the car and he was forced to remove his arm from around her waist.

He could tempt her, Jessica thought, as the cool November air replaced his warmth. "No, I don't think so."

Seth stowed the crutches behind his seat and slid in beneath the wheel. "Have you thought about what I said Tuesday?"

"Yes." But any idea she might have had of accepting his proposal had fled with the remarks in the newsroom tonight.

"And?"

"I can't."

Seth paused, one hand on the keys in the ignition, leaning slightly forward. "Can you give me a valid reason for that answer?"

"Past experience."

"My past experience hasn't shown me that," Seth said, straightening and turning to face her. "What happened in our past that makes you so sure you and I can't be friends as well as co-workers?"

"You and I would not be mere friends." There was something between them that would not lie dormant. The fact that it had for three weeks was amazing in itself. But then, Jessica had constantly struggled to keep the distance between them.

And Seth had helped, she admitted. He hadn't pushed. He had allowed her space and distance, except for a few verbal volleys. He had respected her need to be left alone.

"No, we wouldn't," Seth admitted, his voice gentle bu sure. "What happened to you, Jessica?"

She turned away, staring out the passenger window "It's not something I'm going to talk about." Wearily, she leaned her head against the seat. "It's also not something I'm going to let happen to me again."

"What happened before, Jessica, was between you and someone else. I don't think it's fair to judge me based on another's actions. Do you?"

"I don't think I'm doing that," she protested.

"Aren't you?"

Maybe she was. Maybe she was basing a future on past. "It's possible," she agreed after a moment. "But Seth..." She bit down on her lip, searching for the right words. "Things get misconstrued easily in television."

Seth leaned forward and turned the key, waiting as the engine settled into its natural purring sound. He knew she was referring to the remark he had overheard tonight "Television is highly competitive, kitten. You know that." He reached across the car and took her hand. "People say things out of jealousy or because they feel threatened. You can't let somebody's male ego ruin your personal life."

Jessica looked up. The only illumination in the car came from a streetlight at the corner, but even in the dimness she knew they were talking about the remark Bill had made "Male ego?" Did he really see it that way?

Seth had learned to survive in a highly competitive world and he had learned one of the keys was the ability to laugh "My ego is on very unsteady ground at the moment," he teased, releasing her hand.

"Yours?"

"Mine," he assured her. "I've met a beautiful woman I'd like to get to know and each time she rebuffs me Maybe it's my mouthwash or deodorant."

Despite herself, Jessica laughed at the absurdity of the statement as he steered the car out of the parking lot.

Seth smiled at her laughter, recognizing it for what it was, a release of tension. How far did he dare push? "Try it—tonight. If it doesn't work I'll accept it." They passed a theater and his mind leaped ahead. "We'll go to a movie and then out for that pizza. Then I'll take you home. Just time together like I said, nothing more."

Jessica could have told him how tired she was and how much her ankle ached. She could have protested, but she didn't, even when he turned the car and pulled into a parking space. She didn't protest as he helped her out and then bought the movie tickets. She didn't protest until they were seated in the darkened theater and she realized it was a horror film. "You aren't playing fair," she whispered as the credits rolled across the screen. He just chuckled and laid his arm across the back of her seat.

During the first two frightening scenes Jessica refused to move, sitting still and stiff in her seat, eyes shut tightly. But the third scene was too much and she turned, burying her face in Seth's waiting shoulder. His arm came around her instantly and she felt the warmth of his breath against her hair. As she straightened, he kept her close to him and she watched the remainder of the movie from the safety of his shoulder.

Maybe it was being in such a public place, but it felt right to leave the theater, his arm still around her. It felt right to laugh at his teasing and joke back.

"How about that pizza?"

Jessica paused partway into the car. "I'd like to, Seth, but I really am tired. This walking heel isn't all it's cracked up to be, and I think I just want to go home and put my foot up."

"Home it is, then." Seth drove slowly to her apart
ment, wishing he could think of some way to extend th
evening. "You're sure about the pizza?" he asked as the
reached her door.

"I'm sure I'd love one, but I am tired."

There was regret in her voice and he realized he couldn'
ask for more than that tonight. "Thanks for the movie
kitten."

"Thank you. I enjoyed it."

Seth bent, reminding himself sharply he had promise
no pressure. He kept his kiss light and quick. "Good night
then."

"Good night."

Jessica leaned against the door, listening to his foot
steps fade on the stairs. She didn't move until she heard th
engine start. Straightening, she realized she wasn't tire
anymore, though her ankle did ache dully. After washin
her makeup off she brushed her hair and changed into
baggy sweatshirt and jeans. She padded into the livin
room and turned on the television just as the doorbe
rang.

"If you can't take Mohammed to the mountain yo
bring the mountain to Mohammed," Seth announced a
she pulled the door open. "One very large pan pizza wit
everything except anchovies. I hate anchovies."

"You are one cruel man," Jessica moaned, inhalin
deeply. She stepped back to let him in. "I'll get the plates.'
She paused at the kitchen door. "I think I've got som
wine, would you like that?"

"Perfect," Seth agreed, setting the box on the chrome
and-glass coffee table.

Jessica returned in a moment with plates and napkins a
well as the wine and two glasses. She set everything on th
table beside the box and then eased down on to the floor

pulling a cushion off the sofa to prop her foot on. "I hope you weren't hungry, too," she teased as she handed him the bottle, then opened the box to serve the first two slices.

"I'll fight you for my fair share," he said with a laugh as he poured the wine. After a moment he moved down onto the floor next to her, propping his back against the sofa. "Enjoy it. You deserve it."

"Mmm, stairs won't be any problem at all now, I'll just roll up and down," she retorted around her first bite.

"And you keep forgetting how perfect you are," Seth said and picked up his napkin, gently wiping at a small spot of sauce from her chin. "I don't remember you being this messy," he teased, his eyes laughing as he picked up her hand, cleaning her fingers.

"You've never seen me with real food before," Jessica retorted, thinking of the endless salads she had been eating recently.

"No, it's just harder to make a mess with raisins," Seth said. Her eyes widened slightly as she looked at him and then she dropped her gaze, the thick fringe of lashes shading the green pools and hiding whatever emotion she was feeling. It was so damned hard not to push, not to remind her of what had been and could be. "I'll get some more napkins." Seth got up and hurried into the kitchen.

This was Jessica, he thought as he pulled several paper towels from the roll, studying the small space. The room was filled with life and warmth. Plants covered the window and the top of the refrigerator. The counter held a collection of canisters and a large cookie jar made like a strawberry. Small plaques decorated the walls, and a shiny copper kettle reigned over the top of the stove. The living room, on the other hand, was decorated in cool, pale contemporary furniture. It hadn't been at all what he had expected to find. "The plants are yours, aren't they?" he asked as he came back and settled on the floor beside her.

"Mmm." Jessica accepted one of the paper towels. "It's a jungle in there. There are too many but they keep growing and I can't just throw them out."

"I like them." He looked around the living room again. "Your apartment isn't what I expected at all."

Jessica paused, looking around the room. She had never given the decor much thought one way or the other. "Why? What did you expect?"

"Something warm and soft. This is too cool and reserved for you."

Jessica thought about her bedroom. The furniture was antique and definitely feminine, unlike Emily's sleek contemporary furniture. And the bedroom colors were all evening shades, dusty blues and pale grays with touches of rose and mauve. "The living room is Emily's."

Belatedly he remembered she did have a roommate, one who could come barging in at any moment. One who hadn't been around much either, since she certainly hadn't been here any of the nights Seth had brought Jessica home. Then the apartment had been dark just as it had been tonight. "Don't roommates usually compromise on decorating?"

"Usually. Probably, I guess," Jessica admitted hesitantly. "But when I left Chad it was rather sudden." She swallowed nervously, lowering her pizza to the plate and carefully wiping her mouth. "I just walked out one morning and I needed a place. I called Emily and asked her if I could use her spare room for a while." A while had stretched into two years.

Seth tried to keep his expression noncommittal. "Is all the furniture Emily's?" Had she nothing left from her marriage except memories that upset her?

"Oh, no. My bedroom is mine. There wasn't anything else I wanted from the house." That furniture had been the only thing she had taken into her marriage and the only thing she took from the house. She had let Chad keep everything else, down to the last teaspoon. Jessica picked up her glass of wine and sipped it, wishing he hadn't asked and reminded her of those days.

"I'm sorry," Seth said, leaning toward her. "I didn't mean to revive unhappy memories."

What he had really revived was the memory of all the reasons why she shouldn't be sitting here with him. Instead of telling him that, she forced a smile to her face. "They aren't that bad. Just a little sad."

"It's sad any time love doesn't last," Seth said softly. He lowered his lips to hers, tasting the wine she had just sipped and beneath that the warm sweetness that was her. "That's why I want us to have a chance."

Love? Jessica looked up, meeting his eyes at last. Love? Was it possible he felt that, too? "I think you're leaping ahead too fast for me," she teased, pulling back from him.

"I'm at least one slice ahead of you," he agreed, instantly lightening the mood.

They finished the meal in a comfortable silence.

"You sit still, Big Foot, I'll clean up," Seth said with a smile. He stuffed the napkins and paper towels in the box and carried it to the trash, then rinsed their plates and put them in the dishwasher. He returned to the living room, sitting down next to Jessica again and slipping his arm around her, urging her to rest her head on his shoulder.

Jessica resisted for a moment, but his shoulder was too tempting and with a sigh she allowed herself to relax. The TV filled the silence until eleven when Seth clicked the remote control off. "No news tonight." He bent and kissed her hair, rubbing his cheek against the silken strands a moment. "Has spending an evening with me been so bad?"

A smile teased at the corners of her mouth as she thought about it a moment. "No, it hasn't been bad."

"Then we'll try it?"

"Yes." She looked up into the depths of his eyes only to see the flickering desire hidden there. "If we take things slowly." She wasn't going to fall in bed with him tonight or tomorrow.

"We will," he promised. It wasn't going to be easy to take it slowly, but it was better than nothing at all. He bent to kiss her and only managed to pull back with an effort. "I think I'd better go now. I'll call you tomorrow." He placed one last tiny kiss at the corner of her mouth and left.

Jessica sat for a long time after the door closed. Taking it slowly was going to be a lot harder than she had thought. Her body ached to feel his against it. Her lips burned for his touch again. But it had to be that way.

If it was a salesman she was going to kill him. Literally. To keep ringing the doorbell like that on a Saturday morning was against the laws of nature. People slept late on weekends. She zipped up her caftan and stumbled sleepily toward the door, thinking of every harsh and cruel word she could use and a few she probably shouldn't. Jerking the door open, she froze, mouth open.

Seth looked at Jessica and wondered if he had made a serious mistake. She was covered by a soft, flowing robe. Her hair was a halo of tumbled curls that begged to be touched. Her cheeks were pink and her eyes were still soft from sleep. Everything about her was warm and cuddly and desirable. Rather than take her into his arms, he forced himself to use the light, easy tone he had planned.

"Good morning, kitten. Did I wake you?" Seth stepped around her into the living room and put a box on the table, then turned and took her hands from the door and closed it. "How can you be sleeping on such a beautiful morning?"

"What time is it?"

"Eight."

Jessica groaned in disbelief. "Eight o'clock a.m.?"

"Yes," he laughed.

"Go home and come back at a more human hour." She stifled a yawn. "Humans don't get up until ten on Saturday."

"I'm not human," he teased and then moved to take off his coat. "I'm a big, hairy creature you don't know what to do with."

Jessica nearly choked at the memory his words revived and then he turned. The flannel shirt he had on was open at the neck, revealing the thick mat of hair she remembered so well. She looked up to meet the teasing glint in his eyes. "Well, I've got a few ideas this morning and one of them is murder." She sank down weakly on the sofa. Why was he here so early in the morning? What had happened to taking things slowly? There he stood wearing jeans that hugged his narrow hips and a soft flannel shirt that begged to be touched. "What's in the box?"

"Breakfast."

"It's too early." She really didn't know what to do with him. "You were going to call later."

"Come here," he said, pulling her to the window. He opened the drapes and slipped his arms around her, resting her against his chest. "See that blue sky and bright sunshine? I bet it's the first Saturday you haven't worked in weeks."

Jessica allowed herself to lean back in the circle of his arms, wondering how he had known she had been working weekends. She hadn't seen him at the station. "Yes, and I planned to spend half of it in bed."

"I wouldn't object in the least."

His voice had taken on a huskiness that sent shivers down her spine. "Alone," she added hastily.

"A waste of time," Seth said softly. "Anyway, it's a beautiful day. Much too nice to spend cloistered in a dark, dreary apartment."

"You're right." She sighed. "I don't know what to do with you."

"Yes, you do," he whispered next to her ear. "You give me one kiss, then you get dressed."

She turned in his arms and looked up. "This is crazy, you know that."

"I know." His eyes held hers for a moment. "You are so pretty when you first wake up. Just like a kitten."

"I'm starting to question your tastes again," she joked.

"What's under this thing?" he asked, his eyes teasing as his hand stroked the caftan.

Jessica's face warmed. She had slept in his flannel shirt last night as she did most nights. "That, Mr. Cameron, is none of your business." She stretched up and gave him a quick kiss. "There's your kiss, now I have to go get dressed."

"That wasn't a kiss," he murmured, bringing her closer. "*This* is how you kiss good morning."

His fingers tangled into her hair, tilting her head back as he kissed her, long and deeply. Her arms moved up his chest, pausing as her fingers found the open neck of his shirt before slowly moving up to his shoulders. It was Seth who broke the contact, not pushing her away, just lifting his head until their lips were parted. He smiled down at her, his eyes golden.

"Now, go get dressed," he murmured.

"That has to be the most original line I've heard yet."

Jessica tensed and tried to pull away, but managed only to turn enough to find Emily leaning against the doorway to the hall, watching them. "I'm sorry we woke you," Jessica said.

"Oh, I don't think it was the doorbell or anything," Emily teased. Her clear blue eyes ran quickly over Seth. "I think it was the smell of smoke."

"I'm sorry I disturbed you," Seth said.

"That's all right, though personally I wouldn't mind if she did stay here today." Emily sighed, tightening the sash of her robe. "She won't, though. She'll go to work and wear herself out fighting windmills."

"Not today. Today she's going to have fun—outside in the fresh air and sunshine."

"The very idea seems to have rendered her speechless." Emily straightened and came into the room, extending her hand. "I'm Emily Peterson."

"Seth Cameron," he responded, releasing Jessica only enough to shake the extended hand.

"The news director?" Emily asked.

Seth glanced at Jessica. Hadn't she even told her roommate about their relationship, or at least that he was the man who had helped her?

"Those angel memos you told me about weren't wrong after all, were they, Jessica?"

"What memos?" Seth asked, catching Emily's not quite friendly look and then Jessica's flustered reaction. She looked like a child caught with her hand in the cookie jar. Once again he was reminded of the vulnerable quality he had seen that first weekend.

"It's nothing," she mumbled, again trying to pull away. Sometimes Emily needed to be muzzled.

Though he could feel the tension taking hold of her muscles, Seth kept his arm firmly around her as Emily spoke again.

"What's in the box?" Emily sniffed. "Please tell me it's sausage and biscuits."

"It is. Would you like to share?"

"I'll do better. I'll fix eggs and coffee to go with it. Even grits if you like."

"I'll pass on the grits," Seth said quickly, "but I'll help you fix breakfast."

"The man is a dream, even if he doesn't like grits. Go get dressed, Jessica, You know, jeans, casual, fun."

"I don't think—"

"That's the whole point of the day," Seth said. His voice was light and teasing, but the golden suns in his eyes told her all too plainly what the real point was, whether he admitted it or not.

"One very smart boss— I like your style," Emily put in.

"Support I can use." He grinned. "Point me to the kitchen."

Jessica could hear their talk and laughter, punctuated by the clang of a skillet and other small noises as she went back to her bedroom. Seth had had on jeans so she dressed likewise, then fixed her hair and added a touch of eyeshadow, a light stroke of blusher and some lip gloss.

Standing in the bathroom, she stared at her reflection. "You have gone totally insane, Jessica Buchanan. You know you will regret this the rest of your life."

Seth was busy piling sausage and biscuits on a plate when she got to the kitchen. The table had been set, and Emily was scooping a heaping mound of scrambled eggs onto another platter. "Anything I can do to help?"

"Just sit down," Emily commanded. "You'd only be in the way."

"Gee, thanks. It's nice to feel wanted."

"That's it, I think." Emily set the platter on the table and surveyed the settings. "Oops, your milk."

"Milk?" Seth asked as he sat down next to Jessica.

"She drives me crazy," Emily said. "She won't eat, but she acts like she's committed a crime if she doesn't drink three glasses of milk a day. I don't care what happens, three glasses a day ever since we got back."

"Ever since you got back?" Seth asked, looking at Jessica with open tenderness.

Emily misinterpreted the question and launched into a detailed story of Jessica's recent adventure, an account laced with her own idea of how stupidly Jessica had acted.

"Emily, I don't think Seth is interested in your opinion of whether I behaved sensibly or not."

Emily glanced at her, a momentary apology in her eyes. "So, what plans do you have for the day?" she asked Seth.

"I was hoping I could talk Jessica into showing me the sights."

"You mean like Stone Mountain and the Cyclorama?" Jessica asked. "What have you been doing with your weekends?"

"Working, just like you. Don't you ever take a day off?"

"Do you?" she retorted.

"Starting today I do and so do you."

Chapter Ten

Seth wasn't particularly interested in the sights, but lying in bed, still able to taste the temptation of Jessica's lips on his, he had struggled to think of some reason to monopolize her day. Sightseeing was the only thing he had come up with. It met all the requirements he could think of. It would bring them together, be open and public, and hopefully keep them talking on neutral subjects. As a side benefit it would give Jessica some much needed exercise and fresh air.

Seth hadn't been particularly interested, that is until he tapped Jessica's knowledge of local history and her willingness to argue and defend a point. Since most of the historic sites dealt with the Civil War, it was an easy matter to debate the past with her. And fun, he thought as they drove out on the Stone Mountain Expressway toward the park.

He followed her directions while reflecting that being with Jessica was a refreshing and interesting experience each time, and he had no doubt that in the years to come they would still have lively conversations and heated debates that ended with laughter.

"So, what next?" he asked as he parked the car. The park was large and the brochure included dozens of things to do, but all involved walking, and he didn't want to tire her too much.

"Definitely the top," Jessica smiled, watching the gondola car slide ever upward on its cable. "It's a beautiful day. You'll be able to see forever."

They strolled across the parking lot, pausing for a long moment above the sloping lawn in front of the reflecting pool. Seth studied the carving on the side of the mountain while Jessica told him of the laser shows in the summer, where thousands of people on blankets or lawn chairs filled the huge area.

"Wall-to-wall?" Seth asked, his eyes laughing.

Jessica nodded. "How long did it take to drive from the gate here?"

"Five minutes?"

"During the summer it takes two hours to get out."

"Two hours?" Seth looked back at the grassy slope. "I hope they bring supper."

"They do." Jessica grinned. "But it's worth it."

They continued walking slowly along the uneven path, coming at last to the building that housed the gondola cars. The ride up was breathtaking. Jessica didn't speak as the taped explanation of the size and history of the mountain was played. She stood still, holding on to one of the poles, and watched Seth, enjoying his expression and the feel of his arm around her shoulder.

Once at the top Jessica led the way through the building and out to the mountain. She wanted Seth to see the Atlanta skyline and she moved slowly toward the west side. Again his arm came around her, supporting and helping without comment.

Seth returned Jessica's smile as he admired the view. The granite surface of the mountain was pocketed with shallow holes made by the rain and wind. But on the whole it was smooth. They walked toward the west, his attention more on the woman at his side than on the vistas before him. The wind pushed her hair into a tumble of curls that glinted with golden highlights. It also molded the shirt to her body, outlining the full curves of her figure.

"Isn't it magnificent?"

Seth tore his eyes away from her and gazed in the direction she pointed. The beautiful weather had held and now in the distance the skyline of Atlanta rose like a toy city, the late afternoon sun turning the distant windows into golden fires, reminding him of the rising phoenix that symbolized the city. "Yes. It is magnificent," he agreed.

They stayed on the top of the mountain for a long time. The sun sank slowly in the west, changing the buildings from tongues of flames to golden spires reaching toward a lavender sky. They walked slowly from point to point until Seth noted that Jessica was shivering as the wind whipped across the open granite surface. Earlier the day had been warm, despite the November date, and neither of them had worn jackets. But now, with evening approaching and the exposed rock catching each breath of wind it was easy to remember it was late fall.

"We should consider going back down."

"Yes, it's getting late."

Seth moved to her windward side, blocking as much of the chill air as he could while they returned to the gondola terminal and waited to ride to the bottom. They stopped for a warming cup of coffee before starting back to the car. Sunset had ended and dusk was taking over the world.

"Hungry?" Seth asked.

Maybe it was the fresh air or maybe just the exercise, but she did feel hungry and pleasantly tired. The day had been wonderful. Visiting the sights was something she hadn't done for several years and seeing them through his eyes had been interesting. But she wasn't sure it was wise to prolong their time together.

"We could go somewhere for dinner if you like."

Jessica glanced at her jeans and shirt. "I'm not dressed to go anywhere."

"I know the perfect place," Seth said with a smile. "The atmosphere is relaxed, you don't need to dress up and the food is great."

She knew without asking he was talking about his place, but used the excuse of getting into the car to avoid answering. At the moment the only consent she could give was silence.

Seth slid in beneath the wheel and started the engine, then reached for her hand and placed it on his thigh, close to his knee. When he lifted his fingers from hers she left her hand resting against his leg, needing the contact, the reassurance that simply touching him gave her.

When Seth turned into a subdivision of large houses Jessica looked around curiously and then glanced at the man beside her. She had expected an apartment or maybe a condominium. Why would he buy a home in an area obviously designed for families? The car slowed and she looked out again, totally surprised when he turned in at a two-story house with an attached two-car garage.

Jessica stared at the house. Even though it was nearly dark, she could still see it clearly. Several years before when Neil and Beth had been house hunting, she had spent several weekends exploring with Beth. She had been married at the time and had fallen in love with a particular floor plan. She stared at the house, her heart suddenly feeling very heavy. This was the house of her dreams.

Seth automatically reached for the electronic control for the garage, then paused. "I usually go in through the kitchen. Do you mind?"

"No."

Seth pulled the car in and the door whined closed behind them. Jessica wondered what it would be like to come home in the evening and listen to the door close, knowing the outside world was gone and their own private world waited. Her mind was flooded with questions as she followed Seth into the kitchen.

He had been aware of the tension in the car and of her doubts. He had some doubts of his own. With her hand on his thigh he was acutely conscious of every breath she took, of the warm, fresh scent that filled his nostrils, and he wondered if he had enough willpower to keep the evening light and casual in the private intimacy of his home.

As they turned into the subdivision her fingers had tightened on his leg and he'd looked at her, but she was staring out the window. She had hardly seemed aware of his question about entering through the kitchen. Not that it mattered which way he took her in. The house wasn't ready for company. He should have postponed this until he at least had the furniture arranged and some of the boxes unpacked.

He watched her walk slowly inside. When she paused and looked around the undecorated kitchen he suddenly felt awkward and unsure. He followed her gaze around the room. "I know it doesn't look very good at the moment. I just moved in last week. I hope you don't mind making do.'' He glanced at the curtainless windows and the empty counters, thinking of her small kitchen. It had been so warm and filled with love. "I do have things for supper," he reassured her as he started for the refrigerator. "I had planned to bake some chicken, and there are things for a salad..." Seth trailed off as her silence continued. He opened his mouth to suggest he build a fire when she sighed. "Are you worn out, sweetheart?"

Jessica started and tried to pull her thoughts together, only half aware of what he had been saying. "No." She glanced at the kitchen again, realizing he had been talking about food. "Do you want me to help you with supper?"

Seth crossed the kitchen slowly and stopped just in front of her. Her hair was still tousled from the wind, with strands softly framing her face. He reached out, letting one of the curls twine around his finger, and her green eyes met his. He couldn't begin to decipher the myriad emotions flickering there. He lowered his gaze, pausing to look at her mouth. Her lips were just slightly parted, the lower one trembling as if she were about to cry.

Did she think he had brought her here for some grand seduction scene? Was that what had her upset? He traced the gentle curve of her jaw, tipping her face up to his. "Kitten, what is it?"

Jessica couldn't have begun to explain the complexity of her thoughts and feelings at the moment. She was afraid of the future and haunted by the past. And now she stood in her dream house. She wasn't even aware of the sigh that slipped past her lips. "Why this house?"

Seth glanced around the kitchen and then back at the woman who stood just inches from him. "The first week, before I started working, I spent day after day looking at places. At first I thought I'd get a small apartment close to the television station, but after one day I knew I didn't want to. I contacted a realtor and spent hours walking through houses. When he showed me this one I knew it was right, and I signed the contract before we left.'' Seth paused for a moment. ''I was thinking about you.''

''When did you buy it?''

''The Friday before I started at the station.''

Jessica felt stunned as the meaning of his words sunk in. She had accused him of walking out on her. Until this moment she hadn't realized how much she had needed to know it hadn't been a one-night stand for him.

Jessica looked from the bare window and empty room up into brown eyes. A line of tension had edged across his brow and hardened his mouth. Without thinking, she reached up and gently touched his lips. ''And you were thinking about me?'' she asked with a whisper.

''I think about little else.''

The words held no demand, but the message was clear and unmistakable. Jessica felt every muscle in her body tremble and every bone dissolve with the naked desire she saw. She had known all afternoon this would happen. How could it not when the day had been spent in each other's company, when repeatedly he had taken her hand or put his arm around her, holding her close to the warmth of his body.

But it was all right now. He hadn't forgotten during that long week. It had meant something special to him. He had been thinking of a future—a future that included her.

''Oh, kitten,'' he muttered just before his arms came around her and his mouth heated against hers. ''I'm sorry, but you're all I'm hungry for.''

His lips sought hers, tempting and teasing, until her legs trembled and her knees threatened to buckle.

Seth felt the yearning within her and kissed her again. She clung to him and then her body softened. Her lips parted beneath his and he lifted her into his arms, carrying her down the hall and upstairs.

After laying her on the bed, he stood for a long moment just looking at her. Then he sat down beside her and lightly traced the shape of her face. "All day all I've wanted to do was hold you and touch you and love you." He traced the shell of her ear and then the shape of her lips. "Do you know you haunt my dreams? I wake reaching for you."

"I know," she whispered. "I do, too."

"Do you?" he questioned softly. "Do you wake feeling alone and empty?"

It was exactly how she felt when she woke and he wasn't there. "It's scary," she admitted, unable to look away.

"Oh, no, kitten. Don't be afraid of it." He stretched out beside her, keeping space between them. "Never be afraid of something as beautiful as we have." Lightly he traced one brow. "How can green be compared to fire? Emerald fire. That's what your eyes are. Liquid emeralds."

Melted by the heat from yours, she thought. She couldn't catch her breath, his eyes were so intense. The feathery touch of his fingers sent fevered chills racing along her nerves. She reached up, pulling his mouth to hers. With a groan, he pinned her to the bed, his mouth taking hers in a hot, demanding exploration.

As quickly as the kiss had begun he pulled away, holding her hands at her side. Jessica felt a rush of confusion and doubt sweep away the warmth. "Seth?"

"I've dreamed of this every night, kitten. I don't want to rush and when you touch me that way...." He ended with a slight shake of his head and closed his eyes for a moment. "Even the fire in your eyes makes me feel out of control."

Gently he pulled her to a sitting position and slowly un buttoned her shirt, pushing it off her shoulders befor laying her back again. "You are so beautiful." He sighed tracing the line of her collar bone and then letting his fin gers drift down to the soft swell of her breasts. "I'm going to torture you the way you've tortured me for thre weeks."

It was a playful threat, but one he obviously meant t carry out. He anchored her wrists above her head and be gan a leisurely exploration, trailing warm kisses down he neck to her shoulder, then lower, teasing along the lac edge of her bra. Jessica twisted against him, trying to fre her hands, but he tightened his hold. "No," he whis pered, his breath hot against the silky material. "Not yet.'

It was torture, exquisite tender torture as he stroked and caressed her, kissing her skin at the edge of her bra and panties until she moaned helplessly. "Please," she begged

Seth rolled onto his back, pulling her on top of him "Kiss me," he commanded, freeing her hands at last.

She tangled her fingers into his hair and spent endles moments delighting in the different textures of his face. " miss the curls," she said, running her fingers through hi hair. "I liked it better longer."

"You just like big, hairy creatures," he teased. "Be neath this civilized exterior lives the beast, kitten. I haven' changed."

For a moment they seemed lost in memories. It was chance to put past and present together. It was a time t absorb and unite the two parts of themselves.

His hands roamed over her back to her hips, pulling he firmly against him. His hands moved to release the catc of her bra, then slipped the straps from her shoulders Jessica lifted herself, helping him to remove the garment

A choked moan caught in her throat as the sensitive tips of her breasts brushed the mat of hair on his chest.

Seth turned her onto her back, stripping off his clothes and her panties. Jessica reached for him, but again he caught her hands. "Not yet."

"I didn't do this to you," she protested, arching to meet him, needing him with every fiber of her being.

"Didn't you?" His free hand slipped between her thighs, finding the center of her femininity. "All those times I never heard a word you said because I was thinking of the sweet taste of your mouth." His head dipped to hers for a long moment until Jessica moaned and twisted against him. "Three weeks of watching you from across a desk."

"I can't take *this* for three weeks," she whispered, trying to move against him, needing to feel the hard length of his body against hers.

"Today," he groaned. "Do you know how I felt standing on top of Stone Mountain, your hair blowing against my face, your mouth so close to mine I ached?"

"Yes," she whispered as he finally joined their bodies. She trembled on the edge for a long moment before she felt herself explode in a burst of color. Clinging to his shoulders, his mouth took hers as she felt the answering response of his body.

Jessica woke to light kisses and sleepily opened her eyes. This time it wasn't a dream and with a smile at the man who held her, she snuggled closer to him.

"Oh no, you don't," Seth chuckled. "I'm famished. We're going to get up and fix supper."

"What time is it?" she murmured, still half-asleep.

"Ten."

Jessica giggled. "You're absolutely uncivilized. First you get me out of bed at the crack of dawn and now you want supper in the middle of the night."

"It was your fault I didn't fix it at the proper time," he said righteously. "I was telling you what I had planned when you so rudely interrupted me."

"I didn't interrupt you," Jessica defended herself. "I even offered to help you."

"Well, you can help me now. Up, woman. I'm starving." Seth rolled off the bed and pulled on his jeans. "I'll meet you downstairs."

He already had the chicken in the oven when she got downstairs. While he built a fire she fixed the salad and put some rolls on a baking sheet.

Seth paused in the doorway and watched her work a moment. It was just as he had pictured it. Walking up behind her, he slipped his arms around her waist. "I like this." He kissed her hair. "You look right at home in a kitchen."

"I hope that was a compliment."

"Definitely."

Together they finished preparing the food, then ate their meal sitting in front of the fire. After the dishwasher was loaded they sat side by side on the sofa, enjoying a second glass of wine.

Jessica watched the flames dance over the logs. The only sound in the room was the occasional cracks and pops of the wood. This was not how she had pictured things would go if she met someone interesting. She had always thought it would be more conventional. Beginning to see each other. Slowly working into something serious. Not this cataclysmic thing that had happened with Seth.

"Jessica?"

She turned to him, her eyes drinking in the beauty of his form, the firmly muscled chest and abdomen, the narrow hips, the strong thighs. If they made a calendar of him she would have three in every room.

"Is anything wrong?"

Her eyes skittered back to the flames as she realized what she was doing. "No, I was just thinking."

"Serious thoughts?"

Her gaze went back to him. "Kind of, I suppose," she admitted.

"Do you want to talk about it?"

"There's not really anything to talk about, I guess. I just didn't mean to let this happen tonight. I just feel like I've rushed into things." She turned to look at him, needing his understanding.

It was there in the depths of his eyes, a gentle comprehension that said it was okay to have doubts. But there was also stubbornness in the set of his lips and the angle of his jaw. She leaned her head back against the sofa. "We said we would take things slowly."

Seth studied the slender column of her neck. He had promised her they would, but even the best intentions sometimes couldn't be kept. Rather than try to explain or reason he bent to kiss her, slowly working his way from the corner of her jaw downward. "I plan to," he said huskily. "So very slowly."

Jessica didn't try to resist the familiar warmth that settled deep inside her at the light touches. Instead she let her eyes drift shut as her hand sought his neck, her fingers exploring until she found the nape, pulling him closer. "This isn't exactly what I meant," she protested weakly, her fingers tangling into his hair.

"And what did you mean—exactly?" he whispered against her ear, teasing along the lobe with his tongue.

"I forgot."

"Good, I only want you to think about this."

His mouth was warm on hers. The world and her doubts were lost, unimportant things that had no place in the sensual halo he wove around her. The only world was the one lit by the dancing flames of love that coursed through them until they were one.

"I have to move," she said later, not wanting to break the spell.

"Why?" He held her tighter.

"The cast." It was cutting into her calf where her leg rested on the edge of the sofa.

"Let's go somewhere more comfortable," he said, leading her down the hall. "That was altogether too fast." Pulling her close against him at the bottom of the stairs Jessica was surprised that his desire hadn't been dimmed in the least. "I'm going to have to teach you what slow means."

Jessica wondered if there was such a thing where they were concerned.

Jessica inserted her key in the lock and pushed the apartment door open only to freeze in midstep. Emily lay propped against Jeff's chest, a book open in her hand.

"Hi," Jeff said. "Don't just stand there, come on in and shut the door."

"Hi," Emily said without batting an eyelash, but one brow rose slightly.

"Hello," Seth said, more or less pushing Jessica through the door. "If you're studying we won't be long."

"Emily needs a break anyhow," Jeff said. "I'm Jeff McCall, by the way."

"Seth Cameron."

The two men shook hands, smiling pleasantly. Jessica was astounded at the way Seth had walked into the situation without a blink. He had to realize Emily and Jeff knew she hadn't been home last night, but the idea didn't faze him. It made her decidedly uncomfortable. She hadn't dated anyone, hadn't even gone out very often with groups of friends, and now to come in the morning after was embarrassing. Only Seth's gentle touch and Jeff's easy manner kept her from stammering out an explanation.

"I thought you said you were helping a friend today," Seth remarked, looking at the book in Emily's hand.

"I am," Emily said, reaching for the book and closing it.

"She's so afraid she won't pass the bar she doesn't want anyone to know she's studying to be a lawyer," Jessica explained. "If she's helping a friend that's okay, then she doesn't have to face questions."

"What kind of law?" Seth asked.

"Criminal."

"Prosecution or defense? Jessica, go change. You know all these answers."

"Defense." Emily laughed. "Where are you off to today?"

"Just shopping," Seth answered.

"Up, Emily," Jeff said, pushing her aside. "I'm ready for a coffee refill. Would you like some, Seth?"

"Yes, thank you."

Jessica finally edged her way out of the living room. In the bedroom she stood for a moment in front of the closet debating about what to wear. Jeans seemed the most appropriate. To go with them she chose a cowl neck sweater in a soft rose shade. She sat down at the vanity and combed her hair, then applied a little eyeshadow and mascara and a rose lip gloss that matched the sweater.

"Hey, Jess, is everything okay?"

She glanced up at Emily and smiled. "Yes."

"I take it things went well."

Jessica felt her face flush slightly. "I guess you could say that."

Emily sat down on the side of the bed. "Sometimes things do happen quickly between two people, Jess, I'm not criticizing that." Emily reached out and squeezed her hand reassuringly. "But—"

"You *are* going to criticize," Jessica said, pulling her hand free and turning back to the mirror.

"Jessica, what you did last night was—"

"My business," Jessica said firmly. For a brief second she considered telling her friend the truth, but decided against it. "Emily, I'm old enough to know what I'm doing."

"You also tend to have a short memory," her friend snapped. "You're only going to get hurt again. It's taken you two years to even begin to recover and what is the first thing you do?"

"You don't even know the man, Emily. You're jumping to conclusions."

"I know he's your supervisor and I know from what you said that your job isn't particularly stable at the moment. I—"

Jessica turned on the bench and glared at her friend. "I think you've said too much already." Male laughter filtered into the room. "I'll be out in a moment."

Jessica turned back to the mirror and stared at herself. She knew exactly what Emily was getting at. The others, that nebulous group that Seth had classifed as threatened egos would assume the worst. If she wasn't fired they would simply assume it was for the very reason that had made her walk out that afternoon. If anyone found out she had been out with him both Friday and Saturday nights...

Jessica slumped against the vanity. There was only one thing to do. She would simply tell Seth she had walked too much yesterday. She'd make up some excuse about her ankle and stay home. She wearily pushed herself upright and returned to the living room.

Seth turned and smiled, giving her a warm, caressing look. His eyes were filled with loving tenderness. Jessica decided at that moment to ignore Emily's concerns. It was time to trust someone and at the moment she couldn't think of a better person than Seth.

"I do like you better all cleaned up," Seth said as he crossed to her side. "The sweater is nice, but don't you own any jeans that aren't torn up?"

"Lots, but I can't fit the cast in without ripping the leg open," Jessica grumbled. If it wasn't jeans ripped up one leg it was shoes that didn't match her clothes. "I've looked like a cast-off doll for weeks now."

"Okay, Big Foot, your excuse is plausible, but I thought the effect was more like a homeless orphan."

"Thank you." She grinned.

"Jeff invited us to spend the afternoon here and cook a big pot of chili. He says Emily needs a break. I suggested they come over to the house in a couple of hours. Is that okay with you?"

"Sure." She wasn't sure why he was asking. Did he really want her approval or was he just being polite? It was his house. He could invite whoever he wanted.

"Good. Then we have to add the grocery store to the list. And a big pot."

"You make the chili and we'll bring everything else," Jeff said. "About three?"

"Sounds great." Seth quickly told him the address and how to get there. "We'll see you then." With that he whisked Jessica out the door. He had seen her withdrawal when he announced the invitation, a tension in her posture and a shadowing of her eyes he had seen altogether too often. He let her get nearly to the bottom of the steps before he spoke.

"You aren't happy with the invitation, are you?" She simply shrugged and pretended to concentrate on the steps. "If you didn't want them to come, kitten, you should have said," he said with a frown as she worked her way down the steps.

"In front of them?" she snapped.

"No, I don't suppose you could," Seth agreed. "I thought you and Emily were old friends."

"We are." Jessica paused at the bottom of the steps and took a deep breath. "We just haven't seen eye to eye on things recently."

"I shouldn't have accepted Jeff's invitation." He was pushing her again, though he hadn't meant it that way. "I thought it would be a pleasant afternoon for you, spending time with your friends. Jeff seems like a very nice person."

Jessica instantly felt guilty. Seth was still new in town and didn't know anyone and she was behaving like a spoiled brat. But she wasn't ready to make their relationship a public announcement, which was what he was, in effect, doing. Nor was she sure how Emily was going to behave. "It's your house," she said without looking at him.

"I want it to be our house, kitten."

Before she could begin to sort through the possible meanings behind that statement he had her in the car and was busy listing all the things they would need to get for dinner and to make the kitchen workable.

"Can you think of anything else we need?" he asked as he pulled into the shopping center.

She could think of several things: reticence, discretion and a little less pressure on his part where their relationship was concerned.

Chapter Eleven

When Jeff and Emily finally arrived the chili was simmering in a large pot on the stove and Seth had managed to find enough matching dishes to feed four people. After a flurry of greetings and coat taking, Emily looked around the bare kitchen. "Can I see the house?"

"Sure. Kitten, go ahead and show her."

Jessica could only nod. Seth had told her he wouldn't use that name around anyone, but clearly he thought that promise only applied to work. With a slight shake of her head, she led Emily into the family room, which was bare. The furniture had obviously just been dumped there and left as it stood. Reluctantly she showed Emily through the rest of the rooms, which were mostly unfurnished.

"Decorating early for Christmas, at least." Emily laughed as they rejoined the two men in the family room.

"Beautiful bathroom with green tile and a brilliant red shower curtain. It has a certain—impact."

"Emily," Jeff said with a touch of annoyance in his voice. "Seth's only been in town a couple of weeks. Give the man a chance."

"No, she's right," Seth said, apparently not bothered at all. "I've always had small apartments, with just a living room, bedroom, and a closet-sized kitchen I used to make coffee on the weekends. This is the first house I've owned since my divorce six years ago."

"What's different about this job?" Jeff asked.

"I have greater expectations for my personal life this time," Seth said, watching Jessica. "I want this to be a home, not just where I go to get a night's sleep."

"It's a nice house," Jeff remarked. "I wouldn't mind having one like it at all when I finally talk what's-her-name into settling down."

"First things first." Emily smiled at Jeff. "I can't decorate a house and study for the bar."

"You study and I'll decorate," Jeff said, pulling her close.

Emily groaned. "The man has no taste."

"Neither do I." Seth grinned. "I plan to enlist a little help, myself."

The look he gave Jessica left no doubt whose help he was enlisting. She wasn't sure how she felt about it, but she relaxed a little as Jeff left to check on the chili and make necessary additions to the spices. Seth followed, arguing good-naturedly about the proper amount of pepper.

Despite Jessica's doubts the rest of the afternoon was easy and comfortable. The four of them meshed without trying, constantly talking, laughing and enjoying each other's company even if Emily and Jessica rarely spoke directly. It wasn't until Jeff and Emily mentioned leaving that Jessica began to have second thoughts.

"Jeff, you wouldn't mind taking me too, would you? It would save Seth a trip."

"Uh, no, of course not."

"Kitten, you know I don't mind taking you home," Seth said with a frown.

"I know," she said, avoiding his eyes. "But we both have to work tomorrow and . . . all." And if she stayed she wouldn't go home. She didn't have the willpower to say no to this man.

"Em, why don't we wait in the car," Jeff said, picking up their coats from the stair railing. "Seth, it was a great afternoon. Next time we'll do this at my place."

"I'll look forward to it." Seth waited until the other couple was out the door before turning to Jessica. "Sweetheart?"

"I just need some time. I'm not ready to walk into the station by your side yet."

Seth looked down at her, instantly understanding her meaning. "I don't live my life for the staff, Jessica, and you shouldn't, either." What he saw in her eyes bordered on fear. "Honey, I'll take you home later if that's what you really want." What had happened to make her so uneasy about this relationship?

Jessica looked away, unable to meet his gaze longer. "At the moment I don't know what I want," she admitted. "I'm so afraid we've made a mistake. I really need some time, Seth."

"We haven't made a mistake, kitten." He kissed her tenderly and held her close for a moment, at a loss as to how to reassure her. "We'll talk tomorrow. God, I'll miss you, even for one night."

"I'll miss you, too." And if she stayed in his arms for one more second she knew she would stay for the entire night.

"I'll see you in the morning," he said, kissing her forehead and setting her away from him. He walked her to the car, said good-night to Emily and Jeff again, and kissed the tips of his fingers and laid them against her lips before shutting the car door.

"Why didn't you stay?" Jeff asked as he pulled away from the curb.

"Jeff, that's up to Jessica." Emily sounded irritated.

"Hey, that's all right," Jessica said. "It's okay if Jeff asks." It was okay, but she wasn't sure how to answer.

"The man has really got it bad." Jeff grinned into the rearview mirror. "He can't look at you without lighting up."

And every time he lights up I melt and forget how to stand on my feet, she thought. "He's also pushing," she said quietly. "Too hard."

"He's lonely, Jessica. He's been divorced for years. He's new in town and he's found you. He's what, midthirties? Sometimes men hit a turning point at that age. They want a home and family, and they get in a hurry."

"You aren't making a very good case if you're on his side," Emily said. "You make it sound like he's just a lonely person looking desperately for anyone to fill the gaps."

"All I mean is that Seth is thinking of the future, not just the present. Jessica knows what I'm talking about," Jeff said confidently.

"How could she? She went out with him for the first time this weekend. Sure, she sees him at work, but I see you at work and you know it's not the same."

Jeff chuckled happily. "You keep forgetting, my dear Emily, that Jessica can be a very enigmatic lady. And you know her well enough to know she isn't going to go off the deep end in one day."

"So?"

"So, ask Jessica."

Jessica smiled and shook her head. "Go on, Sherlock, I'm fascinated."

Jeff pulled into the parking lot and made a production of turning off the engine, checking the lights and helping Jessica out of the car and up the steps.

"Okay, Jeff, what is it?" Emily demanded impatiently as they stepped into the living room. "What makes you know so much that neither of us do?"

"I imagine I do know one or two things that you don't," he teased, then ducked the pillow Emily threw at him. "All right, all right, I'll tell." He glanced at Jessica and winked. "The news director at Channel 9 is also the nameless hero of the back trails of north Georgia."

"Impossible," Emily snapped, then caught Jessica's openmouthed look. "Isn't it?"

"No," Jessica admitted. "But how did you know?" Had Seth told him?

"A few little logical deductions." He grinned. "Knowing you and seeing the two of you together I knew it wasn't just this weekend."

"But that's a guess," Jessica persisted.

"Okay," Jeff said. "When we came up to get you that time, I went to the motel office to settle the bill since your credit cards were in your car. The bill had been paid, and that made me curious. I questioned the manager, but all he would say was that it had been taken care of. Then the man began to cross-examine me about who I was and about you. As I was walking out of the office the phone rang. It was Seth calling to be sure we had come and that you were okay.''

"But he had left at least two hours before you got there," Jessica protested.

"The room, maybe," Jeff said and squeezed her shoulder. "But I had the distinct impression he was right around the corner just in case we didn't show up or something happened. I also had the impression he had driven the poor motel manager slightly crazy that morning calling to check on you."

Jessica smiled as she turned to go to her room. She had demanded that Seth leave, but at the same time she had thought he had left her hurting and alone. Only he hadn't, she told herself, happiness filling her chest to overflowing. He hadn't left her alone and he hadn't forgotten.

Jessica had barely gotten to her office the next morning when Amy telephoned her and told her Seth wanted to see her immediately.

Despite the joy she had felt this weekend, the morning had brought cold reality and hard questions. She had carefully tried to keep her relationship with Seth professional. She had rationalized that one weekend, assuring herself they had both been innocent. But innocence no longer applied. She knew who Seth was now and she knew the implications of her actions.

He had argued that seeing each other would make the working relationship easier. She wasn't convinced that was true at all. Her job was still up in the air and if Seth took steps to change the situation, how could she or anyone else be sure it was due to her ability and nothing more? No, things weren't going to get any easier.

Amy wasn't at her desk when Jessica arrived so she went directly to Seth's door and tapped lightly. "You wanted to see me?"

Seth turned from the window and crossed the room to her side. "Yes, I did." He pushed the door shut behind her as she stepped into the room and caught her in his arms. "I wanted to see you all night. I wanted to see you when I woke this morning."

Before she could protest she was in his arms, pressed firmly against the hard wall of his chest. His mouth captured hers in a warm, deep quest that immediately made her forget everything except him. Her arms slipped around his neck and her body molded itself to his as she returned the kiss.

Jessica wasn't sure what brought the reality of the situation back in a cold wave. Maybe it was a sound from the other side of the door, but whatever it was, her body stiffened in protest. "Seth." She turned her head away. "Not here."

Seth refused to let her pull away, though he felt the tension that replaced the soft yielding of a moment before. "Why?"

Jessica glanced around the office. "This is work."

He wasn't surprised by her reaction. After she had left last night he had thought about the day. She had withdrawn as soon as her friends had become aware of their feelings for each other. She had been uneasy inviting them to his house and she had definitely not wanted their relationship made more public.

If he had some facts to work with he might be able to deal with her fears. As it was, all he had to offer her was patience. Seth gently smoothed her hair back in place. "This is *where* we work."

"But the staff."

"They have their personal lives, too."

Jessica twisted away and walked to the window. "This isn't right. If you went out in the newsroom and found two reporters kissing I'm sure you would say something."

"I think that would depend on who was kissing whom." Seth laughed. "Jessica, we aren't standing in the middle of the newsroom. We're in my office."

"And that makes it okay?" she demanded.

Seth went to her side, but resisted the urge to touch her again. "Yes, I think that makes it okay."

"It doesn't and you know it." She could easily imagine what would happen should someone walk in unexpectedly. "There'll be remarks."

"Jessica," he said sharply, "my job is important, but I have a personal life and personal considerations. I won't make all my decisions based on what the staff may think or say."

"I don't do that, either," she protested. "But I do care."

"And what are they going to think if they see us together?"

Jessica turned away. He wasn't stupid. He knew what they would think.

Gently, he turned her back to face him. "Kitten, we are both single, unattached adults. What we do with our private lives is not any of their business."

It was difficult to argue when his statements were so logical. But Jessica knew that logic didn't always play a part in relationships. "You said you could keep the personal and private part of your life separate," she accused. "This isn't."

"Kissing you in the privacy of my office is not mixing the two. Spending a few moments with you, even if it includes something personal, is no different for us than for you to talk with Diane about shopping or a movie in your office. I can't, and won't, turn my feelings off like a light switch," Seth said firmly.

He was right. She couldn't deny anything he said, but even as she admitted that to herself, the last morning of her marriage replayed itself in her mind. *There's only one way a woman ever makes it.* The harsh, hateful words reminded her of the risk she was taking and the indelible line she had already crossed.

She wanted a chance with this man, a chance to make the relationship work and she didn't believe she would have that as things stood. No matter what he said, outside influences could and would color their lives. "Seth, would you please accept my resignation now?"

Seth felt as if someone had splashed him with a bucket of cold water. "Your resignation?"

Jessica plowed ahead desperately. "When you first came you said when things had settled down a little—"

"And you call the way things are out there settled?" he demanded.

She knew her timing was all wrong, but she tried again. "You said we could talk about it." The warmth that had greeted her and the tender questioning that had been in his eyes faded to be replaced by flint. The firm line of his mouth hardened and the angular line of his jaw changed into granite as he looked down at her.

"Fine, we'll talk," he agreed, gesturing toward the chair. What he really wanted to do was shake her until the truth tumbled out. He wanted to clear the air and get to the bottom of whatever it was that kept holding her back. Instead he flicked the intercom and told Amy to bring two cups of coffee.

As they waited, Seth tried to contain his anger and bring some order to his thoughts. Jessica didn't speak, but he could tell she was upset. When Amy brought the coffee in he nodded and told her to hold any calls. Only then did he return his attention to the woman who sat across from him.

He was totally confused by her reactions. Friday she had been hesitant, but Saturday she had relaxed and opened to him again. And Saturday night she had wanted him. He hadn't forced her in any way. But then last night she had begun erecting a wall once more. After three weeks he had no clues about her feelings except that she felt it was impossible to mix her private life with work. Nothing she had said in the mountains or since he had been at the television station gave him any concrete reasons for her repeated demands to quit.

"First, you agreed to wait a month—"

"It's been three weeks," Jessica interrupted.

"Which is not a month," Seth said firmly. "Second, things have not settled down around here. Diane quitting last Friday and Jacobs starting today do not make for a restful tribe. I'm sure even you can see that."

Jessica flinched at the sarcasm in his last statement. "Yes," she agreed.

"We've covered the reasons from a business point of view," he continued relentlessly. "Now, we'll go into a few more personal ones. Do you have another job?"

Jessica shook her head. "Whether I work or not is not your concern, but no, I don't have another job." But she would start looking this morning. She would make a few phone calls and let people know she was interested in a change.

"Then your request is denied," Seth said firmly. He wasn't going to let her quit until he had some answers. Speaking more gently, he looked across the desk. "Jessica, you were making an emotional request when you asked just now."

She had, but his initial reaction had been emotional, too. How, in the few minutes it had taken Amy to bring in the coffee, had he managed to marshal his emotions and thoughts into such an organized attack? She knew her request had caught him off guard at first. "Partially."

"And what part wasn't?"

For just a second she considered telling him how unhappy she was or how afraid she felt that what they had would be lost. She had told him that weekend about her loss of interest in her job, but he had turned the conversation away from emotional issues. "I still think I'm a handicap to you, Seth. I can't help but feel as if you're protecting me." Jessica took a deep breath and looked up. "And I can't help but feel it's because of..." She trailed off, unsure what words to use. Emotional involvement sounded too strong and relationship sounded trite.

Seth sat back in his chair for a moment. "I don't deny that my personal feelings probably do color my decisions," he admitted. "But I'm still not ready to accept your resignation and that is not purely personal." Realizing he needed to give her some leeway, he went on, "If you do have a job offer you are considering or when things have settled down here and you still wish to discuss it, we will. In the meantime, the subject is closed."

Jessica nodded helplessly and rose. She wouldn't bring it up again, but she was going to get out of television, Seth or no Seth. In the meantime she wouldn't go out with him again. She couldn't risk it because she had no control where he was concerned. "I'd better get to work."

"Jessica, there was a reason I wanted to see you, other than to say good morning," Seth said as she reached the door.

"Yes?"

"Jacobs is to have the lead in the news. Every night."

She couldn't read anything in his expression as he issued the order. A dozen questions sprang to mind but she simply nodded and left the office.

She knew she had handled the discussion poorly from the moment she walked out the door but she also knew she couldn't easily mix these two parts of her life again. The memories and the pain left over from her first marriage were still too strong to make it something simple. She trusted Seth, but there were others she didn't trust, others that could hurt both of them.

She made a few phone calls when she returned to her office, letting several people know she was considering making a change. Then she resolutely turned her attention to the day's work. It was midafternoon when she looked up to find Seth standing at her office door.

"Got a few minutes?"

"Of course."

"Not too near the deadline?"

"No, everything's fine."

She watched as he stepped into the small room and closed the door. Her office wasn't large, but with Seth in it, it felt even smaller than usual. He sat down in the chair by her desk.

"I've been thinking about what you said this morning."

Her heart thudded nervously against her ribs as she waited for him to continue.

"You're right, I have been protecting you. You should be upstairs in the evenings."

Her heart stopped its thudding and fell into her stomach. Upstairs was the last place in the world she wanted to be. "Seth, I—" Had he misunderstood her? Did he think resigning was just a threat in order to be included again?

"No, you were right." He smiled gently. "You were right, I don't think anyone can always make impartial decisions." Seth saw the tension lines forming around her mouth and at the corners of her eyes.

How impartial was this decision? How impartial could any decision be after this weekend? "Why today, Seth?"

"You're a good producer, Jessica. You need to be there."

She had been a good producer all along. And she had needed to be there all along. Why now? her mind demanded, why today? Her mind had an answer already formed, but it was her heart that really wanted to know. "That's not why I asked you to accept my resignation." If she had had any idea he would have taken this step she certainly wouldn't have spoken this morning.

Seth's brows raised slightly in surprise. "I never even thought that."

And I believe him, she thought. I believe he didn't see it as anything but an emotional outburst. And it was my emotional reaction that caused him to analyze his and take this step.

"You don't want to be there, do you?" Seth asked, interrupting her thoughts.

"Not really."

"Starting tonight I expect you upstairs." It was an order, given in a firm, steady tone.

"I think I'd rather quit," she said weakly.

"Jessica, what happened between you and Daniels?"

"Nothing," she denied. "I'll be there."

Seth rose, but paused at the door. "You can talk to me, you know."

About that? She couldn't talk about that, especially not after this weekend. "There's nothing to say."

Jessica was as tense as a wound spring by the time it was time to go to the meeting. She had double and triple checked the newscast. With no excuses left to delay her, she went upstairs to the executive offices. Seth was waiting for her in the hallway.

It was obvious from the moment she walked in that Gerald Daniels had not been aware she was coming and it was equally obvious that he was furious with Seth. She was even more shocked at the harsh criticism leveled at the newscast. The only good thing he had to say was about Jacobs. She wished with all her heart she hadn't brought up the issue of her resignation that morning. The tension that had been with her all day coalesced into a throbbing headache midway through the newscast. When it was finally over, she excused herself quickly and left the office, her only thought to get away.

But her plans of escape were useless. Neil was nowhere to be found. Jessica returned to her office and sank wearily into her chair. The thought of waiting for a cab was almost more than she could bear. Her head pounded dully as she reached for the phone to call a taxi.

"Ready to go?"

She looked up at Seth. "Did you tell Neil not to wait for me?"

"Yes."

"Why?"

"There was no reason for him to wait when I had to stay," Seth said reasonably. "It's no problem for me to take you home."

"I don't appreciate having my life arranged for me," she snapped.

"I'm not arranging your life, Jessica," Seth said softly. "I simply told Neil I'd give you a ride."

"If I wanted to ride with you I would have told Neil myself."

"I don't think this is the place to discuss this."

Slowly she stood up and pushed her arms into her coat. "I'll go home with you, but that's all."

Seth studied her a moment. "No problem," he agreed. "You don't mind if I stop for some take-out, do you? I'm not in the mood for chili tonight."

Jessica sighed. She was too tired for a confrontation now. She never seemed to win with Seth, anyway. Somehow he made all her statements seem inconsequential. And she couldn't argue unless she gave him facts she wasn't ready to share.

Only Emily knew the truth about her first marriage and the divorce. Only Emily knew the things Chad had said and only Emily knew what Daniels had suggested. It was why Emily had been so sharp and critical this week. And now she had been proven right.

What was the first thing Seth did? Force her upstairs and take over her life as if he had earned some territorial right.

"Come on, kitten, it's been a long day and you're tired." And definitely angry, Seth thought, but he wasn't sure why. He only knew it was more than just the fact he had told Neil not to wait this evening.

Jessica leaned her head back and closed her eyes, not even bothering to open them when he stopped for food. She didn't want to talk because she knew Seth would start probing again. It wasn't until she heard the whine of the garage door that she sat up and opened her eyes. "I said I wanted to go home," she protested sharply.

"This is home," Seth said and was out of the car before she could say anything else.

"I meant my apartment," she said when he opened her door and reached to help her out. "I'm tired, Seth."

"I know you are, kitten." He gazed down at her rigid body a moment. "You take everything in life too seriously."

"Someone has to. You certainly don't."

"I take you seriously and I'm not dropping you off at a dark, empty apartment where all you'll do is sit and brood."

Jessica glared at him. "I don't like you when you're so high-handed."

Seth grinned. "I like you even when you're contrary."

Jessica sat silently on the sofa while Seth built a fire, fixed her a cup of hot tea and brought plates and napkins to the coffee table.

"Hope you like Chinese," he said as he opened up the white cartons.

"Is he always that way?" Jessica asked abruptly.

"Who? Daniels?"

"Yes."

"Don't let him upset you." Seth handed her a plate. "Eat."

Jessica forced a bite into her mouth, but she had no appetite. "Is he?"

"So far," Seth said casually.

"Doesn't it bother you?" Daniels had always been critical, but tonight his comments had been harsh and biting. They hadn't been directed at her personally, but she still felt stunned.

"There was nothing wrong with the newscast," Seth said, glancing at her untouched food. "It was a little rough around the edges, but it'll take a few days for the on-air personalities to mesh. As far as the stories, the coverage and the lineup went, it was a good show."

"How do you stand it every night?" she asked, setting her plate down.

"I take the source into consideration," Seth said with a rueful smile. "He'll calm down eventually." Seth shrugged. "I was shoved down his throat by the corporate offices," he explained after a moment. "And Gerald Daniels obviously doesn't like having anything shoved down his throat."

No, he doesn't, Jessica thought. No more than he liked being refused something he wanted.

Seth finished eating and cleaned up, then came back into the den and sat down beside her on the sofa. "Let me hold you, please," he said, taking her in his arms without waiting for a response.

"It's getting late. I should be going home." The protest was halfhearted.

"I just want to spend some time with you," he said. "Nothing more."

That was what he had said about this weekend, too, but Jessica couldn't help relaxing into the warmth of his arms. "Things haven't been easy for you, have they?"

"They never are at first," he said and for the first time she could hear the fatigue in his voice.

Jessica looked up and then smoothed his hair back. "I'm sorry if I've made your job harder."

Seth nuzzled her neck a moment. "You haven't." Having her there, having something to think about other than the crazy conflicts with Daniels had been a relief.

Jessica smiled ruefully. "Oh, I don't know. I haven't been your most cooperative employee even when I knew the things that happened weren't your decision."

"Like what?" Seth asked, settling back and pulling her more comfortably against him.

"Like Jacobs replacing Diane." Jessica let her head settle onto his shoulder as he looped his fingers together and rested his hands just below her breasts.

"I knew you understood and that helped." Seth smiled. "But it sure makes it nicer to spend the evening with you."

But just the evening, nothing more, Jessica promised herself. "Has it been harder than other places?"

"In some ways," Seth admitted after a moment. "I knew about what to expect from Daniels, but the staff in general seems very indecisive."

"Alex Smith couldn't stand up to Daniels. They're a little afraid to trust you yet."

"Do you think they will?"

Jessica smiled to herself. "I can't imagine why they wouldn't."

"I can." Seth sighed tiredly. "Diane is one good reason."

"When they cool off they'll realize it wasn't you, Seth." Jessica sat up and turned to him. "They'll calm down and think in a few days."

Seth turned her back and settled her against his chest again, resting his cheek on her hair. "I hope so. God, I hated doing that."

They sat talking quietly. Jessica could hear the edge of tension leave Seth's voice as he discussed some of his frustrations. They fell silent after a while. She hated to disturb him and drag him back out to drive her home. He was as tired as she was. Jessica promised herself she would ask him to take her home in a few minutes.

Seth felt the tension slowly ease from her muscles. She shifted slightly and he smiled as her head settled into the hollow of his shoulder. After several minutes he looked down. She had gone to sleep. Gently, he lifted her into his arms and carried her upstairs. In the morning she would probably raise hell. Tonight he would at least have her by his side.

Chapter Twelve

This is getting ridiculous."

There was more than a little impatience in Seth's voice this morning. The first week he had said nothing, but for the last week his irritation had been getting more obvious. "It's you who refuses to bring me home in the evening," Jessica retorted. Not that she protested that strongly, she added to herself as she fit the key into the lock. "If you'd just bring me home you wouldn't have to do *this*."

This was getting her home in the morning so she could shower, do her hair and be dressed in time to ride in with Emily. It meant he had to get up and then either go to work at least an hour early or find some place to waste the time.

The whole thing was silly, she admitted to herself, silly and immature. It was immature to play games and pretend she was not seeing Seth except at work. It was silly and unfair to expect him to crawl from a warm bed and bring her home in the morning. She knew he was right to be annoyed, but she needed the space and the protection it gave her.

"It's one thing for you to take me home in the evening since we both have to go to late meetings," Jessica continued as she tossed her purse and coat on a chair. "It's altogether different for us to arrive together." She turned and glared at him. "You know the first thing everyone would assume."

"The truth," he said with a chuckle. "Don't you think they already think that way, anyway?" He saw the instant loss of color from her face and backed off a little. "What would be wrong with us being together, Jessica? I've told you before I won't make all my decisions based on what someone else may think or say."

"You aren't a woman," Jessica retorted.

"You certainly didn't seem to mind that I wasn't a woman last night." Seth knew he had pushed too hard almost as soon as the words were spoken. Quickly he crossed the room and took her gently in his arms. "Kitten, I'm sorry." For a moment he held her, sheltering her from whatever hurts held her so tightly in check. In the privacy of his house she was warm, vibrant and passionate, but as soon as she crossed the threshold she changed. "Please, just think about it."

"I've got to get dressed," she said, her voice too quiet.

Seth watched her leave the room. He was fighting unseen, unnamed ghosts. He was fighting shadows with no identity, and there were moments when it was exhausting.

It had been one of those days, Jessica thought as she scrambled to get the last of the six o'clock show in order. First there had been round fifteen with Seth. Then the noon producer had called in sick and she had had to take over for him as well as tend to all her regular duties. Jessica wasn't sure she had sat down since she had walked in that morning, and her ankle hurt. The cast felt like it had gained twenty-five pounds. For the first time ever the thought of the meeting in Gerald Daniels's office sounded nice. At least she would be off her feet.

Any thoughts of sitting down died a quick death as she walked in to Daniels's office. The phone rang and with a scowl, he handed it to her. Jessica took the receiver and listened.

"Are they ready?" She nodded at the answer, already spreading papers across the desk. "Then we'll start with it. Get me Tyler. He'll have to lead in."

"What in hell are you doing, Buchanan?" Daniels demanded. "Jacobs leads the newscast every damned evening."

"Jacobs can't ad lib and I don't have time to write the words for him," she snapped without thinking. "Tyler? You've heard? Right. We'll give you thirty seconds and then cut over." As the intro music began Jessica turned to Seth. "We've got an airliner down. There's a crew on the scene, another nearly there and one on the way to the airport." She turned back to the papers almost before she finished her explanation, glancing at the lineup. For every second they used live on the plane crash an equal amount of time would have to be pulled from the planned schedule. Her eyes scanned the sheets, deciding which stories could best be pulled when she spotted two commercials for airlines. "And I've got to pull these spots," she said over her shoulder to Seth in between giving orders to the booth.

"Cameron, damn it, do something," Daniels yelped. "We'll lose money if we don't run those commercials."

"Gerald, this is her job. Shut up so she can do it," Seth snapped.

If putting three minutes into a newscast was hard, pulling one completely apart and putting it back together while they were already on the air was nearly impossible. She glanced up at the row of monitors as Tyler turned to the crew at the airport. Broken pieces of a plane filled the screen. People milled about, obviously stunned and in shock. The first rescue units arrived just as the report began. She half smiled as Tyler asked pointed, incisive questions. The reporter on the spot, who had initially appeared as stunned as those behind him, began to distance himself and respond.

Seth pushed a note in front of her as they finally broke and went into the next story. She glanced down and a little of her tension eased as she realized he had been timing the live segment for her. She began to reorganize the material in front of her.

They worked perfectly as a team. Seth didn't try to take over, but he was there, helping, seeing her needs before she spoke, and then filling them. They finished five seconds short. Sighing, Jessica started to gather up the papers she had strewn from one end of Daniels' large mahogany desk to the other.

"You are fantastic!" Seth yelled.

"I—" He picked her up and swung her around in a circle, his arms tight around her waist. She started laughing. "Seth, put me down." The room whirled past her again before she was slowly lowered to her toes.

"You are great." He grinned and kissed her soundly.

She totally forgot about where she was or who their audience was. She had scored a victory and he was proud of her. "I am, huh?" she asked, grinning back at him.

"Absolutely. The greatest."

"Almost," she agreed with a laugh. "I mistimed that last segment by five seconds."

"So, who's counting?" Seth teased. He lowered her to the floor, but kept his arms around her. "It was a fantastic job. I wouldn't have changed a thing."

"You helped. If you hadn't been timing those first live reports I could have lost it all."

"If we can call a slight pause to the mutual admiration society," Daniels cut in coldly, "I'd like a few explanations."

"Of course," Seth said with a wink at Jessica. "Before you is a man who can't be happy when we just outdid every television station within five hundred miles."

"I thought I had made it plain Jacobs was to have the lead. You let her pull him without batting an eyelash."

"First, he has had the lead every night until now," Seth said. Jessica glanced up at the steel in his voice. "Second, Jessica is right. The man can barely read, much less ad lib an intro and then follow up with the pointed questions Tyler did." He glanced at Jessica and smiled. "I don't interfere when my staff knows what they are doing. We have one of the best producers I've ever had the good fortune to work with on any level." Seth paused for a moment. "If you want her to go, Gerald, then you've lost me, too."

"That can be arranged," Daniels said coldly.

"Gerald, when you get to your favorite watering hole tonight and the boys from 4 and 7 are eating their hearts out over this one try to remember who pulled it off."

Jessica didn't know what she had expected of Seth, but his jumping to her defense felt wonderful. As they entered the newsroom he gave a thumbs up sign to everyone there and then began speaking to all the staff, sometimes

in groups and sometimes individually. He managed to chat
with all of them, from the control booth to the crews at the
airport, and let them know how proud he was of the work
they were doing.

The newsroom was humming with activity, even though
it was well into the evening. There were continual reports
coming in, along with demands from the networks for
feeds and information. The late-night show had to be re-
worked.

A little later someone pushed Jessica toward a table
spread with sandwiches, pizza, soft drinks and fresh coffee. She overheard someone mention that Seth had had it
brought in and wondered how he had pulled it off at that
hour of the night on such short notice.

Jessica took a short break, sipping a steaming cup of
coffee while she watched and listened. Everyone was elated
at the job they had done and Seth seemed proudest of all.
He wasn't out to steal the glory for himself, either, and
Jessica was thinking that maybe she had been wrong all
along. Maybe she was still hiding from a past that she had
never dealt with fully. Then someone called to her and she
set the coffee down and turned back to work.

It was almost midnight when Seth put her coat around
her shoulders. "Come on. Time to go." She glanced
around the room. Everyone was beginning to leave. A
skeleton crew would stay on, but for the moment the crisis was over. She turned, more than willing to go home.
She leaned heavily against Seth as she went down the steps
to the parking lot.

"I know one very tired lady," Seth said softly as he
helped her into the car.

"Yes," she admitted. "I am."

"Then it's home and to bed with you," he said, pausing to kiss her cheek.

Jessica sighed, leaning her head back against the seat and closing her eyes. Home and to bed was exactly where she wanted to go. She didn't pay any attention until the car stopped and Seth cut the engine. She opened her eyes and stared out the windshield, not quite believing where they were. She had been thinking of his home and his bed. She had been thinking of sleeping curled in the warmth of his arms. She hadn't thought he would bring her to her apartment.

She found herself fighting back tears as she climbed the stairs and fumbled through her purse for her keys. Was this his way of saying it was over? Had he decided this morning he was tired of playing games? As she reached out to put the key in the lock, she paused. "Why here?"

Seth was glad the darkness hid the anxiety he was feeling. He had been afraid she wouldn't even ask that much. "You're tired, kitten. This way you can sleep a little later in the morning. You need it."

Jessica stood very still. Was that the only reason? "Seth?"

"Yes?" He hardly dared to breathe, afraid even that much disturbance would change her mind.

"If I got some clothes would you...I mean is it really..." Swallowing, she turned and looked up into the shadowy planes of his face. Even in the dark she could picture each feature clearly. "I'd rather..." Again she trailed off, almost afraid to speak. "I'd rather be with you."

Seth caught her in his arms. "I'd rather you were with me. I'll help you pack." Her lips were cold when his first touched them, but they quickly warmed to the sweetness of sunkissed berries. Her body molded itself to his, even through the coats they both wore. "Let's pack."

Seth carried Jessica up the stairs once they reached his house. She protested mildly, but it was obvious that she was exhausted and equally obvious that her ankle was hurting. He helped her change, then put her into bed and held her until she was sleeping soundly.

Sleep did not come as easily for Seth. He was happy she had finally admitted she was willing to have a public relationship with him, but he was still troubled by the doubts that kept holding her back, doubts she never talked about.

She moved against him and he wasn't sure if the soft sound she made was a whimper or a sigh. He turned, watching her, searching for answers. Since he had been at the television station she had appeared to be tired most of the time. He knew the day had been long and hard, but her fatigue went far deeper. Was it only the ankle?

Seth frowned into the dark, shaking his head. Where he and the rest of the news staff had been exhilarated and proud tonight, her response had been weariness and tension. She hadn't seemed to find any joy in meeting a challenge.

For the first time he began to question her motives for wanting to resign. When they had talked in the mountains, when there had still been some distance between them, he had told her she didn't love her job and she had agreed. But when she had submitted her resignation he hadn't been thinking about that at all. Seth turned and studied the face against his shoulder, lightly touching a curl that lay against her cheek.

The next time she brought up the subject—no, the next time he could safely steer the conversation in that direction—he was going to have to do some probing into her reasons. He had, perhaps selfishly, assumed her only reason was him. She was obviously uncomfortable with the fact they worked together, which was another issue he planned to probe. But after this evening he couldn't help but wonder if he wasn't the catalyst, not the cause, for her repeated attempts to resign.

Seth straightened, pushing the mound of paperwork aside. The building always seemed empty when Jessica was out. He glanced at his watch with a frown. She should have been back long ago. Had the doctor found something wrong with her ankle? It had been seven weeks and the cast was still on. She never said more than it was doing fine, but then he had learned that Jessica rarely said little about what was on her mind. Now. Once she had talked freely and openly. Once she had dared to share her dreams.

Stretching, he walked to the window. Raking his fingers through his hair, he opened the blinds and glanced out. It was a gray day. Rain had been predicted and the sky hung leadenly against the building-studded horizon. Maybe it was just the weather that he found depressing. A car pulled up and a foot in a very familiar cast was extended. His mood instantly lightened. She was back.

The sigh of relief that had filled his chest exited in a whoosh as a man ran around the car and helped her out. Jessica laughed at something the man said, a free, easy laughter he rarely saw. Her eyes were alight and filled with an excitement he hadn't been able to put there in a long time. The many nameless things that had been nagging at him turned into anger as he watched the interchange. The man laughed, leaned forward and kissed her.

Jessica was ecstatic as she climbed the steps to the lobby of the television station. Yesterday she would have sworn life couldn't get better, but today it had. First the doctor had promised, almost guaranteed, that her cast would be off next week. But the joy of having her leg back had been totally eclipsed by her lunch meeting.

Jessica paused, her hand on the stair railing. Seth might not like the idea initially. In fact, he might be furious, but once he understood how much she wanted it and how important it was, she was sure he would be behind her all the way. Wasn't it Seth she had to thank for everything else in her life being so wonderful? Seth, with his patient strength and quiet encouragement, had given her back the confidence she had lost in the last few years. She glanced down at herself and smiled. Yes, it was Seth she had to thank and he would understand. She couldn't wait to tell him.

Seth glanced up at the knock on his door and turned as Jessica came in, as close to dancing as she could get while still walking with a cast. Her eyes sparkled and her face was flushed with excitement. Something twisted painfully inside him. He wanted to be the one to bring that look to her face, that happiness to her smile.

"Oh, Seth, wait till you hear," she said, crossing the room and throwing her arms around his neck. Jessica leaned against him, the steady beat of his heart and the warmth of his body making her world complete. She wanted to reach up and kiss him, but she felt self-conscious about being demonstrative at work. Even with the door closed she hesitated to do more than offer a quick hug.

"Hear what?" That she had found someone else, someone that made her laugh and someone she felt free to kiss in public?

"First—the cast comes off next week. He promised. Well, almost, but for Dr. Bertram that's a guarantee." Again she laughed. "You won't have to live with a Big foot anymore." Jessica settled on the edge of his desk and looked down at the cast. "Just imagine. Walking and jogging and tennis and living again."

"You said first?" Seth asked after a moment, tension knotting his stomach. For a moment Jessica sobered a little, but then the sparkle in her eyes was back.

"Yes. I had called an old college professor a while ago and he suggested that I talk to Michael Campbell, who's starting up a small magazine, and express an interest in an editorial position. Today I talked with Michael and he offered me the job. I can't believe it's practically fallen into my lap like this."

A job? She hadn't mentioned looking for a job. "I didn't realize you were going for interviews." He glanced at the window, remembering the interchange outside that had ended with a kiss. Some interview that must have been.

"I wasn't, not really." That was part of what made the whole thing so unbelievable. "I had made a few phone calls, but I hadn't really followed up until this came along yesterday. It's just the most fantastic thing that's ever happened. Michael wants me to start immediately, but I told him I'd have to give you notice."

"Does that mean you've accepted the job?"

"Yes, I accepted it. I couldn't possibly not and maybe let someone else take it. It's just what I've always wanted."

"I thought we had agreed to discuss this before you made any decisions." Evidently he had thought a number of things that she hadn't. He had assumed that any decisions affecting their future would be discussed and the decision reached as a couple.

She realized too late how reserved he had been ever since she walked in. Only now, with the cool tone of his question, did she note the tension that had tightened his shoulders. He hadn't returned her hug, much less tried to steal a kiss as he always did. "Seth, I'm so excited." She glanced at him with a smile. "I think I need to start over. I left out all the details."

"I'm sure you don't need to talk to me, Jessica. You've made your decision."

She wasn't sure exactly what he was angry about. Could it simply be that she hadn't dropped the idea of getting out of television? "Seth, I know we haven't talked about it, but I was serious about quitting. You knew that, didn't you?" Surely he knew she'd been serious. It was the only thing she hadn't changed her mind about ten times lately.

"I was also serious about discussing this before you had made a decision. I thought you understood that."

She tucked her hands under her legs, wishing she had sat down in one of the chairs instead of on his desk. "But we did. I guess that was weeks ago, but, Seth, this was just too good to pass up."

"And what about your agreement to stay until things had settled down here?" He paced the narrow space, knowing he was being unfair. Things had settled down throughout the department. In fact, things were going far better than he had hoped for at this point.

Jessica swallowed and slipped from the desk, moving to one of the chairs as an excuse to give herself time to organize her thoughts. "Things have settled down, Seth." She spoke quietly, then sat down, carefully folding her hands in her lap. "You have everyone's support and respect." The night of the plane crash his praise and hard work had won him the admiration of the entire staff.

"And you? You're fulfilling all your duties now, aren't you?"

"Yes." She couldn't face him, but she wouldn't cower in her chair, either. Slowly she raised her eyes and met the coldness in his. "But you know that wasn't the real issue."

"And what is the real issue?"

"I don't want to stay." She lifted her chin fractionally and stood her ground. "You knew that too, Seth. I'm not turning down this offer. It's the perfect job for me."

Jessica watched as Seth paced across the office several times. There was nothing he could say to change her mind, not with the job that had been offered. "Seth, I—" She had wanted to tell him about the job, to share her excitement with him. But something had gone terribly wrong between the time since she had walked in the door.

"I don't think we have anything further to discuss, Jessica. You've made your decision."

"Yes, I have," she said quietly. She rose and started toward the door, then turned, wanting to ask what was wrong. Thirty minutes ago she had been the happiest person in the world and now she watched helplessly as the most beautiful part of her life broke, splintering into a million tiny shards. But he had turned his back on her and rather than ask why, she left without speaking.

Seth slumped into his chair as Jessica left his office. He had done exactly what he had promised himself he wouldn't do. He hadn't tried to find out the underlying issues, or anything else. He had simply attacked her. She had pulled the rug out from under his feet and he had attacked.

This past weekend he hadn't pursued the subject. He had been concentrating on other things. His shoulders sagged as he remembered their time together. It had been riddled with mild disagreements over Jessica's constant refusal to make his house her home. He had wanted to go shopping for furniture. Jessica had refused. He could have forced her to go along, but he wanted her participation, not just her presence.

He hadn't understood what was holding her back. Now he did. The lines she had drawn in their relationship were because she had known she wasn't staying. She had moved most of her winter clothes and a few small personal items to his house, but she refused to bring anything more. She had clearly planned on it being a temporary arrangement.

As six o'clock approached Seth paced restlessly about his office. The only decision he had reached all afternoon had been to accept her resignation without dispute. He dreaded the ordeal this evening. Sitting in the same room with Jessica, wanting to talk and yet knowing that, even had they been alone, talk would be pointless because he wouldn't get any answers.

And it made no sense. None. When they had been strangers she had talked to him. It had been part of her charm. She had talked openly and honestly about her job, her life. But since he had been here she had carefully and rigidly kept all those thoughts and feelings silent. She had locked herself away and he had no key to the puzzle.

He went up to the second floor several minutes early and told Daniels that Jessica would be leaving. The news delighted the station manager. Jessica entered the room a few minutes later and took her usual seat apart from them, looking pale and unsure. Seth wanted to hold her and tell her they would work it out, but he wasn't sure if it was a promise he could keep. He wasn't even sure he wanted to try anymore.

"I was told you've resigned, Jessica," Daniels said.

Jessica glanced up at Gerald's remark, then looked at Seth. She hadn't put it in writing yet and she hadn't told anyone, except Seth. She had wanted him to know before it became common knowledge. So there was only one way Daniels could have found out. "Yes, I have." There was relief but no joy in the knowledge that this time Seth had decided to accept her decision.

So she hadn't told anyone else, Seth thought as the surprise flickered in her eyes a moment. If it was the perfect job and she was so thrilled about it, why hadn't she told several people?

"That really surprises me," Daniels commented a few minutes later.

Seth didn't move or look at either of them directly, but he was aware that something was going on he didn't understand. There had always been undercurrents between them, but this was something more, something Daniels thought he could use to his advantage.

Again, Jessica looked at the two men. Seth hardly seemed aware of the conversation. She turned back to Daniels. "My resignation?"

"Yes," Daniels mused. His eyes ran over her slowly, a considering look that left her feeling degraded. He glanced at Seth and chuckled softly. "I've really been impressed by you recently."

That was news to him, Seth thought. All he had heard was how incapable and uncooperative Jessica was. And the tension in her voice, though it stayed level, alerted him that she knew Daniels meant more than he said.

Jessica swallowed and glanced at Seth. Icy fingers teased at her spine. His attitude had changed. He hadn't moved, and she doubted that Daniels was aware of the shift, but she knew Seth wasn't missing one nuance of their talk.

Carefully, she framed a response, hoping to diffuse the situation. "I'm glad my work has been satisfactory."

"Your work has always been satisfactory." Daniels laughed softly. "More than satisfactory. No, I'm impressed at how well you learned to play."

"I haven't been playing."

Play? Seth listened carefully. There were pieces missing, pieces he didn't understand. Then Daniels laughed again, a knowing sound that turned Seth's stomach.

"You've played, and I assure you, you did quite well."

If the glimmer in Daniels' eyes hadn't been enough, Seth's cold detachment would have driven the truth home. Unconsciously, Jessica thought suddenly, she had done exactly as Daniels was suggesting. That was the only explanation for Seth's behavior today. She had learned the game and she had played it.

No! No, she hadn't! She looked quickly at Seth's impassive expression. Or had she without realizing it? That was the only explanation for his anger this afternoon, for his silence tonight.

Jessica looked down at her hands, forcing herself to untangle her tightly twisted fingers. She hadn't, not intentionally. She had believed that Seth was different. She had trusted him, but with Daniels's words everything fell in place. The movie after he had helped Diane. Being reinstated to her "full duties" after spending the weekend with him. She had fallen into the trap, consciously or unconsciously, and now she would have to pay the price. The realization came with a wave of nausea so strong she thought she would be sick on the spot.

"Yes, you've learned," Daniels continued. "There's no doubt about why you kept your job for the last few weeks."

Seth wanted to punch Gerald Daniels' white teeth down his throat. He wanted to tell Daniels Jessica had kept her job because she was an excellent producer. He wanted to refute the remarks, but something made him hold his silence a moment longer.

Seth hadn't said a word. Tears stung the back of her eyes. No! Seth was not that kind of man. Seth would not— But this was the second time he hadn't defended her, the second time he hadn't responded when someone had attacked her. Her head throbbed and her stomach churned. Things had gotten just as complicated as she had feared, more so even, because, despite everything, she loved him. She loved him and she had let that love blind her to reality, and she hadn't considered the consequences of her actions.

She rose from the chair, not looking at the two men. She lifted her chin and squared her shoulders. "You were an excellent teacher, Mr. Daniels."

Seth had his key. He had it. Now he understood why she had walked out and what she had been afraid would happen. He started to speak, then stopped. Words wouldn't penetrate with a man like that, but actions would. He rose from his seat and crossed to Jessica's side. "I think you fail to realize, Daniels, that this is a double resignation." He had the satisfaction of seeing the station manager look shaken. "You've said before you wanted her out and I told you then if she went, I did too." He slipped his arm around

Jessica's waist. "I won't work at a place where there's sexual harassment of the employees."

"I don't think you know what you're talking about, Cameron."

"I do," Seth assured him, his voice deadly in its calm. "And you can be sure I'll inform the board fully when I talk with them."

"I think you're being a little hasty in your judgments, Cameron," Daniels said, looking decidedly nervous.

"I think I've been slow in my assessment of the situation," Seth retorted as he turned Jessica to the door.

"Why don't you think about it overnight? You're throwing away a good future. And for what?"

"For something you would never understand, Daniels," Seth said.

Chapter Thirteen

It took Jessica a few moments to absorb everything that was happening. She had been standing alone and then Seth was by her side, his arm around her, his voice harsh with anger. But it wasn't anger at her. His condemnations were directed at Gerald Daniels. He was defending her.

As they crossed the receptionist's office the two men's final words penetrated. Seth was quitting and Daniels was right, he was throwing away his career. She couldn't let him do that.

As they entered the hall Jessica stopped and looked up. "You can't quit, Seth. It's wrong."

"It would be wrong to stay. I'm going downstairs to call the board president."

Jessica reached out, laying her hand on his arm. "At least talk about it before you make an irrevocable decision." She couldn't let him throw away his entire career because of her.

Seth turned sharply. "Talk? You, of all people, suggest I talk? You've kept your life one big secret. Now you tell me to talk." He raked his fingers through his hair and shook his head as if he couldn't absorb the meaning of her words. "Oh, what the hell. Let's get out of here. I'm sick of it." He grasped her arm firmly and started for the stairs. "I'm sick of all of it."

Jessica noted the openly curious looks as they entered the newsroom. Seth walked straight to her office and tossed her her coat, pulled her purse from the drawer and then turned her toward the door again. The room had fallen very quiet in those few moments, Jessica thought, as she struggled to keep up with his long strides. Too quiet.

Seth said nothing on the drive home and didn't look at her once. Jessica didn't know what to say, so she sat quietly, aware of the anger and tension that filled the interior of the car. She had seen him angry at work when a story was ruined. But this was something much more, much deeper.

As he turned into the drive and waited for the garage door to close, his words echoed hollowly through her mind. *I'm sick of all of it.* She followed him into the house and watched as he went to the bar and poured a very stiff bourbon, then sat down, his back to her, seemingly unaware that she was even present.

Jessica turned back to the kitchen, thinking she would fix herself some tea or possibly start supper. Suddenly the room seemed hollow and empty. She stood in the doorway and stared at it as if seeing it for the first time. *I'm sick of all of it.*

There were still no curtains at the windows, no pictures or plants, nothing to show that the room was used, lived in, loved, a part of anyone's life. Glancing over her shoulder into the family room, it was the same. No drapes at the windows, and the bookshelves held only a few stray items that Seth had unpacked. *I'm sick of all of it.*

Feeling slightly ill herself, Jessica glanced at Seth's still, withdrawn figure. Turning, she walked down the hall and upstairs to the bedroom. Slowly she crossed to the closet and took down her suitcase and carried it to the bed. She had wanted a miracle. She had a miracle, only she had been so busy fighting ghosts she had pretended it wasn't there and had held herself back until Seth had been left with nothing. She had been so busy waiting to prove him guilty she had stripped away all the beauty that could have been.

She had no idea why he had even put up with it as long as he had. Other than a few evenings she had never given him the time and thought he needed. She had refused to become a part of his life, to make his house her home, their home. Jessica turned and went to the dresser, lifting out a stack of lingerie and carrying it to the bed. Tears burned the back of her throat as she turned to the closet and removed an armload of clothes, then put them on the bed.

Seth stood in the doorway, wondering why he felt the rug had just been pulled out from under him again. He was a fool to feel surprised that she was packing. She had never wanted to be here, never wanted to be a part of his life. Why she had, even temporarily, he wasn't sure. Yet the sight of her methodically folding a sweater and laying it in the suitcase was like a blow to his midsection.

Anger filled him. He had just given up fifteen years of work and planning for this woman and she was walking out. He welcomed the burning, hot feeling that replaced the iciness even the bourbon hadn't touched. "What are you doing?"

Jessica started at the harsh question. She hadn't heard him on the stairs and hadn't seen him stop at the door. She picked up the sweater she had dropped and carefully began refolding it. "Packing."

"I figured that out." Seth's voice dripped with sarcasm. "Why?"

For just a moment hope sprang to life, but the coldness of his eyes quickly blew out the tiny flame. Jessica studied him briefly before turning back to her task. He deserved some answers. But she didn't know how to talk to him. "I can't be the woman you need," she said after a moment.

She could have, Seth thought furiously. At one time she could have been the woman he needed—open, trusting, strong, determined. But only if she had wanted to be. The qualities he had longed for were there. She just wouldn't let them out, wouldn't share those parts of herself with him. He crossed the room and reached out, pulling her away from the suitcase. "Can't you?" he taunted, his hand stroking deliberately across her breast. "Do you think I need more than this?" He deliberately teased her, watching the passion flare to life at his touch, feeling the trembling under his fingers.

Jessica knew she deserved his anger. She deserved his sarcasm. She didn't deserve this. Her own anger flared, hiding her pain and her need for him. She twisted out of his hands, her throat aching with the tears she refused to let fall. In desperation she lashed out. "All we've ever had is what happens in bed."

"You're right, Jessica, all we do have is what happens in bed. It was enough for a start, but it had to go somewhere after that and it hasn't." Her head came up sharply and the pain on her face was almost more than he could bear. "I wanted someone to share my life with me. I haven't found that in you."

His heart thudded heavily as she wrapped her arms about her waist, holding herself tightly. She wasn't going to fight back. She was going to sit there until he had said his piece and then— What had happened to the woman he had first met? What had happened to the woman who met every challenge?

He stepped back, then turned and walked across the room to the window. He couldn't let go. He couldn't just let her walk away. Not without a few answers. Seth crossed his arms over his chest and watched her. "I've figured out several things. You walked out because of Daniels. And you didn't want to be seen with me because you thought everyone would assume what he suggested tonight." His voice became harsh and condemning. "You are determined to quit this job because of that, aren't you?

"Am I right about the reason you want to quit?" he demanded when she didn't answer. She nodded and Seth gripped her shoulders, jerking her around to face him. "And what kind of treatment do you expect to get from that redheaded octopus?"

"Redheaded octopus?" Jessica repeated blankly.

"The man who brought you back today," Seth snapped. "I assume he's Michael."

And then she remembered. She and Michael had stood at the bottom of the steps a moment, talking, and Michael had kissed her. A friendly kiss of thanks on her cheek. "Is that how we gather the news now? Peeping from windows?"

"I have to gather it somehow," Seth sneered. "You certainly aren't going to tell me a damned thing." He turned and pinned her with a cold look. "What has all this been for you? Were you playing house until the right job came along? Has it all just been a game?"

Jessica dropped the skirt she had been holding as she turned to stare at him. "I never, never did that." She took another step backward. The tears she had been fighting were threatening to completely overwhelm her.

"Didn't you?" Seth knew he was pushing, but he took one last chance, using the only clue he had. "You walked out because of Daniels. You said yourself you got so upset you broke your ankle. Men play hardball, Jessica. You should know that by now." He paced across the front of the window, raking his fingers through his hair. "You claim not to like all these little games."

"I wasn't—" She had struggled to hold everything in since early afternoon and now the tears choked her, cutting off further words, making speech impossible. She turned, thinking at least she would fall apart in the bathroom rather than dissolve in front of him.

"Weren't you?" he demanded harshly. "I don't think standing on the steps kissing your new boss supports your statement."

Jessica straightened angrily. "Michael kissed my cheek."

"Today your cheek, tomorrow—"

"You've made up your mind, Seth. You've made up your mind and nothing I can say will change it."

She was wrong. Seth knew she wasn't the type of woman to do what Gerald Daniels had suggested. He remembered her initial shyness and hesitancy. There had been a vulnerability about her, one that spoke of a woman who wasn't sure of herself sexually. But he didn't tell her that.

He pushed one more time. "I've been asking you for weeks about Daniels. Tonight I finally got the answers."

"I didn't," she shouted. "I really didn't. I don't care what he says—I never did."

"You didn't what?"

"Sleep with..." It was too much. She couldn't say it.

"Why would I even think you had?" Seth challenged. He couldn't look at her. The pain on her face was more than he could stand and he had to get this out so they could go on.

"Chad did. He said it. He told everyone at the newspaper it was the only way I could have gotten the promotion. He said there was just one way a woman made it."

Silence descended on the room with her words. Jessica blinked against the tears, but they fell anyway, not that Seth could see them. His back was to her, his arm against the window frame, his forehead resting on his forearm.

Seth understood at last. At least most of it. Anger boiled through him at the thought of what her husband had done to her. How could the man, any man, possibly believe Jessica was that type of woman? Jessica was not—

Seth turned when he heard what could only be described as an hysterical giggle. Tears were streaming down Jessica's face as she stared at her foot. His anger evaporated, leaving only an aching despair. Slowly he moved to her side. "Kitten?"

Jessica wasn't really thinking any longer. He knew every deep, dark secret she had. At the gentle touch of his hands she shuddered, fighting back a fresh flow of tears. "Michael kissed me because I helped him with his children." Seth turned her to him, but she didn't look up. "He has five children and three of them have chicken pox. Melissa, his wife, had to take the baby to the doctor and we couldn't meet at his office. My college professor called just before I was to leave and then Michael called and I said I'd meet him. But then he couldn't go to the office so I met him at his house and helped him fix peanut butter sandwiches and feed the kids. He just kissed me because I helped. Even Melissa kissed me when she got back."

"Kitten, I'm sorry about that remark."

"I deserved it."

"You did not deserve it," he said sharply.

"It's true, isn't it? The only reason I've kept my job is because I did have an affair with you. You didn't mind baby-sitting as long as I..." Jessica fought back tears. "But as soon as I accepted another job... I'm sure the staff thinks the only reason I've kept my job is because of you. Because I—" She just couldn't say the words.

"No, Jessica. No, it isn't." Seth gripped her shoulders tightly. If he had had any idea about her past maybe he would have handled the situation differently, but the damage had been done. "I don't think you slept with Daniels or anyone else, Jessica. I don't believe it. I never even thought it."

She wanted to trust him. She wanted to believe him more than she had ever wanted anything, but she couldn't. "Why not?" she challenged. "I certainly dropped into bed with you fast enough."

"Don't, Jessica. Please don't." Seth walked across the room, his back to her. "I took advantage of you that weekend. I started out with good intentions and I pretended to take care of you but, God, kitten, you were hurt and tired and in pain. You were so vulnerable and I took advantage of that. I can never make that up to you, not in a million years."

Jessica stared at him. From the back, his head bent, his shoulders slumped, he looked defeated. Slowly she pushed herself from the bed and reached out. "You never took advantage of me."

Seth stared out at the dark, wet street below. He could feel the cold through the window, a cold that would soon be part of his life. "You were hurt. That damned hospital never even considered admitting you, though you were probably suffering from shock. They never asked if you had anywhere to go. No one seemed to care."

"You cared," Jessica said softly.

"Yes, but then I let my hormones get in the way."

Jessica took a hesitant step toward him and then another. Finally she touched him, but he didn't move. The muscles of his arm were hard and tense. "You never took advantage of me."

At last he turned. His eyes were dark with emotion and his face was drawn. Jessica reached out and stroked the face she loved. She traced the angle of his jaw, feeling the rough texture of his beard beneath her finger.

"Why did you, Jessica? Why did you 'drop into bed' with me?"

"Because I had already fallen in love with you," she whispered at last. "I love you." How many times had she bitten back those three little words? How many times had she stopped, burning to say them, but holding herself back? She looked at him now, not sure if she had won or lost him, but glad she had at least said the words. "I love you, Seth Cameron."

Hope bloomed where a moment ago there had been only a hollow emptiness. She hadn't told him she loved him before. "Then why are you quitting? Why have you held me at arm's length?"

"I—" Jessica shrugged and sighed. "I knew you'd heard the rumors, the remarks. After I practically threw myself at you I thought..." She let the explanation trail off, unable to say the words.

"I don't." Seth's voice was strong and sure.

"And every time you did something I assumed..." Again she trailed off. "You aren't like that," she added, shame making her unable to meet his eyes. "But the timing was so bad."

Seth closed the short distance between them and wrapped her in his arms. "I was trying to make things easier for you," he said after a moment. "I didn't know what had happened, but I was trying to protect you from it. I had your job and I thought—I'm not sure I was thinking. I just didn't want you hurt anymore."

Jessica leaned against the solid warmth of his chest. "He tried to make it look like I had slept with him." The words were whispered, but Seth heard them.

"You didn't."

Jessica twisted away from him, but, afraid to see the look in his eyes, she hung her head and went on. "Everything had become so tangled up, I was just struggling upward, clawing my way forward because that was what I was supposed to do." Seth's hands settled on her shoulders, not demanding but offering her the strength she knew so well. Jessica took a deep breath and went on. "I walked out and then I spent one beautiful afternoon talking to a Yeti who made me see how hollow my life was, how empty my achievements were."

"I'm still the Yeti," Seth said, turning her back to him. "We talked then, so why can't we now?"

Jessica felt the tears welling up again. "But it was all tangled up. I knew you were helping me, I just wasn't sure why." Seth's arms tightened around her.

"I was busy protecting you from my own guilt," Seth said, his mouth against her hair. "When you flew out of the meeting that evening and then turned in your resignation the next morning I thought you saw what had happened as a one-night stand and regretted it. I knew it was more and I just wanted a chance to show you."

Jessica looked up. "And I was terrified that because I'd been so easy you would believe the remarks." But one little doubt lingered in her mind. Taking a deep breath, she met Seth's eyes. "But you can't quit because of all this, Seth. You can't."

Seth held her closer. "Words aren't going to penetrate with Daniels. It takes action."

"Aren't there any other actions you can take? Isn't there anything else you can do? You've worked for years with Garver Broadcasting and rumor is that you're in line for a corporate position. You'll lose all that over this."

"And aren't you worth that loss? I think you are."

"No," Jessica said firmly. "I'd just start feeling guilty again. Please Seth, do something else."

He smoothed her hair back and smiled. "Okay. I won't resign yet. I may still decap all Daniels's perfect white teeth, though." Seth's expression lightened and became teasing. "Stick around awhile and you'll get to see what happens next."

Jessica wanted to cry again. "I'd like to stick around, but not at the television station, Seth. I really want this new job."

Seth's heart pounded against his ribs as he tried to interpret the answer. "Okay, not at the station, but you will stick around?"

"Oh yes." Jessica laughed, tears welling up as she reached up to kiss him.

His lips were warm and firm against hers, his arms strong and hard around her body. Jessica pulled his head more firmly to hers, and Seth lifted her into his arms. He laid her on the bed, never breaking the kiss.

Sometime later she stirred lazily, stretching out one leg and arching her back before snuggling against his shoulder, her hand playing in the thick mat of hair on his chest. "Seth." His chin nudged the top of her head as he drew her closer.

"Mmm."

"I'd like to tell you about the job."

Seth looked down at the tumble of curls against his shoulder. He still wasn't sure it was right to let her quit. She was reacting to emotions she hadn't completely dealt with, but then so was he. "Okay."

Jessica could feel the slight increase in tension with his response. "It's a small literary magazine. I'm getting in on the ground floor. It's being started to give new authors and poets a place to publish their work. I'll be the editor." She had been away from that type of thing for so long, but her college teacher had given her a glowing recommendation and so had her old boss at the newspaper.

"It sounds risky, Jessica. Something like that could fold after the first issue."

"Yes, it's risky," she admitted after a moment.

So he hadn't been wrong. She wasn't sure. Seth drew her closer, gently stroking her shoulder. "Kitten, you're good at what you do. You have a solid future in television. Don't throw it away because of one man." Suddenly she sat up, pulling the sheet up around her bare breasts.

She had to make him understand. Somehow she had to make him see her side. "Seth, do you remember when we were talking and you asked me why I had gone into the field I had?" She turned and watched him, waiting. He nodded. "I liked print. I had been put in book reviews at the paper. I loved it. That was just at the time when things got so bad in my marriage, but then it seemed more important to try to salvage the relationship."

Jessica turned away, staring down at her lap. "I was wrong. You shouldn't settle for something just to please another person. That's what I did. I settled for television news to try to please Chad when what I always wanted was what I had." She turned back, her eyes pleading for his understanding. "I want this chance. I want to take the risk."

"Then you should," Seth said after a long moment. "If you're sure you aren't just reacting to the situation at the station."

Jessica smiled at him. "Maybe I was at first, but now I'm sure."

"Then do it," he said and pulled her back down to him. "I'll be here if it falls through."

Before she could say anything he claimed her mouth in a warm, long kiss.

Jessica sat up sleepily and rubbed her eyes. All the clothes she had dumped out of the closet and dresser were now lying in a heap on the floor, the open suitcase on top. "What a mess I made," she moaned softly, thinking of trying to find something to wear to work.

"I think you straightened everything important out," Seth said, running his hand up her bare back.

"I hate cleaning up messes, though."

"I can think of much better things to do," he said, pulling her down onto his chest. "And much more fun."

"I didn't realize Yetis were insatiable," she said laughing. "After last night you want more?" The angry words and hurt had been healed repeatedly in each other's arms.

"More and more," he said huskily. "And only from a blond, green-eyed Big Foot."

"I won't be a Big Foot next week," she reminded him hesitantly. Then his hands began their familiar caressing of her body.

Seth watched the doubts fade as the heat built in her eyes until finally he touched her intimately, eliciting a moan. "Only green-eyed kittens who purr that way," he said, rolling her over.

Suddenly he captured her wrists as he had their first night in the house together and held her still beneath him. "Jessica, I said to take the risk, that I'd be here to catch you."

She nodded.

"As your husband. Will you marry me?" For a long moment she just stared at him and then he began to re-awaken her with slow, teasing touches, his eyes never leaving her face. "Will you marry me?"

"Yes." Jessica wrapped her arms around his neck. "Yes, but I think our vows should say love, honor and talk."

"Later," he growled softly against her lips. "First, love."

Epilogue

Jessica laughed happily at Neil's latest story. After years of trying he and Beth had finally had a child and each event was special to him. She smiled as Beth rolled her eyes.

"If he had to change every diaper on that child," Beth said, "it wouldn't be as exciting."

"I think it's great," Jessica said. "All that love and joy."

"It is," Beth agreed sheepishly. "It's just that to hear Neil tell it, no one else has ever had a child before."

"That's the way every father should feel," Seth said from behind Jessica and then she felt the familiar warmth of his hand on her back just before his arm slipped around her waist. "With every child they have."

"When are you two going to grace the world with one?" Neil questioned teasingly.

"As soon as I can," Seth said and gave Jessica a wicked look that caused her to blush and made both Neil and Beth laugh.

"Newlyweds," Beth teased.

"Six months isn't very new," Jessica protested.

"New enough," Neil said.

"It's just that Seth doesn't understand the meaning of slow."

"I'm learning," Seth said with an understanding smile. "It just takes time."

Jessica tensed involuntarily as she saw Gerald Daniels moving toward them through the crowd. The annual television awards were always an event and this year no less so. Except that she didn't have to be knotted into a pretzel worrying about her job. She only had to be knotted worrying for Seth and it seemed much more pleasant that way.

She felt Seth's arm tighten around her as Daniels approached. She would never like the man and she would certainly never trust him. They chatted for several minutes. Gerald told her how much they still missed her and she smiled and thanked him. Only after he moved on did she start giggling, nearly spilling the glass of champagne in her hand.

"Share the joke," Seth said with a quizzical look.

She shook her head. "It's just that one of the reasons I wanted out of television was so I didn't have to be nice to people like him, yet every time I'm with you I do."

"The price of love," Neil said with a chuckle.

And worth every minute of it, Jessica thought, gazing up at Seth.

"We have to take our seats," he said with a gentle smile. "Brace yourself, we're sitting with Daniels."

Slipping her hand into Seth's, she followed him into the large ballroom. "Daniels, huh? Been holding out on me again?"

"Afraid you'd chicken out," he teased as he led her through the maze of tables to one immediately in front of the stage.

"And miss a front row seat?" Jessica asked. As Seth held her chair she glanced around. They were seated with top executives from the station. At the table to her left were the top people from 4 and to her right those from Channel 7. "Such exalted company I keep now," she whispered mischievously.

"You never know where you'll find big, hairy creatures," Seth teased as he sat by her, laughing as she blushed.

The dinner was long and tedious, and as Jessica ate, she thought about the past.

Seth had talked to the board of directors, and had reported the harassment. With her support as well as that of many others at the station, Daniels had had to answer for his actions at last. He had nearly lost his job; however, in the end he hadn't. But, despite his big talk and grandiose schemes, everyone knew he was only in a figurehead position now. The real decisions were made by others.

At last the presentations began. It was a long drawn-out process, and Jessica stifled a yawn. She glanced sidewise, hoping Seth hadn't noticed, but he had. He smiled at her and draped his arm across the back of her chair, but his eyes were concerned.

"How is that little magazine of yours coming?" Gerald asked during a lull in the ceremonies.

Seth watched as she answered, enjoying the bright sparkle in her eyes. She loved her work and its challenges. It was a job that really suited her.

"Not the same as television, though," Daniels said. "Don't you miss all of the glamour and glitter, like tonight?"

Seth felt her tense beneath his arm and gently touched her shoulder. Jessica wasn't the only one with reason to despise the man. In fact, if it hadn't been for her continued pressure and unwavering support at times like this he probably wouldn't have stayed on. But he knew in the long run it wasn't a decision he would regret and in the meantime he had Jessica to talk to about it in the evenings and Jessica to make nights like this bearable.

The time for the last presentation finally arrived. Jessica felt Seth tense beside her and she reached out to him, laying her hand on his thigh. This was the award for best overall news program, and winning would mean a lot in promotion and advertising. With a silent prayer to the powers that be, she crossed her fingers.

"And the winner is—WAKQ, Channel 9, Seth Cameron, News Director."

The room erupted into a near riot of whoops and shouts as all the people from the station rose to cheer for themselves. It was the first time in six years Channel 9 had taken this award home and all the credit went to Seth. Jessica realized she was crying as he walked up to the podium to receive the coveted statue.

"I just want to say the only people to thank are the staff who do the work. Without them we wouldn't have a news program. I thank all of you for your support and help."

* * *

Jessica lifted her head from Seth's shoulder as the garage door whined closed behind them. After the long presentations everyone had gone to a nearby bar to celebrate, and the party hadn't stopped until the wee hours.

"Come on, kitten, let's get you to bed," he said as he helped her from the car. "You can sleep as late as you want tomorrow. It's Sunday. In fact, you can spend the whole day in bed if you want."

"A waste of time." Jessica sighed.

"Not if you're not alone." Seth chuckled.

Jessica followed him into the kitchen, glancing around the room. The house was a home now, not just because it had pictures and curtains and furniture. It was where they lived, where they shared their day and began their mornings. It was where they went to be together and to talk about their dreams. "Neil sure is crazy about that baby, isn't he?" she asked as they started down the hall.

"You should hear him at work," Seth agreed, holding her tightly against him. "Every day we get a blow-by-blow account of the kid's actions."

"What are you going to do when we have one?" she asked as they started up the stairs.

"First, I'm going to practice some more how to get one," he said, picking her up. "That is, if I can keep you awake long enough." He stopped at the top of the steps and looked at her. "What is it with you and sleep recently? I've never known you to be so tired out."

"The doctor said it was perfectly normal and shouldn't last long."

"Doctor? Are you sick? What's wrong?" Seth demanded anxiously.

"I'm not sick," she said laughing, trying to wriggle from his arms. "I think it's just nature's way of making up for all that sleep you're going to miss at two o'clock feedings."

"Two o'clock feedings?" His eyes widened. "Kitten, are you . . . are we . . . do you mean . . . ?"

Jessica laughed, finally managing to escape his hold. "I am, we are and I do mean."

"You're really going to have a baby?"

"*Our* baby."

"Oh, kitten, that's wonderful." He hugged her tightly, then quickly loosened his grip, touching her as if she would break. "When?"

"Ah, Mr. Cameron," she teased. "This time you can't hurry anything. Nature decrees it takes a full nine months. How does January sound?"

"It sounds perfect," he declared, swinging her into his arms again and carrying her to the bed. "I've always loved January." He paused, then smiled. "And that's only seven months," he laughed. "It won't be long at all. I wonder what you get when you cross a kitten and a Yeti?"

"That depends on whether it's a boy or a girl," she laughed, pulling him down with her. "If it's a girl she's certain to be an angel. If it's a boy he'll probably be the Abominable Snowman."

"Jessica," he said hesitantly, "I want to make love to you." He laid his hand on her still flat stomach. "I don't want to hurt you, though."

She laughed softly and pulled him closer. "Oh, you big Yeti. You won't hurt me or the little snowman, either."

They made love gently and tenderly, holding each other for a long time afterward.

"Seth, are you happy? Really happy?"

"Do you need to ask?"

No, she thought. She could see it in his eyes and feel it in his touch. "I just like to hear the words sometimes."

Seth stroked her back gently. "I'm happy, kitten. Happier than I've ever been in my life. I just wish I could make a dozen more mistakes like you."

* * * * *

Silhouette Desire®

CHILDREN OF DESTINY

A trilogy by Ann Major

Three power-packed tales of irresistible passion
and undeniable fate created by Ann Major to
wrap your heart in a legacy of love.

PASSION'S CHILD — September

Years ago, Nick Browning nearly destroyed
Amy's life, but now that the child of his
passion—the child of her heart—was in danger,
Nick was the only one she could trust....

DESTINY'S CHILD — October

Cattle baron Jeb Jackson thought he owned
everything and everyone on his ranch, but fiery
Megan MacKay's destiny was to prove him wrong!

NIGHT CHILD — November

When little Julia Jackson was kidnapped, young
Kirk MacKay blamed himself. Twenty years later,
he found her . . . and discovered that love could
shine through even the darkest of nights.

Silhouette Special Edition

COMING NEXT MONTH

AVAILABLE THIS MONTH: